michele jaffe

BAD KITTY

harpercollinspublishers

Bad Kitty
Copyright © 2006
by Michele Jaffe
All rights reserved. Printed in the
United States of America. No part of this
book may be used or reproduced in any manner
whatsoever without written permission except in the case
of brief quotations embodied in critical articles and reviews.
For information address HarperCollins Children's Books, a division
of HarperCollins Publishers, 1350 Avenue of the Americas,
New York, NY 10019.www.harperteen.com

Library of Congress Cataloging-in-Publication Data

Jaffe, Michele.
Bad kitty / Michele Jaffe.— 1st ed.
p. cm.
Summary: While vacationing with her family in Las Vegas, seventeen-year-old
Jasmine stumbles upon a murder mystery that she attempts to solve with
the help of her friends, recently arrived from California.

ISBN-10: 0-06-078108-4—ISBN-13: 978-0-06-078108-8
ISBN-10: 0-06-078109-2 (lib. bdg.)—ISBN-13: 978-0-06-078109-5 (lib. bdg.)
[1. Las Vegas (Nev.)—Fiction. 2. Racially mixed people—Fiction.
3. Humorous stories. 4. Mystery and detective stories.] I. Title.
PZ7.J15342Bad 2006   2005005733
[Fic]—dc22   CIP
AC

Typography by Sasha Illingworth
2 3 4 5 6 7 8 9 10
❖
First Edition

For Dan,
My Superhero

This book could never
have existed without the
inspiration and assistance of:

Meg Cabot
Susan Ginsburg
Dan Goldner
Abby McAden
The Desert Passage Shops
The Forum Shoppes (especially Phase III)
The Grand Canal Shoppes
The Shops at Mandalay Place
The Via Bellagio Shops
Tacos
TiVo

I thank you all for being
so super fabulous.

One

I believe everyone has a superpower. My friend Polly can name the designer, season, and price of any garment on any person (knockoffs too) with flawless accuracy. Roxy can eat more food faster than anyone I've ever seen, has a perfect sense of direction, and over one spring break she built a working TV out of an old toaster. And her twin brother Tom can imitate anyone's voice and pick any kind of lock.

Still, I've never been able to figure out what my superpower is. Dr. Payne, my dentist, says my teeth generate plaque faster than anyone he's ever seen. And I have an incredible ability to be in the wrong place at the wrong time, without fail. But I'm not sure either of those count. I guess the only thing I've got going for me is that cats like me.

But if that is a superpower, you can have it, because it's the reason I got into this whole mess.

It had started out as such a nice day too.

I was relaxing on my chaise lounge at the Venetian Hotel pool in Las Vegas after a grueling fifteen minutes of water aerobics with my stepmother, Sherri! (Actually, she just recently stopped writing her name with the exclamation point after it. Now she just puts a heart over the i.)

Sherri! and I had just finished our "exercise," which mostly consisted of me flailing my arms around like I was telling some hovering space aliens, "Over here, come this way," and Sherri! naming the different brands of breast implants on display around us in the pool. Sherri!'s breasts are real, but since almost all her friends from the ABA where she works as a hand-breast-thigh body double, are "enhanced," she's become kind of an expert. (ABA stands for All-Body Agency, supplying body doubles to Hollywood since 1984, not the American Bar Association, which is what my aunt Liz thinks.)

That's not her superpower, though. Sherri!'s superpower is that it's impossible to hate her. I know, you're thinking that is not a superpower, but in the case of Sherri!, believe me, it is. Because it's not just men who don't hate her. Everyone doesn't hate Sherri! Even I can't hate her, which, if you know anything about stepmothers, is really very wrong. We are *supposed* to hate each other; it's in the natural order of things. And that does not take into account the special circumstances of me vs. Sherri! Which are:

Sherri!:
Boobs: C-cup, real, perky
Eyes: sky blue

Skin: peach sorbet

Face: could totally launch a thousand ships.

     Even rockets.

Figure: she's a body double for Hollywood stars.

     Need I say more?

Height: perfect (5'6"; 5'9" in heels)

If her hair were a character in a horror movie, it would be:

     the pretty girl who always looks tidy yet sexy even when

     running for her life from the scary unpredictable murderer

Dream: to invent a line of comfortable, safe, and attractive seat

     belts for small dogs

Age: 25

Me (Jas):

Boobs: nonexistent (like my superpower)

Eyes: grass green (from my Irish father)

Skin: chocolate milkshake (from my Jamaican mother.

     Along with my dimples.)

Face: could launch, maybe, a science experiment

Figure: stick bug

Height: King Kong

If my hair were a character in a horror movie it would be:

     the scary unpredictable murderer who sometimes looks

     perfectly normal and then other times reveals an inner

     demonic self.

Dream: to have a boyfriend I can look up to. Literally. While

     wearing my cowboy boots. Oh, also to fight crime and

     make the world a safer place.

Age: 17

Yes, that is right, my stepmother was eight when I was born. Don't even ask how old my father was when she was born; it's upsetting. And yet, despite that, I cannot hate her.

Since she and my dad got married a year ago, Sherri! has been nothing but excellent. She doesn't take my dad's side in our arguments, and she uses logic on me to get me to do what she wants. Like, "If you use the car without permission, you'd better remember to fill the gas tank. You have money for gas, right? If you don't, you might not want to go." I mean, that's helpful. Plus, she has never tried to give me menstruation tips, or tell me how *lucky* I am because my *exotic* coloring opens up a whole *palette* of eye shadow colors most women can't go *near*, or point out that some boys like to date women a foot taller than them, or advise me about guys at all.

Not that her advice would work anyway, since her experiences as a seventeen-year-old and mine have nothing in common except that we are both the same species. And I'm not even sure that's true. I mean, Sherri! could well be some new, improved form of *Homo sapiens* designed to end hatred and bring voluptuous beauty to the world. The way the really cute guy sitting at the pool's Snack Hut looked in our direction as she perfectly "Right arm, jab! Left arm, jab!"ed her way through water aerobics made this very clear.

My plan for the afternoon was to lie around far, far from Sherri! and Dad and their cooing, trying to come up with something to write in my summer Meaningful Reflection Journal for school. It seemed like a good time to start, since school was beginning in two weeks and so far my journal was empty. So I decided I would just write down whatever I wanted. Like this haiku:

Cute guy at Snack Hut
Why won't you remove your shirt?
It's so hot (you too)

The point of the Meaningful Reflection Journal, according to Dr. Lansdowne, the college counselor at the Westborough School for Girls, which I attend, is to encourage us to compile thoughts and reflections and take stock of all the little life lessons we learn each day. (Translated, that meant that it would force us to practice SAT vocabulary words while helping us come up with something that sounded deep in our college essays.) Young people, Dr. Lansdowne said, experience so much and process so little; the journals would change that. He can get away with saying things like that without choking on his tongue because he looks like Hugh Grant did when he was young, complete with British accent.

(I wonder if that could count as Little Life Lesson 1: If you have to say something that would be better printed on one of those posters with a photo of a kitty hugging a tree branch, say it with a British accent. Being the only cute male at a school of 480 girls might also help.)

Dr. Lansdowne says we should aim to learn sixty Little Life Lessons, "or approximately one each weekday of summer vacation." Talk about a depressing calculation. I mostly try to do what Dr. Lansdowne says, not only because he has dedicated his life to helping us get into college when he could be making a lot more money as a teen sex icon, and I think that deserves validation, or because I have what Polly calls British Accent Stupidity Syndrome, but really because college is my only chance of escaping from my father. But despite being highly motivated, I still could not bring myself to write anything in my journal all summer. And not for lack of trying. The truth was, I didn't learn anything in those three long months. Unless of course you count the random facts and quotations I picked up playing Dixie Cup Trivia during my breaks with the receptionist and nurse's aide at my uncle's office.

I'd had a really fantastic summer internship lined up working as a junior criminalist in the Los Angeles Sheriff's office, but my father refused to let me take it. For some reason he thought being an assistant's assistant in his brother's medical practice would be more educational. And who could blame him, really? I mean, when it comes to developing skills I will call on again and again in my future life, how can knowing how to sequence DNA possibly compare to being able to say, "Please urinate in this cup and leave it here for the doctor," fluently in English and Spanish? Right, no contest.

(In case you're wondering, that's *"Favor de dejar un especimín en este copa para el doctor."*)

(Also, in case you're wondering, the cute guy still had his shirt on.)

My uncle Andy was the reason we were in Vegas. It was his and my aunt Liz's turn to choose where we would take our annual End-of-Summer-I-Know!-Let's-Torture-Jas-by-Making-Her-Leave-All-Her-Precious-Pals-and-Spend-Time-with-Her-Family Vacation, and they'd decided on the Venetian Hotel. To which I could only say: Bless you, Uncle Andy and Aunt Liz. Because even *sans* little pals and *avec* embarrassing family members, the Venetian Hotel? Yes, more or less my definition of heaven.

In fact, I was kind of bummed we weren't staying longer. We'd arrived the night before and would be there through the weekend. Even though it was a Thursday, the pool area was full and the people-watching was mind-boggling. There was everything from two really pale punk girls with dyed hair (one hot pink, one bright blue) wearing black cutoff cargo pants, black combat boots, black studded leather wrist cuffs, black lipstick, and black suspenders over white tube tops small enough to show off their navel art; to a woman wearing huge diamonds and fancy matching bathing suit–robe combo; to a man with a tattoo on his back of a parrot saying, "Doobie or not doobie, that is the question."

And there was the cute guy at the Snack Hut. I had gotten a good look at him earlier when I went to order a root beer float for breakfast, and they made me wait a long time while they found the ice cream (apparently some people do not consider ice cream a breakfast food. I shudder for them). He was sitting at the table *reading* a copy of *Spin* magazine, not just flipping through it like I would have been, which showed he was a deep intellectual soul, as well as interested in music. Even better, as I casually ambled by him on my way back to my lounge, I could tell that he was admiring my root beer float. Clearly we were destined for each other.

I was just thinking that between the presence of my Destined One, the green marble bathroom with the steam shower, the Krispy Kreme doughnut bakery, and the outstanding people-watching, I could happily live and die at the Venetian, when I heard a menacing *crack crack crack* from my left and smelled the sugary scent that could only mean one thing.

Do not look up, I told myself. Maybe if you don't look up, the frightening creature will slink away. Or you'll suddenly be invisible. That would be a very helpful superpower. Do not look up do not look up—

I looked. And there it, or rather she, was, perching on the lounge chair next to mine like an Abercrombie and Fitch version of a praying mantis: my perfect cousin, Alyson (superpower: ability to turn people into gnats with just a look, or at least make them feel like she has).

Alyson and I are the same age and go to the same school and presumably share some strands of paternal DNA since her father and my father are brothers (not that I'll ever be able to sequence it), but that's pretty much where the resemblance ends. She was with her Evil Hench Twin, Veronique, who is not her real twin like Roxy and Tom are, only her twin in terms of darkness of the soul, clump-free mascara application, perfect glossy straight brown hair, and that kind of thing. They were wearing coordinating rainbow bikinis, rainbow heart-shaped necklaces, and rainbow-striped newsboy caps, looking (it pains me to say) quite cute doing it. The only difference between them was that their caps were skewed at slightly different angles, and Alyson had a pack of sugar-free Bubble Yum stuck through the elastic part of her bikini bottoms, while Veronique was using that prime real estate to store her chapstick.

I forgot to mention that Alyson has another superpower, which is that she can blow the largest bubbles you've ever seen with chewing gum. When we were in third grade, Alyson won a bubble blowing contest and I don't think I've ever seen her without Bubble Yum since then. It's her signature scent.

Alyson blew a huge, perfect bubble, let it snap back, and said, "Look, it's Calamity Callihan. Didn't do your journal this summer, Calamity? Did being a receptionist-slash-loser in my dad's office take up too much of your time?"

Because her thoughts are quite lofty, mere words are not sufficient for my cousin Alyson to express herself and she must string them together with slashes. Alyson and Veronique high-fived each other in honor of this recent slash, and Veronique went, "That was so MasterCard."

I couldn't help myself. I had to ask. "MasterCard?"

"Duh," Alyson said, popping a bubble. "Like the ads? You know, 'priceless.' Gee, Calamity, get out much?"

There were about a thousand excellent things I could have said as a comeback to that, but I couldn't think of a single one of them.

It's one of the great galactic mysteries how Alyson's father, who is among the kindest men in the world and would provide medical care—not to mention summer employment—to any stray who wandered in off the street, and her mother, my aunt Liz, who hand-sews clothes for her teddy bear collection and bakes "Welcome to Our Blessed Block" cakes for new neighbors, ended up with a daughter whose idea of kindness to others is to wear a push-up bra and smile occasionally. But I was under strict orders from my father to be nice to "your sweet cousin Alyson and her friend," and since I am above petty things like bitterness that she got to bring a friend on our FAMILY vacation and I did not, and since I noticed that Alyson had bitten the acrylic tips off her nails which meant something was *really* bothering her, and (to be perfectly honest) since I'd just remembered that the last time Polly saw anyone wearing a newsboy cap she said, "Holy Time Portal to last year, Batgirl!," I smiled at the Evil Hench Pair and said, "So, how was your summer?"

"Totally Visa," Alyson gum-cracked. Then like she was speaking to a five-year-old she said, "You know, it was everywhere we wanted to be."

"I read a lot," Veronique volunteered.

"Anything good?" I asked to be polite.

"*Macramé for Dummies* was pretty good," Veronique said. "And *Rabbits for Dummies*. Those were probably the best ones." She nodded to herself, then fixed me with a Hench gaze. "Is it true that you had to stick your finger in old people's butts working in the doctor's office?

Alyson said you did, but I told her even you wouldn't."

Now that was touching. I said, "Why, Veronique, thank you for that kind-slash-unexpected show of support."

This seemed to really confuse her and she looked at her Evil Hench Mistress for guidance. Alyson rolled her eyes, then said to me, "You're not going to go all freaky and do anything embarrassing to ruin our vacation, are you?"

I pretended to think about that. "Would it really bug you?" I asked, then laughed girlishly. "Just kidding. Of course not."

She sneered, said, "Good," and I agreed, and at the time I said it, it was totally, completely true.

As well as for the approximately nine minutes that followed.

Two

I'd hoped that after this fascinating conversation, the Evil Hench Twins would wander off to pick up some lifeguards or small animals for one of their midnight sacrifices, but I was out of luck. Instead, they settled in on the lounges next to mine and got lost in an intellectual discourse over a copy of *InStyle*, which went:

"Cute."

"Cute."

"Cute."

"Cute."

"So cute."

"Totally cute."

"Cute."

I think it might be a tonal language. Then all of a sudden Alyson said, "Cu— Oh, my god. Do you know who that is?"

And Veronique said, "Who?"

"Over there in the cabana," Alyson said, pointing with the bill of her cap. "That's Fiona Bristol."

"No way. Wait—which one is Fiona Bristol again? Is she the one who wore that red dress to the Oscars?"

"Hello, SatCom to Veronique. Fiona Bristol is the model-slash-yogi-slash-former-kindergarten-teacher who was discovered on a playground in Los Angeles by that famous photographer, who she married. Remember? And there was that big scandal last year because—"

And then, just like her Evil Hench Self, she started whispering. Which was so unfair because I'd had to listen to all that other stuff and now when they were finally saying something that could at least be interesting, I couldn't hear.

To make it clear to them that I didn't care what they were saying, I picked up my Meaningful Reflection Journal and tried to meaningfully reflect. This what I came up with:

Who shouts what is dull
But whispers what might delight?
Evil Hench Twins do!

(P.S. Veronique:
Please lean back in your lounge chair;
you're blocking my sun.)

A double haiku! That, I decided, was more than enough Meaningful Reflection for one day, so I put down the journal and moved on to intently studying my copy of *Modern Drummer* magazine in preparation for my career as a drummer in a kick-ass angry girl band. My eye kept being drawn to the cute guy at the Snack Hut, though, who was still sitting there in all his splendor. He looked like he might be tall, too. He was definitely Visa.

I decided to try some secret mind control on him and implant a message into the core of his being. The message I settled on was: "You're growing very, very warm. You wish you were not wearing your shirt. Stand up to your full height and take it off."

In case you're wondering, the way you use mind control to stare into the core of someone's being is like this:

Apply lip gloss.
Apply sunglasses.
Stare.
Stare really, really hard (but without furrowing your brow
because this could cause wrinkling and can make you look,
according to Polly, like the Incredible Hulk taking a poo).

Mind control is another superpower I don't have, so I was really surprised when, all of a sudden, it seemed to be working. The cute guy was looking in my direction! Our eyes—through our sunglasses—locked! He started to stand up!

I should have been suspicious. Seriously, why would anyone pay attention to an "exotic-looking" girl with no boobs when there were plenty of buxom supermodels scattered around the pool?

Good question! If you find yourself in that situation, here is the answer:

They would pay attention if an enormous orange cat with only three legs were leaping through the air onto the girl's (boobless) chest, baring its claws. Believe me. Because that is exactly what happened, and let me tell you, I suddenly got a lot of attention.

Then I got a lot more when I shouted a really bad word at the top of my lungs. Because attached to the cat was a silver metal leash, and silver metal leashes get really hot in the desert sun, especially when they whip around your leg. Try it sometime. They get so hot that you don't even notice that a cat is sticking its claws into your chest. Or even stop to wonder what a cat is doing at the Venetian pool. And why it's on a leash.

Once the mists of pain cleared from my mind, though, I am sure I would have thought of all those things. Only I didn't get a chance because when I tried to lift the cat off of myself, he dug in with his claws, causing pain to shoot through my body like I was being stung by a thousand million bees. Which I took as a subtle message from the cat that he wasn't going anywhere, at least without a large amount of my skin under his claws. I must have been light-headed from the pain because all I could think was that if this were a murder case, and the cat were the killer, boy would that skin under its nails be incriminating evidence. I was about to warn the cat about that when a huge shadow fell over all of us, and the cat went very still, but dug in harder.

"I take the animal now," the shadow told me, only he said "de" instead of "the" in that kind of accent Arnold Schwarzenegger has made so popular. And really, if you'd been trying to cast a comic book villain named the Fabio-inator (which, okay, why would you be, but still) you could not have done better. He was about eighteen feet tall and had long dark hair and a fake tan and a square jaw and biceps that bulged out in forty-three different directions. Which were visible because all he was wearing were small, tight, black swimming trunks. And a gun.

I'll have to ask Polly, but I'm pretty sure that's a fashion don't.

Anyway, since the cat seemed to be adhering himself to me with super strength, I said, "He's holding on pretty tight. Maybe if I just pet him for a moment he will calm down." Which I thought was both polite and very wise.

The Fabinator just glared at me and said, "Now. I take pussy from you now."

I swear.

And not only did he say that, he said it loud, and as he talked, out of the corner of my eye I saw the cute guy taking off in the opposite direction, fast. This allowed me to collect Little Life Lessons 2 and 3:

Little Life Lesson 2: A good way to ensure you will never have a boyfriend is to have a large armed man with an uncertain grasp of English heckle you in public.

Little Life Lesson 3: If for some reason the guy might still be interested, following up by having your father rush over right afterward screaming, "Jasmine, you know you are not allowed to talk to strangers!" as though you were six will nip it in the bud. Oh, and it helps if your father is wearing a safari suit. With shorts. And knee socks. Because this is his idea of what you wear in the desert.

Now you know why I want to be in an angry girl band.

Anyway, on the one hand there's the Fabinator with his gun and his Speedo. On the other, there's Crocodile Dundee threatening to send me to my room and wash my mouth out with soap. And on the third hand, or rather paw, there is the cat trying to burrow under my skin. I guess I was pretty close to losing it then so, when out of nowhere a strawberry-blond little boy with tears streaming down his face came running toward me yelling, "Don't let them have my kitty! They're going to hurt him! Run!," I did.

Little Life Lesson 4: Do NOT take orders from an eight-year-old.

Where I ran, with the cat still adhered to my chest, was toward the part of the pool that was less crowded. I ducked under a velvet rope and headed behind this sort of pavilion thing, where I discovered another smaller pool. And a wedding.

Or the beginning of the wedding. Because as I came around the corner, the bride was walking down the red carpet on her dad's arm, and everyone was standing and the band was playing, "Here Comes the Bride." I stopped running and started backing up, which is not that easy in flip-flops, but I couldn't stop looking at the bride, because she looked so happy. And so did her dad.

Then I made myself turn and I was almost around the edge of the pavilion when I felt myself get jolted back and I heard a kind of clanging, then a kind of screeching, and I realized that the cat's leash had gotten caught on a chair and was dragging behind us. And before I could try to get it off, the chair snaked around and got stuck on the edge of a table.

A table with a cake on it. Or actually five cakes, because it was a five-tiered wedding cake. With real flowers. And I bet it was expensive because when the bride saw the table going over and the cake starting to slide, she pulled away from her dad and leaped to save it.

Which is why they both hit the pool at the same time.

The groom just stood there staring. He didn't make a single move to save either the cake or the bride. Personally, I would not marry someone who stared at me as I floated in the pool in my wedding dress rather than jumped in the pool after me and pretended the whole thing was some great joke and we meant to do that so the guests would think it was funny. But that is only because the chances of me falling into a pool are very high and I have to protect against that. Although the chances of me ever finding anyone who could put up with me long enough to want to marry me are, as my father points out whenever I practice the drums while he is at home, very low, so maybe it doesn't matter. But anyway, here was the situation:

Bride: wet
Cake: demolished
Groom: stunned
Cat:

Ah, yes, that's an excellent question. "Where was the cat in all this?" you may well ask. And the answer SHOULD have been, at my side, faithful witness to all he had wrought. But no. As soon as the mayhem started, the cat jumped off of me and padded off into the bushes. So that when Security came up and started screaming at me, and I said, "It wasn't me, it was the cat's leash," they could stare at me and go, "What cat?" And mean it.

You see what I mean about being attractive to cats being kind of a sucky superpower.

That is when I discovered that the only thing more embarrassing than having a cute guy nearby while a large man and your father yell at you is being escorted away from a pool by two red-coated security men while wearing nothing but a bikini. Five million people, or however many were at the pool, all stopped to stare at me. And all probably saw the place behind my knee that I missed shaving. Plus, I am sure my nipples were showing through my top. My one consolation was that the cute guy was not there to witness my walk of shame.

My other consolation was that, instead of walking through the casino, the security men led me to this secret doorway that went into some bat-cave part of the hotel. Only when it slammed behind us did I begin to wonder what the laws were in Nevada. My father had been going on and on during the flight to Vegas about how Nevada still seemed like part of the Wild West, which did not give me a warm, relaxed feeling. Like, I was pretty sure running by the pool was against the rules, but by Wild West standards, was it the kind of thing that required execution? What if they were taking me to some special, secret electric chair? Would it work better because my bathing suit was still a little wet from water aerobics? What if this was the underground lair of a super bad guy? Who wanted to use my cat powers to spread evil in the world?

One of the guards pushed me through the door toward this hard-looking metal chair that was standing next to a hard-looking metal table. I said, "What is going to happen now?" and I admit it, I stuttered. Because I was scared.

"What is going to happen now, miss," he said, wagging a stubby square finger at me, "is that you are going to get in a lot of trouble."

Then he closed the door. And locked it. Giving me a chance to add Little Life Lesson 5: When you go to prison, try not to be wearing a bikini. (Especially a damp one.)

Three

The main difference between where I was and real prison, as far as I could tell, based on what I'd learned as a faithful viewer of Court TV, was that they let me keep my watch and they didn't give me an orange jumpsuit. Which meant that by using the second hand to time my pulse, I could come up with a really good record of the rate at which I was freezing to death sitting there in my bikini. I calculated that if it kept up at the same pace, I would die in forty minutes.

Then the air conditioner came on. This was so not Visa.

It was probably all for the best, since even if I did make it out alive, my father would kill me. It's one thing to occasionally find yourself in the middle of other people's difficulties like I sometimes do (but never on purpose. And, in case it comes up, I really was *not* responsible for the altercation-slash-riot in the food court at the mall that time. I even got the GOLDEN CHOPSTICK CERTIFICATE OF APPRECIATION ENTITLING THE BEARER TO ONE FREE EGG ROLL EVERY MONTH for my help. Plus, it was two years ago), but that's nothing compared to destroying a wedding. That is someone's cherished memory! And weddings are expensive. Who knew what a place like the Venetian charged for a five-tiered cake?

There were other questions too, like: Would they give me an installment plan to pay it off? Or would my father just cut up my body and sell the different pieces for scientific research? Could you get a lot of money for that?

My only hope was that my father would somehow have had one of his epiphanies. He's a professor of anthropology and a genius—a certified one; he was given one of those Macarthur genius grants and everything. I don't know about all geniuses, but when my dad gets an idea, he becomes totally absorbed in it and forgets about real life around him. (Which is another reason it's so great to have Sherri!. When I was twelve, my dad decided to do a book on ritual worship, so we spent a year traveling around Europe looking for all the pieces of St. Catherine's body. Which was cool, but my dad completely forgot that I might have to go to school. I had a lot of making up to do when we got back. Sherri! would totally not let that happen.) Maybe, if something had triggered an especially super idea, my dad would be too distracted to notice what had happened. If he could forget about a whole year of school, certainly he could miss one little decimated wedding—

The door slamming open to reveal my father pretty much crushed those bold girlish dreams. I wish I could say that he strolled or sauntered or skipped into my cell, but I'm pretty sure the right word here is stalked. Or maybe marched.

If I thought things were grim before, I was wrong. You haven't seen grim until you've seen a six-foot-six sunburned man dressed like a British tourist in India at the turn of the last century stalk-march toward you, stop, and say, "Do you know what you have done this time, Jasmine?"

I took the "this time" to be a bad sign, suggesting he was not only aware of what had just happened, but was also, in fact, remembering that time in the food court. Or the other time at the circus. Or—

I swallowed hard. "I saved a cat's life."

"Bah," he said. "That cat was in no danger."

"Really?" I asked. This was good news. "Then why did the little boy say—"

"Be quiet!"

Yes, he was definitely remembering the food court.

"The hotel has asked us to leave," he said, leaning over me. "You, Sherri!, and I. As well as your uncle and his family."

I probably should have seen that coming, but hadn't. And if I felt bad before, now I felt awful. I wasn't just destroying my vacation, I was destroying everyone's. "I'm so sorry," I said. I stared at the table. "I didn't mean to ruin anything."

"Why must you always surround yourself with mayhem, Jasmine? Why can't you just interact in a normal manner with others?"

I braced for the "like your cousin, Alyson," that usually came after statements like that, but fortunately he didn't say it. Or maybe unfortunately. Because he didn't say anything, just gave a long sigh and stared at me with this sad look on his face that told me I'd let him down again. He ran his hand through his hair and said, "Do you have any idea what it is like to watch your only daughter be escorted away by Security?" His voice was soft and kind of sad.

I decided it wasn't the right time to point out that, whatever else I'd done, teen pregnancy wasn't on the list, and I didn't have a daughter. I said, "I'm sorry, Dad. I don't know why these things always happen to me."

"Happen to you?" he exploded, suggesting maybe I should have mentioned the absence-of-a-teen-pregnancy thing. "Blast all, they don't just happen to you. How can running into a wedding just happen?" He hit the table in front of me, making me and it jump. "No, Jasmine, you've got to stop pretending to be a passive participant in all this. You are not a child anymore and have got to start taking responsibility. How can you be trusted to drive a car if you can't be trusted to not ruin a wedding?" This is the kind of logic that makes sense to geniuses. "As of today," he said ominously, "be prepared to pay the price for your actions."

"Are you going to sell my body parts to science?"

"This is not a joke."

"Who would joke about something like that?" The way he was looking at me, it was fully possible.

"You will leave here and apologize to your uncle Andrew and your aunt Liz. Then to your cousin and that girl she has with her. Then to the couple whose wedding you ruined. When you have finished doing that, you will return to our suite where you will pack your bags. The hotel has kindly agreed to let us all stay tonight, provided you do not leave your room. When we get home, you will be grounded for the foreseeable future except to go to school."

Weighed against apologizing to the Evil Henched Ones, having my body cut up and sold to science didn't sound so bad. Really.

I had forgotten how cold I was while basking in the heat of my father's anger, but as soon as I tried to stand up and found that my knees were frozen in place, I remembered. I'd just pried myself off the chair when there was a commotion outside the door and Sherri! ran in, holding a robe out toward me.

Bless you, Sherri!, I wanted to say.

Then I wanted to shout it when she smiled and said, "It's all taken care of. Everything is fine. We can stay in the hotel."

How totally MasterCard is my stepmother?

My dad and I were staring at her and she said, "Wait, here he is," and held out her arm like a game show hostess.

A man wearing a double-breasted gray suit came in. He was hand-some in a high-end-men's-catalog kind of way, with a square jaw and brown hair graying at the temples. He had slight crinkles around his eyes and his face was tan except for a triangular patch around his hair-line. He walked with a spring in his step, like an acrobat or a long-distance runner, and even though he was featuring white socks with black shoes, a definite fashion no-no, I decided I would give him the benefit of the doubt if he was there to free me.

He had a nice voice as he said, "Hello, Dr. Callihan. I am L. A. Curtis, the head of security for the resort." Then he looked at me and said, "This, I presume, is Jasmine."

I nodded. "Yes, sir." I couldn't help thinking he looked more like someone who should be welcoming guests to Fantasy Island than a security chief. "I am very sorry, sir, for everything that—"

He put up his hand and gave me a smile that almost blinded me, it was so white. "Stop, young lady. In fact, the Venetian Hotel would like to apologize to you and your family for any inconvenience."

Had I passed into a parallel universe? I looked around quickly.

L. A. Curtis *was* wearing white socks with black shoes, which was suspect, but everything else—father steaming; Sherri! beaming; me cold—was just as I expected. Finally I managed to stammer, "Are you sure?"

Mr. Curtis laughed like I'd said the funniest thing in the world. "Yes. We would like you to continue your visit with us. And the hotel would be delighted if you would allow us to cover the cost of your rooms."

This was really weird. "Um, thank you."

My father's eyes sort of goggled and he started to say, "That won't be necessary, we—" but Mr. Curtis cut him off with the words: "We would also like to extend the use of one of our limos to you at any time."

Oh, hello. Hotel limo? I was definitely in a parallel universe. Or one of those *Candid Camera* shows. That was it. And you know what? Who cared! They were giving me my own limo!

Of course a limo wouldn't really be any good to me if I were grounded. I said, "Does this mean I'm not in trouble?"

"There will be no record of what happened today at the pool. You have been fully exonerated."

Everything in my brain at this point said: Jasmine, do not speak. Keep quiet. Pretend your two lips are but one. Do what Helen Keller would do.

But I couldn't stop myself. I said, "Why?"

Mr. Curtis and my dad both gave me the same look. And let me tell you, it was not a look that said, "What a delight it is to have such an inquisitive daughter, let's join hands in merry revelry!"

To clarify, and because I was not yet completely gagging on the foot I'd inserted into my mouth, I went, "I just mean, what happened to change everything?"

My dad continued with The Look, but Mr. Curtis flashed me another smile and said, "These things are complicated, Miss Callihan. Let's just say—"

At that moment there was a knock at the door, and when it opened, who should muscle in but the Fabinator, the large gentleman with the small bathing suit and the gun.

Which he was still wearing. As I could clearly see beneath the turquoise mesh muscle shirt he'd slipped on.

Oh, yes. He went there.

"They want see the girl," he said, demonstrating an admirable command of short words.

L. A. Curtis gave what looked to me like his first genuine smile as a little boy appeared behind the Fabinator. He was the boy from the pool. Not the cute one who wouldn't take his shirt off, the little one. The one who had told me to run.

Demon child, you might call him. In light-up Spider-Man sneakers. And with a runny nose. Definitely sinister.

Standing next to him was the most perfect-looking woman I had ever seen besides Sherri! She was medium height with long blonde hair, wearing a black-and-orange silk wrap over her bathing suit. The only thing not quite perfect about her was that she had a black smudge shaped like a lightning bolt on the toenail polish of her left big toe. Honestly, that was the ONLY imperfection.

L. A. Curtis cleared his throat and said, "Miss Callihan, I'd like you to meet Fred and his mother, Ms. Bristol."

The perfect woman was Fiona Bristol! The yogi-slash-kindergarten teacher-slash-model-slash-scandal-haver. She must have been my savior. Why why why couldn't the Evil Henches have talked louder so I would have known what Ms. Bristol's scandal was?

Ms. Bristol pushed her son forward and said, "Fred, don't you have something to share with the lady?"

Fred took a step toward me and then said to the floor, "I'm sorry I got you in trouble." At least, I think that's what he said. He talked like someone angling for top prize in a "Don't Move Your Lips or Else Alien Ants Will Crawl into Your Mouth and Eat Your Brain" contest.

I understood, though. Parents. I said, "You didn't do anything wrong. Is your cat okay?"

Only then did he look up at me. I'd read in some of Sherri!'s Buddhism books about people with old souls, but I'd never really gotten what they meant until I saw Fred's face. He had cheeks and stuff like a little boy, but his eyes looked like they'd seen way more than most eight-year-olds. He nodded. "He's fine. We found him in some bushes."

"What's his name?"

"Mean And Dangerous Joe. We call him Mad Joe for short."

"That's a good name for him," I said, meaning it.

"He's a watch cat," Fred informed me, wiping his nose on the back of his hand.

His mom decided to cut in here. She said, "Sweetheart, we use Kleenex for that," and then smiled at me apologetically. "I'm sorry, he's got a mild case of the sniffles. I wanted to thank you also for chasing after Mad Joe. He's been a bit spooked lately, and I don't know what we would do if something happened to him." She put her hand on Fred's shoulder when she said that and he didn't even try to shrug it off. He was one unhappy kid.

"I'm glad everything has worked out all right."

Then there was one of those silences where everyone studies the carpeting like they've never seen such a remarkable substance before—

carpeting! Wonder of wonders! It's like hair! For the floor!—until L. A. Curtis stepped in to rescue us. Turning to Ms. Bristol, he said, "Why don't you two go back up to your suite while I finish up with the Callihans?"

My father stood up as they left, then turned to Mr. Curtis and said, "We'll be going as well. Thank you for your help."

"Before we leave, I was wondering—" I started to say, but my dad put on a weird smile and went, "Wouldn't you rather stop asking questions, Jasmine, and go enjoy yourself?"

Only the way he said it, it wasn't a question. It was more like a threat. Slash order. So I agreed.

Then there was another round of handshaking all around and a good deal of bonhomie (if that means goodwill between my father and L. A. Curtis) and we moved to the door. I couldn't get rid of the feeling, though, that despite him being very nice, none of this was Mr. L. A. Curtis's idea of a fun afternoon. In fact, I got the nagging sense that his version of an ideal world was one with fewer Jasmine Callihans in it. And I thought I knew why.

As I went by him to leave, I said, "I'm really sorry you had to be called away from fishing because of me. I hope you can go again tomorrow." I kept going, but he put a hand on my wrist to stop me.

He looked at me quizzically. "What a strange thing to say. What made you think that?"

"Well, I noticed—"

"Jasmine," my father's voice said behind me, "we are going. Now." And he grabbed my arm. For a minute I thought my dad and Mr. Curtis were going to play Stretch Armstrong with me, but Mr. Curtis let go, and my dad dragged me behind him.

While we were riding up to our adjoining suites in the elevator,

Sherri! said, "Jas, were you just guessing that he was on a boat?"

"No. His face was tan except for one corner of his forehead like he'd been out in the sun wearing a cap at an angle, he had a groove on his thumb where he'd been pressing it against something for a long time, and I guessed that something was a fishing line when I saw his cufflinks were fishing hooks. He was pretty nattily dressed, but he was wearing white socks with a gray suit and black shoes, which made me think he'd gotten dressed quickly to come to work. I bet Thursday is a quiet day at a casino, so it would be a good day for him to take off."

Sherri! said, "I think it's so cool how you can do that. I only noticed that he'd recently had his teeth done at BriteSmile. What about Ms. Bristol? Did you notice anything about her?"

Which made my dad growl and go, "Don't encourage her." Then he growled at me. "How many times have I asked you not to play your little detective games in public?"

"Eleven?"

More growling. "I'm serious, Jasmine. They are both disconcerting and troublesome. You embarrass people, and they don't like that. I'm sure I don't have to remind you what happened that time at the aquarium."

Okay, that was five years ago. More than a quarter of my life ago. I was sure my father would not want to be held responsible for things he'd done a quarter of a lifetime ago. I was going to point this out, but he kept right on talking, saying, "I really thought that if nothing else, what happened today would have taught you to mind your own business."

To which I said reasonably, "Actually, Dad, according to child labor laws, it's illegal for me to have my own business, at least in California."

My father sighed. He gave me the same sort of sad look I'd gotten a strong dose of earlier, the one that prophesied for me a lifetime of holding cells and clammy bikinis and being a huge disappointment to him. Part of me was mad at how unfair that was—because it was not like I had been *not* minding my own business. Did I summon the cat? No, I did not. And did I end up being THANKED and getting a limo? Yes, I did—but a bigger part of me just wanted it to stop. I decided at that moment that for the rest of our trip, I would be a Model Daughter, the kind you read about in Hallmark cards and see on TV ads (not the ones about how bad drugs are, the other ones). There would be no more "happenings" for me. Not so much as a thought about Ms. Bristol or why Fred seemed so sad or how important you had to be to get to keep a bodyguard with a gun at the pool, not to mention a "watch cat." I would take my dad and Mr. Curtis's advice and mind my own business and enjoy my vacation and not get into any trouble. With a limo at my disposal, how hard could that be?

Oh, yes. I actually thought that.

four

But being a Model Daughter did not exactly come naturally to me. I blame my father for that. In addition to being a genius, my father's superpower is to take your deepest and most precious desires and use them against you.

I call him the Thwarter. In my head I mean, not to his face. Usually.

This is how it works: Most of my friends' parents applaud and encourage it when their children evince an interest in some new hobby or subject. They see it as a precious spark to be nurtured and cultivated and blown on so it might one day blaze into—well, a blaze.

Not my dad.

Although he worked two jobs to enable his younger brother to follow his dream of becoming a doctor, my educational dreams are meaningless to him. As his behavior in the elevator made clear, my dad wants nothing more than to take the spark of scientific inquiry burning inside me and douse it with fire extinguisher foam. Then maybe stomp on it.

He says it's for my own good. Just like his suggestion that, instead of the topics that interest me, I should focus my attention on, and I quote to demonstrate how very, very sound of mind he is, "Things like combustion engines and needlepoint and maybe baking." Oh, certainly, Father, right after I make my own soap and perhaps dip a few souvenir candles from my 1888 girlhood! Curses, I got tallow on my pinafore!

Seriously, if he could lock me up at home without getting in some kind of trouble with the law, I really believe he would. My father is so overprotective he makes the Secret Service look like a bunch of slackers. Part of it has to do with the fact that my mom died in an accident when I was six, and I guess in some ways, until Sherri! at least, I was all he had. But it's one thing to be overprotective and another thing to be the Thwarter.

Ever since my mom died, the only thing I've wanted to be is a police detective. Not to go on a quest or try to solve some Nonexistent Mystery Surrounding Her Death, but because that was when I learned about how people leave things behind, even when they are gone from our lives.

When my mom had her accident, our house filled up with detectives and police officers asking questions and talking to my dad. One of them, this nice lady officer, took me aside and taught me how to find fingerprints on doorknobs and light switches. For months afterward I went around the house covering every surface with all my mom's old eye shadow and blush, looking for any prints of hers that might still be there. I guess in retrospect I can see why that sort of freaked my dad out, but the way he dealt with it—taking all of my mom's fingerprints I had carefully lifted and saved on paper and throwing them away and telling me never to do anything like that ever again OR ELSE—didn't really make me want to stop. Him being overprotective because my mom died, okay, but even as a first grader I knew that was no way to parent.

Like all good radicals, I took my cause underground. In second and third grades I would go over to Polly's house after school and we would play Barbie Crime Scene. Polly liked it because she got to dress Barbie and Ken and Skipper up in the right outfits for whatever scenario we were doing—like beachwear for "Tropical Paradise Turns into Bloodbath" or party clothes for "Massacre at a Charity Ball." We would pose them like crime victims and leave "evidence" around, and then the Spice Girls and My Little Pony would come and figure out what happened. Polly's mom thought our game was so cute she even had their housekeeper make a lab coat for Posh Spice that said CORONER on the back. (She didn't like it as much when Skipper offed Barbie and Ken and tried to cover up the evidence in "Night of Kasbah Passion Turns to Night of Horror" by setting a small fire. On an antique Persian rug. But that was kind of understandable.)

One day my dad came to pick me up when we were presenting our evidence in court (the Honorable Hungry Hungry Hippo presiding)—not even reconstructing a crime or doing "Courtroom Shootout Takes Down Key Witness" or anything—and his head almost peeled open to let Weebles come dancing out. It was unhealthy for us to think about murder, he said, waving his arms around. It was unnatural for us to reconstruct crimes, and, more than that, we could be putting ourselves in grave danger!

Yes! Grave danger! Playing Barbies! (And he wasn't talking about us developing eating disorders due to Barbie's unrealistic portrayal of the female anatomy, either. Or Achilles tendon injuries from walking on tiptoe. Or the fact that if you looked really close, Barbie's eyes did seem a bit CrAzY.)

I know he meant well. That he was just trying to protect me from . . . well . . . something. Something only he could see. Which is called, in the world of non-geniuses, Mental Illness. Anyway, from then on, Polly and I were only allowed to play Non–Crime Scene Barbies. For some reason my father saw no problem with us playing "Barbie and Ken Go to Hawaii to Save Their Marriage by Picking Up Another Couple for Sexy Good Times," but if Barbie and Ken had gone to Hawaii to "Rescue Another Couple from a Crazed Kidnapper," that would have been wrong.

I know. It's a wonder I grew up as normal as I did.

And nothing has changed. In fact, I think it's gotten worse. He still gets all red in the face if he sees the teensiest dusting of eye shadow on a surface, even if it just spilled while I was attempting to apply it to my eyelid. And okay, why I would be doing that in the kitchen is a bit of a mystery, and maybe I *was* trying to lift prints off the pitcher to see who had left the orange juice out AGAIN, but that could not in any way count as being dangerous. Or if I accidentally use the verb "to detect"—for example, in the sentence, "I detect that we are out of milk"—he goes cuckoo. Milk! Dangerous! It's like a mania or something. In my gentle, daughterly way I have even suggested that he talk to a professional about his problem, but surprisingly, he does not take kindly to this idea. "This is not a joke,

Jasmine," is what he says. And I totally agree. Any man who is afraid of Barbies and milk needs serious help.

Apparently, however, the problem is all mine. I am the one with "unsuitable, dangerous, and unhealthy" hobbies. Which is why, if I went to him today and asked for a few thousand dollars to set up a meth lab in the pool house, the chances are higher that he would give it to me than if I asked for a $400 advance against my allowance to buy a new microscope so I could replace the one from the Strawberry Shortcake Chemistry Kit I've been using since I was five. (Yes, that one has sentimental value, since my mom bought it for me before she died, but I really feel I am ready to move on to a microscope that is more than a tube of pink plastic with a magnifying glass at the end. And possibly even one that is not strawberry scented.) What kind of parent thinks this way?

The Thwarter does.

But I am stronger than he knows. I could not be so easily stomped into submission. It was my deep familiarity with the overprotective-slightly-unbalanced-fire-extinguisher-foam part of his personality that led me, as soon as I got back to my room, to log on to the Web so I could make sure that no one had gone in and interfered with TiVo recording *Forensic Files* while I was gone (Ha! Foiled again, Mr. Thwarty-Thwart). Even a Model Daughter could do *that*. While I was online I checked my email and found five messages from Polly.

To: Jasmine Callihan <Drumgrrrl@hotmail.com>
From: Polly Prentis <madamebovarywasframed@ hotmail.com>
Subject: Y

HAVEN'T YOU WRITTEN TO ME YET? YOU'VE BEEN GONE 23 HOURS. AM LANGUISHING HERE. LANGUISHING AND, um, watching TV. But there is nothing good on. So write to me. Also downloading country music. Yes. COUNTRY MUSIC. Do you feel guilty now? The Step-Dude has declared that we can only eat raw food and all anyone around the house can talk about is that Madison can say, "My shoes and purse don't match."
Write to me before things get desperate.

>airkiss< >airkiss<
Polly

Madison is Polly's two-year-old half sister, which makes it pretty impressive that she can coordinate accessories. And suggests that even she has a superpower—being a Baby Gap consultant before she even had real teeth.

More proof that everyone has a superpower but me.

To: Jasmine Callihan <Drumgrrrl@hotmail.com>
From: Polly Prentis <madamebovarywasframed@hotmail.com>
Subject: U so sad

Have now downloaded 4 country songs. One of them rhymes "bouffant" with "want." This is your fault. In case you forgot: I am the main lyricist for the band.

><
Polly

●●●●●●●●●●●●●●●●●●●●●●●●●●●●

To: Jasmine Callihan <Drumgrrrl@hotmail.com>
From: Polly Prentis <madamebovarywasframed@hotmail.com>
Subject: a picture is worth . . .

Me, with a bouffant, waiting for you to call:

```
        ( 0 )
       ( ( ( ) )
      ( ( ( ( ) ) )
       ( | >*< | )
        ) .  . (
          -
        <  |  >
         /\ | /\
          |\
          | \
        </ |  |\>
```

Still waiting:

```
              ()
            ((0))
           ((( ())))
           (|>*<|)
            ). .(
              -
          `\/ | \/`
            /_\
             |\
             |
          </|  |\>
```

Languishing . . .

```
              ()
            ((0))
           ((( ())))
           (|>*<|)
            ). .(
              ^_____
            \ /\
             \/ |\>
```

. . . and dreaming of . . .

```
              @
            (>*<)
           @@@@@
           @@@@@
          @@@@@@@
           @@@@@
           %. .%  <help! It's alive!
          ~  O  ~
          \/|\/
           / \
          /___\
          |: :|
          | |
          |: :|  |: :|
          </|    |\>
```

. . . you with a bouffant!

Ha! Take that. CALL ME! And, friendly reminder: I am also the main costume designer for the band. (At least I gave you your cowboy boots. But I can take those away at any moment. Tick tock.)
Yours truly, P

. . . .

To: Jasmine Callihan <Drumgrrrl@hotmail.com>
From: Polly Prentis <madamebovarywasframed@ hotmail.com>
Subject: Fine. I can take a hint. You don't like me anymore

Bye. Forever. Find yourself a new best friend.

. . . .

To: Jasmine Callihan <Drumgrrrl@hotmail.com>
From: Polly Prentis <madamebovarywasframed@ hotmail.com>
Subject: I mean it this time
!
p.s. Should I get bangs?

The answer to that was "no." Polly and I have a signed pact to not allow each other to get bangs. We've been down that path before and it's never pretty. But the fact that she was even considering it showed how desperate things had become for her.

That and the country music.

I had just started to write back to Polly when she IMed me.

PrincessP: RU OK? I called your dad's cell and Sherri! told me what happened. She said you tried to save a cat and went to jail and that FIONA BRISTOL bailed you out! What does she look like?

DrumGrrrl: Nice.

PrincessP: NICE? That's it?

DrumGrrrl: Yes. I don't think you should get bangs, P. And I think the band should stick with our current format. No country.

PrincessP: Okay, but what about Fiona Bristol??

DrumGrrrl: I told you. She was nice. I don't want to talk about her.

PrincessP: Come on, Jas. You know who Fiona Bristol is, right? She's the one whose husband

DrumGrrrl: NOT INTERESTED

PrincessP: killed her lover and

DrumGrrrl: NOT INTERESTED NOT INTERESTED

PrincessP: was arrested but before he could go to trial he escaped and

DrumGrrrl: DON'T CARE NOT INTERESTED DON'T CARE

PrincessP: What did they do to you there?

DrumGrrrl: Nothing. Why does it have to mean something is wrong with a person just because she doesn't want to hear gossip about people she doesn't know?

PrincessP: Or because she has begun speaking of herself in the third person?

DrumGrrrl: Don't we have anything more interesting to talk about than other people's problems?

PrincessP: Hello, Evil Jas. Can you please bring back Good And Nice Jas? Thank you.

<SheRox logged on>

<MrT logged on>

SheRox: JAS! Are you okay, sweetie? Tom and I just heard from Sherri!.

DrumGrrrl: Yes, Roxy, I'm fine. No big deal.

MrT: We hear you tussled with the Man. And won. Nice work.

DrumGrrrl: Thanks, Tom.

SheRox: Excuse me, no big deal? Can't you see they

must be covering up something huge to just let you go like that? Something having to do with Fiona Bristol? Did you see anyone who looked like they were in the Russian Mafia? It would not surprise me if they were involved in this.

PrincessP: Don't waste your time, Roxy. Jasmine has no interest in life's little mysteries any longer. Our little girl is growing up.

SheRox: What is Polly talking about?

DrumGrrrl: She's just mad because I don't want to hear gossip about Fiona Bristol.

SheRox: You do know there is a murder involved, right? And bounty hunters. There is even a million-dollar—

DrumGrrrl: DON'T CARE NOT INTERESTED

SheRox: Oh my God. Now, Jas, sweetie, I want you to think back. What exactly did you eat and drink while you were in custody? If we can figure out what they used, we can get an antidote and

DrumGrrrl: NO ONE DRUGGED ME!

PrincessP: Personally, my money is on them paying her for her silence. Or using electric shock therapy. Jas, do you have any unusual marks on your body?

DrumGrrrl: I am so not responding to that.

MrT: You tell them, cowgirl.

SheRox: They might have used an experimental hypnosis technique. It would leave no outward signs. The government is pioneering them. I read about that in *Know the Truth Weekly*.

MrT: Isn't that the same fine publication that ran a cover story about how Cabbage Patch dolls are actually secret recording devices made by aliens to see into American homes and learn our ways?

SheRox: Who but aliens would come up with a doll that is half vegetable, half human? It's completely plausible. As is the use of hypnosis on Jas. Or gum. Did they give you any—[1]

DrumGrrrl: I'm fine. It's just none of my business.

[1] Polly: Roxy? Pssst, over here.
Roxy: Hi, Polly. What are you doing down here?
Polly: Trying to get your attention stealthily.
Roxy: I love stealth!
Polly: Look, I'm worried about Jas. I was—
Roxy: Shhhhh. They might be listening.
Polly: Who?
Roxy: THEM. Her overlords. BE STEALTHY.
Polly: Um, Rox, I don't think—

	And I have decided I am going to mind my own business.
	Hello?
	Are you still there?
	Breaker breaker good buddy?
SheRox:	Sorry about that. Of course you're fine, sweetie.
PrincessP:	Right. Well, I've got to biplane. Tango class with Roberto. Can't keep him waiting or he gets hot behind the ears.
MrT:	I believe it's under the collar.
PrincessP:	He won't be wearing a collar. He dances without his shirt on. Ciao for now, cupcakes.
<PrincessP logged off>	
MrT:	WHY WON'T SHE GO TANGOING WITH ME?
DrumGrrrl:	Because you don't wax your chest and then apply baby oil to it until it attains a glassy sheen?

Roxy: Uh-oh, Jas is getting restless! We'd better go back up there before she gets suspicious and gives the game away.

Polly: What game? What are you talking about?

Roxy: Nothing to see here, nice overlords. Not a thing. Tra la la. (Call me later, P.)

44

SheRox: No way. Roberto doesn't do that.

DrumGrrrl: Cross my heart, not my fingers.

SheRox: Wow. Isn't that kind of messy?

MrT: You guys, I'm serious! I love her. What should I do??

DrumGrrrl: You know you have nothing to worry about with Roberto. He's just a dance partner to her and besides, Polly is the girl whose idea of intimacy is an air kiss.

MrT: Isn't that cute?

DrumGrrrl: If by "cute" you mean "strangely psycho."

SheRox: Maybe if you ever asked her out this would go better.

MrT: True. But how do you ask your dream woman to go out with you?

DrumGrrrl: "Hi, Polly? It's Tom. Would you like to go out with me?" might work. Just, like, for openers. Although you might want to say "Tom Hernandez, Roxy's brother" to make sure she knows who you are. Since she's only known you since we started going to school with Roxy in 6th grade and sees you, like, every weekend.

MrT: Thanks for the hot tip, Jas. So what are you

going to do now? Any retirement parties you
can take down? Or are the MIND-ALTERING
DRUGS still coursing through your veins?

DrumGrrrl: Why, Tom, I'd love to stay for more of this
witty banter, but alas, I've got to go. I have
callers.

SheRox: The Russian Mafia already! Do you want me
to call Sherri! and alert her?

DrumGrrrl: Actually, it's just room service.

SheRox: Okay, but be careful. The Russian Mafia
are all over that town. And the man was
murdered with a —

I logged off without reading the rest. It was seriously unfair of my friends to taunt me like that. Being a Model Daughter was going to be hard if I did not have a supportive peer group. But I was going to persevere in minding my own business. What I needed was sustenance, in the form of the grilled cheese sandwich with fries, ice cream sundae, and apple pie à la mode that was waiting for me on the other side of the door.

Or supposed to be waiting for me.

Because when I opened it, it wasn't the room service man standing there. Not by a long shot.

It was trouble.

Five

I should have expected it.

"Hi, Jas," Alyson said, using up all of her community service hours by giving me a big smile. "Can Veronique and I come in?"

"This is a really nice room," Veronique said.

"Don't they all look like this?" I asked.

"Um, well, our TV is on the other wall," Veronique said lamely.

Okay, I admit that by now it should have been clear to me what was going on, but I plead nerves ragged by the contest between my father, my friends, and my better self. It's not easy to be a Hallmark Card Model Daughter when you haven't trained for it.

And on an empty stomach.

I said, "Did you see the room service man outside when you came in?"

"No, are you hungry?" Alyson asked. "Because that's what we came about. To see if you wanted to have dinner with us."

"Why?" I asked.

"Duh, Calam—Jas, just to, you know, hang out."

"Your hair looks really nice like that," Veronique said.

That was when it clicked. "You want to go somewhere and you want to use my limo."

Alyson got all matter-of-facty. "It's not really your limo. Technically, you wouldn't even be here if it weren't for us. And if you weren't here, you wouldn't have the limo. And also, you know, the psychic scars from your actions? Well, we have them too."

"Really?" I asked. "Can I see them?" Because who wouldn't be interested in that?

Apparently she thought I was kidding. That is always the way. She said, "Whatever. There's this totally cool club on the top of the Rio, and Veronique's dad can get us on the list there so we won't need ID. Everyone will be there. We thought the three of us could go over and, like, have dinner and then maybe meet some guys. Do you want to come or do you want to be a loner-slash-loser and sit alone in your room all your life?"

Hmmm, two appealing options. While sitting in my room loner/loser style getting a little restorative Vitamin TV was at least guaranteed fun, the prospect of going out with Alyson and Veronique and watching them have to be nice to me because they wanted my wheels had its appeal as well.

And since in the backwards world I inhabited, to my father, me going out in a strange city and picking up men older than my stepmother would be better than me sitting at my computer and doing a Google search for Fiona Bristol, it was clear that the Hallmark Card Model Daughter thing to do was to cancel my room service order and go out with Alyson and Veronique.

Plus, none of the pay-per-view movies looked good at all.

Which is how I found myself, an hour later, wearing my gold Betsey Johnson dress, my "hot stuff" underpants, and my favorite brown cowboy boots with horseshoes embroidered on them, sitting in a limo with Alyson and Veronique on our way to the Voodoo Café and Lounge on the top of the Rio Hotel.

For the record, I do not think I am "hot stuff." Polly gave me the underpants as a joke and I only wear them to gym, but the Evil Hench Twins were rushing me and that was the pair on top.

Little Life Lesson 6: If you're going somewhere with Evil Hench People, take the extra time to find a non-embarrassing pair of panties. Really. Trust me on this.

In the limo Veronique adjusted her bra beneath her pink-and-purple lace camisole and said to Alyson, "If Miles could see you right now, he'd—"

Alyson shot her a look, and she immediately shut up. Even I would have shut up. Alyson had gone very Evil Hench Mistress, wearing a black leather miniskirt, black mesh top, black leather knee boots, and a black leather cap, and she looked scary.

But the chance that Miles was the reason Alyson had bitten her nails off was too good to let pass. "Who's Miles?" I asked innocently.

"No one," Alyson hissed, giving me the *Queen of the Damned* look. "Okay, Girl Scouts, it's time for the ground rules." She held up a finger with a black-painted nail on it, and I was glad to see that while I'd been worrying about my life behind bars, she'd had time to change her nail polish to match her outfit.

"First," she said, "no more than two dances-slash-drinks in a row with any one guy UNLESS you push your hair behind your ear with your right hand, which means, 'make an exception.'" She put up another finger. "Second, if you push you hair behind your ear with your left hand, it means, '911, cut in now.'"

"Cut in?" I asked.

"Yeah, you know, come over and pretend you have a crisis. Duh, Jas."

Okay. Right hand good. Left hand crisis. I said, "Should we be wearing Kevlar bulletproof vests or something? Or carrying black jacks?"

She ignored me.

On the way up in the elevator she added, like an afterthought, "Oh, and never leave your glass on the bar. Someone might put something in it."

Neat! I'd never been to a social gathering before where I was supposed to distrust everyone and be prepared to wrestle myself or others away from them. This was really going to be a learning experience.

And it didn't stop there. At dinner I gathered another Little Life Lesson.

Little Life Lesson 7: My definition of food (food) and other people's definition of food (lettuce, air) are not necessarily the same.

I got really excited when Alyson said, "And now, time for dessert," but I should have known better. In unison she and Veronique reached into their purses and pulled out their flavored lip glosses.

After that delicacy, we moved from the restaurant into the bar area. Everything was purple and red, and there were voodoo dolls and candles everywhere, so it seemed cool, and its coolness was confirmed by the fact that the bartenders appeared to be way hipper than the patrons.

There were a lot more men than women, most of them like the guys who hung around the keg at the UCLA fraternity parties I'd been to, slouching in jeans and untucked shirts and baseball caps, giving each other the occasional high five and appearing pretty much all the same. The bartenders, on the other hand, were wearing an assortment of black leather items and had piercings in all different places. The best one was a woman with really pale skin and dark hair wearing a black lace-up corset, black leather pants, a studded black choker, and a matching black leather wrist cuff. All the other bartenders seemed to kind of defer to her, as though they too felt her supreme excellence and honored her as their Queen. Or maybe she was just their boss. I sat on a stool in her section, hoping some of her coolness could ooze in my direction. Acting on Alyson's advice I ordered a bottle of water and a straw.

Before I could really start enjoying myself, Veronique popped up onto the stool next to me, her back to the bar, facing the room. At first she just sat quietly twirling her hair on her finger, with a little frown, but after a while she said, "I totally don't get it."

"What?" I asked, because I had to.

"Why all these guys are into you. They're fully eye-humping you."

Eye-humping. Why thank you, Veronique, for searing that image into my brain for all time.

And she wasn't done! She looked at me and wrinkled her nose. "I never would have thought you were so bacon."

"Bacon?"

"You know, sizzling hot?" Her expression changed to genuine confusion. "Do you and your friends speak Braille or something?"

"Yes, yes we do," I admitted. "When we're not speaking Esperanto."

"Oh." And she went back to scoping out the room.

I decided, despite the eye-humping, I kind of liked Veronique. I mean, how could I *not* like someone who believed I spoke Esperanto? And at least, unlike my so-called real friends, she didn't treat me like I had been the subject of a secret government experiment. Or if she did, it was nothing new.

As a gesture of friendship I went, "I'm sure the guys are all staring at you, not me." Plus, I was pretty sure it was true.

"No. I can fully tell when a guy is running my plates—I mean, checking me out," she added for the Braille-speaking crowd. "I have this, like, psychic ability to sense when guys are getting ready to put the moves on people. Like that guy over there in the cargo pants? A minute and ten seconds, he'll be over to ask me to dance. I bet his line will be something about numbers."

As we counted down the seconds, I said, "Who is Miles? In the limo you said he was a friend of Alyson's?"

"Sort of. He's this guy that Alyson—I mean, he's no one. I'm not supposed to tell about him."

"Please?"

But before I could get her to spill, time apparently ran out. The exact guy she'd said sauntered over, put one elbow on the bar, and said to her, "Can I borrow your cell phone to call 911? You're so hot you're setting this place on fire."

Which meant that now Veronique had a superpower as well. Great.

As she went off with Mr. 911 she pointed to a group of guys across the bar and said, "One of them will be over to talk to you in two minutes, tops. He'll bring up love."

I guess the odds were sort of in her favor, since a girl sitting alone at a bar is probably fair game, but I was still surprised that she was right again. Well, almost—it was two minutes and eighteen seconds. But the guy's line was, "Do you believe in love at first sight?"

"No."

"Me either. That's why I want to see you again tomorrow."

"Thank you, but I'm busy," I said, and developed an enormous interest in my water bottle.

"What about the next day?" He put his finger under my chin and turned my face toward his and I got a big whiff of cologne. "I just can't get enough of those dimples. Come on, what do you say?"

The cologne must have had some special brain-numbing power, because my mind went blank, and I said the first thing I thought of. Which was, *"Favor de dejar un especimín en este copa para el doctor."*

"What?"

"She told you to pee in a cup," the ultra cool Queen of the bartenders said. "I think that means get lost."

When he was gone I caught her eye and said, "Thanks."

She shrugged. "Don't mention it. What's your name?"

"Jasmine," I said.

"Listen, Jasmine, you've got to be direct with these guys. Don't beat around the bush. And don't worry about hurting their feelings—God knows they're not worried about hurting yours." (Little Life Lesson 8)

She had the kind of scratchy voice that suggests a lot of serious life experience, much of it occurring late at night in smoky bars. I felt like I had been taken under the wing of a Sage Master who would teach me the ways of the Cool and Jaded and protect me from evil. It was an extremely comforting thought.

Only I forgot the part about how somehow whenever the student faces a Supreme Test of Strength, the Sage Master is on a cigarette break.

So I was on my own when Bachelor Number Two sat down next to me and murmured, "Excuse me, don't I know you from somewhere?"

I said, "No."

He looked at me with his eyelids half lowered and went, "Now I remember, it was in my dreams. Want to make a few of them come true?"

Be direct, I heard my master's voice whisper. I said, "Does that line really work?"

Number Two went, "You're talking to me, aren't you?" And winked.

That was when I noticed he was about five times as big as I was and wearing a T-shirt that said UCLA WRESTLING, which didn't look borrowed. I decided the not-beating-around-the-bush thing to do, at that point, would be to get away. So I said, "No," took my bottle of water, and walked to the only place I knew a woman would be safe from a man.

As usual, there was a line in the bathroom.

Standing in the line at least gave me a chance to hear Bachelor Number Two pound on the door of the bathroom behind me and say, "Who do you think you are walking away from me? I'll be waiting for you, tall bitch." And not in, like, a cooing voice.

I was pretty sure that being followed to the bathroom by irate wrestlers was not the kind of behavior that Model Daughters engaged in. That or responding to the name "tall bitch." So I decided that as soon as I got into one of the five bathroom stalls I'd just stay there and never come out. That's why. Not because I am a coward.

Much.

But the thing is, it's kind of boring to sit in a bathroom stall.

Especially one at a fancy place, where no one has written anything instructive on the walls, like what number to call for a good time, or who is H-O-T-T. Once I'd read the label on my bottle of water, then shredded the label on my bottle of water, there really wasn't anything left to do.

Well, okay. I could ponder the failure of my Model Daughter scheme. Because I was pretty sure Model Daughters didn't find themselves hiding in bathrooms while a guy shouted, "Hey, tall girl, I'm still here," every time the outside door opened. I even found myself wishing I'd brought some dental floss so at least I could be doing something to deal with my plaque production superpower while I waited. (Little Life Lesson 9: Always carry dental floss with you. You never know when it could come in handy.) Truthfully, I was starting to feel a little sorry for myself.

Then I heard someone sniffling in the stall beside me. Model Daughters do not eavesdrop because they're too busy minding their own business, but my business had pretty much ground to a halt, and I couldn't help myself. Especially after the sniffling turned to a voice, which said, "I just want it all to end. I can't live this way anymore."

Who wouldn't listen then? Are Model Daughters supposed to be heartless as well? I don't think so.

Especially not if they think they recognize the voice. And if, happening to look beneath the wall between the stalls, they see a foot with a black smudge shaped like a lightning bolt on the nail polish of the left big toe.

It was Fiona Bristol. Crying.

And talking on the phone, I realized, when she said, "You have no idea what it's like. I'm terrified all the time. Terrified for myself, even more terrified for my son. I know what you think, but I have no choice. Every day asking myself what if, what if, I can't go on like that, I—"

There was silence broken only by her sniffles until she said in an angry whisper, "How can you promise that? You don't know. He might come at any moment and take us by surprise. And God knows what he will do. He's capable of anything. This is the only way."

Another pause. Her toes were pointed in, like she was pigeon-toed, and I pictured her slumped back hopelessly. I wondered where Fred was. Maybe the Fabinator was baby-sitting. Poor Fred.

Like she was reading my mind she said, "You know I hate leaving Fred, even just for a few hours. He's not feeling well and he gets so scared, and today, after what happened with the cat . . ."

I listened to see if she would mention me, but she just said, "Maybe. But it's too late now. I've made my decision. More than anything, I just want this to be over. I want to be able to go home. I want us to be done with this charade."

What charade?

She listened to the person on the other end of the phone for a few seconds before taking a deep breath and saying miserably, "God, why does doing the right thing have to be so much harder than doing the wrong thing?"

Silence again. I heard the scrape of a lighter and smelled cigarette smoke. She said, "Yes, I'm positive. And I'm grateful." Crossing one leg over the other, she said, "I don't know what I would do if I didn't have you, darling, I really don't."

Darling? Did she have a secret boyfriend?

There was a long pause while she listened to whoever was on the other end of the phone, and when she spoke again she sounded resigned. "I know. But having to talk to you on the phone like this instead of— Thank you, Alex," she said curtly. "I hardly need to be reminded of that."

Alex. That was "Darling"'s name.

There was another pause, and then she said, "Knowing you're on my side, that you're there for me, will be there for me the whole time no matter what, means everything. Listen, I'm going to get out of here. No, I won't do anything drastic." The cigarette butt fell to the floor, and she crushed it under the heel of her shoe. "Yes, I promise. Love you too."

I heard her push the OFF button on her phone. For a few moments she sat very still. Then she took a single ragged breath, pushed herself up, and walked out of her stall.

I wish I could say I had a moment of indecision about what to do, that I took into account the whole Model Daughters Are Own-Business-Minded thing, and Bachelor Number Two on the outside waiting to pounce on me. But I didn't. And not (just) because I am nosy. Or because I owed her for being my savior earlier that day. There had been something in Fiona Bristol's tone when she said she wouldn't do anything drastic that sounded like maybe she'd had her fingers crossed. And we were on top of a forty-five-story building.

No part of the Model Daughter job description could possibly involve letting someone plunge to their death, I reasoned, so I bolted out of the bathroom after her as soon as I could.

Or anyway, that was my plan. By the time I threaded my way through the line of women applying lip gloss, teasing up hair, squinting at themselves in the mirror, and waiting to use the bathroom, she was gone. The corridor the bathroom gave on to was empty— Bachelor Number Two must have given up, I noted, not exactly shedding any tears—but then I thought I saw someone just beyond it. I was so distracted looking ahead of me that I didn't notice the man coming toward me until I almost bumped into him. Which shows I must have been preoccupied because he was wearing a long white caftan and had a huge beard. Kind of hard to miss. In fact, he looked a lot like Polly's mom's Kabala teacher, except this man had a longer beard and a gold watch. (Polly's mom's guru is strictly anti-time-keeping. He says watches interfere with the body's rhythms.) Even with that concession to the modern world, he was not exactly the kind of person you'd expect to see at a place like the Voodoo Lounge. His breath didn't smell like he'd been drinking, but he seemed a little unsteady on his feet. I said, "Pardon me," and moved to the right, but he did too, and then we both went to the left. He gave a half smile and mumbled, "I hadn't planned on doing any dancing tonight," and it fully would have been funny, if I hadn't been trying to get anywhere. Finally he stepped to one side and I stepped to the other and went by him. But it was too late.

Fiona Bristol was long out of sight. I headed for the place I'd choose if I were going to harm myself, the outside balcony that was on the corner of the building, to look for her. I pushed my way through the packed crowds and for once I was glad to be tall. I walked all around the balcony twice, but I didn't see Fiona anywhere. If she wasn't outside it meant she wasn't going to hurl herself to a dramatic death. At least not right then.

Still, I wanted to be sure she was safe. I went back inside and stood at the edge of the dance floor to see if I could spot her there. I was standing on my tiptoes trying to see over the packed crowd when a male voice behind me said, "Excuse me. Don't I know you?"

No. Please, no. Not again.

A wise voice in my head rasped *be direct*.

Without turning around I said, "That arctic blast you're feeling? It's the chill coming off my cold shoulder." Snappy and direct. Done and done.

There was silence, which I thought meant mission accomplished, but before I could pat myself on the back, the Male Voice returned, closer behind me this time. It said, "Do you have a copyright on that? I think that's the best line I've ever heard."

Not only did Male Voice say that, but it said it in a British accent. One of the really fancy ones.

I turned around and found myself face to chest with a Greek god. At least if his pecs, which I could see through his well-fitted—but not tight—white linen shirt, were anything to go by.

Then I looked up.

six

I swooned.

No, I didn't, but I fully could have, because his face was even better than his voice or his pecs. And it was a face I knew: the face of the cute guy from the Snack Hut at the Venetian pool!

And he was smiling at me. And was cuter up close.

Better-than-ice-cream cute. Super-duper-deluxe-supersize-that-please-ma'am cute. Who-cares-what's-on-TV-I-can-just-stare-at-you-all-night cute.

Yes, *that* cute.

Suddenly I *did* believe in love at first sight. Because there was the proof, all wrapped in a dark-haired, lightly tanned, moss green–eyed, worn-in jean-ed, green suede Adidas-ed, white-shirted package—that was at least four inches taller than me.

My one true love.

He smiled more—he had really nice teeth—and said, "I thought it was you. I saw you at the Venetian pool this afternoon. With the cat."

And because there are monkeys that live in my head and always make me say the wrong thing, I said, "Ah. If you saw my moves there, I guess you're not going to ask me to dance."

I'm pretty sure the vocabulary word to describe that is "suave."

Unsurprisingly, he looked at me like I was a lunatic and sort of seemed to choke for a moment before recovering speech. "Actually, I wanted to ask if you were all right. It looked like things got a bit rough for you."

He came to see if I was all right! My limbs were all hot and cold and my heart was so loud in my ears I felt like I was on some kind of medical show. I said, "It was nothing. I just feel bad for those people whose wedding I interrupted."

"I think they're lucky—at least their wedding will be memorable. Not just another boring ceremony. Although I really felt the groom should have jumped in the water as well."

Like he had read my mind. Soul mates, that was what this was called. I couldn't speak.

He nodded toward the dance floor. "I didn't mean to interrupt you if you were looking for your friends, Miss—"

"Callihan," I stammered. "But you can call me Jasmine. Or Jas." Or Snookums. Honeybunch. Hotsie Totsie Cowgirl. My Little—

"It's nice to meet you, Jasmine. I'm Jack."

Is it me, or do Jas and Jack sound really, really good together? They do! The monkeys in my head thought so too, chiming in to sing "Jas and Jack, sitting in a tree, K-I-S-S-I-N-G" as we shook hands.

His hand was strong and warm and soft. I did not want to let go.

His superpower, it became clear, was to use his smile to debilitate anyone who came close to him and erase their memory so they could not think of what they meant to say, or who they were, or anything besides, "Wow is he hot, I wonder what his favorite flavor of ice cream is." Which is what I was thinking when I realized he was talking again.

"Are you the baby-sitter?"

"The what?"

"The baby-sitter. For the boy with the cat?"

I laughed. The idea of me baby-sitting, given the kind of rapport I had with children, was very funny. "Um, no."

He looked confused. "Then you're a friend of the family's?"

"No. I'd never met them. I mean, before. I have now. They introduced themselves afterward."

He said, "How were they?" and for a moment his voice sounded different, more intense. Then he shook his head. "I'm sorry. What I meant to ask was, were they, ah, grateful?"

"Yes. Mostly they seemed relieved." Which was very different from how Fiona Bristol had sounded in the bathroom talking to darling Alex. Meeting the Man of My Dreams had momentarily distracted me from looking for her, but I was on a mission. I made myself remove my eyes from Jack and glance around the dance floor, toward the bar.

Weirdly, after all my unsuccessful looking, she was now the first person I saw. She was standing there with none other than the Fabinator, who had changed his swim trunks for a pair of jeans and a jacket that no doubt concealed his gun. But more astonishing—more astonishing even than the fact that the Fabinator had tied his hair back with a black bow. A BOW! Way to show fashion who's the boss of it,

Fabinator! You go!—was that Fiona Bristol was leaning against a stool next to him, laughing and smiling. Looking happy. As if there were nothing wrong.

As if she had not been sobbing and saying she was terrorized and sounding suicidal just a few minutes before. Hadn't she?

It didn't matter, I realized, since she looked fine now. I should have felt relieved but I was more confused. Something must have shown up on my face because Jack said, "Are you okay?"

My eyes went back to him and I almost said, "no," because the way he was gazing at me, DOWN at me, made me feel woobly and tingly and like I wanted to bare my soul to him. But I didn't want to move too fast—probably a bare foot was a better place to start—so instead, I tried for a smile that I prayed didn't make me look stupid or young (dimples do that) and said, "Yes, I'm fine. I, um, thought I saw one of my friends. But I was wrong."

He said, "Good. I'd be sorry to lose your company."

"You would?" I asked.

"Of course. It's not often one meets a genuine good Samaritan."

That was not exactly what I'd hoped he'd say. "I'm more like a disaster attractor-beam. Ask my father. I'm no good Samaritan."

"I beg your pardon. As I understand it, you ran off with the cat simply to be nice. Because the little boy shouted at you."

I shrugged and then I heard my mouth reply, "I guess I'm just a sucker for boys." Which was 100 percent not what I meant it to say. Uh, monkeys? You're so dead.

But I decided it was okay when he laughed. This really, really nice laugh that made me think of maple syrup melting on hot waffles. He said, "Thank you, Jasmine. It's been a long time since someone has made me laugh that way." Like he really meant it and was harboring some deep inner trouble, which only I could help him out of.

Preferably while helping him out of his shirt.

His face got serious, and he cocked his chiseled, cheekboned head to one side. "But I thought you were the keeper of the cold shoulder. You seem very warm to me for an ice maiden."

"I am. I mean, I'm not. I—" I'd looked away from him again, hoping that might allow me to speak like a human being, but instead I caught sight of Alyson on the other side of the dance floor, furiously pushing her hair behind her ear with her left hand.

Was left good or bad? I couldn't remember. From the way she was leaning away from the guy, I guessed it was bad. Which figured. I meet the man of my dreams, act like an utter moron, and then have to leave him without having a chance to redeem myself. I said, "I'm sorry, but I've got to go."

"Of course. It looks like you spotted your friend. It was a pleasure to meet you."

"Ditto," I said, and headed for Alyson.

Ditto? What was I, seventy? And why was I helping Alyson, anyway? She would never have helped me. Especially if she were talking to a guy.

And what a guy. I looked back over my shoulder. Jack was still standing at the edge of the dance floor where I'd left him, but he was staring intently off to one side and kind of frowning. He was even gorgeous as he frowned. Be still my heart.

Then I noticed these two really pretty girls in the corner staring and pointing at him (did I mention he was hot? Like "Get the ice pack, I've got a first-degree burn" hot?), and I realized he was out of my league.

Plus, Alyson needed help. And she did look pretty grateful when I tapped her on the shoulder and said, "Hi, Allie," even though I know she hates to be called Allie.

"Jas. Nice of you to drop by."

"Yeah, well—" How did one butt in? "I'm having a crisis."

The guy with Alyson, wearing wire-rimmed glasses and a button-down shirt said, "Can't you see we two players want to be alone?" He looked like a wannabe Bill Gates, but talked like a wannabe hip-hop star. Which is not exactly a combination I'd recommend if you were placing an order at 1-800-Dream Date. He added, "'Less you're interested in making it a threesome, sweet thang?"

"No," I said. "Thank you anyway." I spotted Veronique nearby and I flagged her over. "There's our other friend. We've got to go. Come on, Alyson."

The guy reached out to stop me, holding my dark arm next to Alyson's paler one, and said, "You sure? A little chocolate on vanilla action. I could get into that."

"I beg your pardon?" I asked. *Model Daughter*, I told myself. *Be a Model Daughter.*

"Oh, yeah. Have me some hot chocolate with whipped cream on top." Veronique had wandered over by then, and he licked his lips, said, "Make that a double portion," and pulled us closer to him.

Alyson said, "*Eeeeeew.* Let go of us!"

And for once I completely agreed with her.

Even when she balled up the fist of her free arm, reached up, and punched him in the nose.

Little Life Lesson 10: Violence is not the answer.

Little Life Lesson 11: However, in books where it says punching an assailant in the nose will debilitate him, it's true.

seven

People are always surprising you. Take Alyson. She hadn't seemed to like the guy that much when I walked up to them, and when we got in the down elevator she said, "I've never been so grossed out-slash-insulted in my *life*."

I nodded. "I know what you mean."

That's when she looked at me like I'd grown extra heads. "Um, excuse me, what do YOU have to be grossed out about? I mean, he went from hitting on me to hitting on *you*. That is MORTIFYING."

Veronique nodded vigorously. "I was just telling Jas how surprised I am that guys—"

"Uh, Veronique?" Alyson interrupted. "Were my lips moving?

They were? Right. When my lips move, yours don't." She looked down at her hand. "Great. My knuckle is bleeding and I broke another nail. This is all your fault, Jas."

Now *that* was MasterCard.

And then there was her nerd boyfriend, DJ Jazzy Bill Gates. He didn't really look that likable to me. But it turned out, moments later in the lobby, that he knew a lot of people. People with muscles and thick necks. Including Bachelor Number Two from the bar. Who was now with a pack of like-minded individuals, following us through the lobby shouting, "You made a mistake, tall girl."

The three of us stayed slightly ahead of them to the front of the hotel. Where, mercifully, we found our limo waiting.

Limo, yes. Driver, no.

Screaming hordes? Right behind us.

Alyson and Veronique took refuge in the back of the limo and hit the LOCK button, rolling down the window to say, "Go find the driver, Jas."

I should have left them there right then. Headed for the hills, made a life for myself as a mountain woman, living off the land, yodeling for tourists, and milking yaks. Or at least hopped in a cab and gone back to the hotel.

But for some dumb reason, I felt like it would be wrong to leave them there. Plus, if I did, Alyson would tell her father who would tell my father and the Model Daughter scheme would be dead and gone. Deader and goner than it already was. So I turned around, praying that when I did, by some miracle, I'd see the driver. What I saw instead was one of the Screaming Horde Of Guys (SHOG) shoving a burly valet parker out of the way like he was a popsicle stick. Deciding this was the G-rated preview of the NC-17 treatment he had in store for me, I ran to the driver's side of the limo and tried the door.

It was unlocked. And the keys were in the ignition.

I decided it was a sign.

My plan, as I peeled out of the Rio driveway leaving the SHOG in my wake, was to go straight back to the Venetian.

Only limos? While completely stocked to answer all your crystal decanter needs, are a bit light in the map department. Sure they have one of those electronic GPS direction locator units. But those are kind of finicky, it turns out. Like, one wrong button push and *whammo!*, they only speak Chinese.

Oops.

Little Life Lesson 12: If you have your cousin and her friend stand out the sunroof of your limo to give you navigational instructions, be sure that they aren't facing backward to wave at the cute guys in the Porsche behind you when they tell you to go left or right.

Little Life Lesson 13: Making U-turns in a limo requires some form of advanced super-driver training they don't give you in regular driver's ed. At least not at my school.

Limos are kind of fun to drive, though. They have a smooth ride and much better pickup than you would think. Their brakes are also quite good.

Which comes in handy if you find yourself surrounded on all sides by police cars and are forced to pull over onto the gravel shoulder of the highway.

It turned out our limo driver had just gone to the bathroom, and boy was he surprised when he came out and found his ride gone. Surprised enough to call in a favor with a friend on the police force who issued an all-points bulletin on us.

(For the record, at no point while extending the use of a hotel limo did Mr. Curtis specify that it was only for riding in. So there would really be no technical basis for a grand theft auto charge.)

(And I seriously don't see why I was threatened with a resisting arrest charge when I was not the one who, as the police report states, "promised to 'give you cops a makeover you'll never forget' while menacing the officers with a pack of Bubble Yum and a cuticle scissor.")

(Nor was I the one who "attempted to inflict grievous bodily harm against Officers Knightly and O'Bannon with a pointed high heel, size seven, and a cell phone." Since, among other things, I am the only potty-trained person in North America not to have a cell phone.)

(And I wear a size ten.)

Yes, Fates, I know. Ha ha. Get your laughs now.

I would have said, once Officers Knightly and O'Bannon let us go merely with a warning to "never make yourselves visible to us again," after a long cell phone chat with Veronique's father—whose superpower, apparently, was to get his daughter both into clubs and out of legal jams—that this was one of the worst days of my life. I could not think of a way it could have been worse. I mean, I'd been mauled by a cat, a security guard, and some strangers at a bar. I'd almost died in my most embarrassing underwear. I'd been arrested two times. My attempt to be a Hallmark Card Model Daughter had been pretty much of a failure. And I had humiliated myself in front of the man of my dreams. Twice.

But as I put on my Hello Kitty pajamas and got into bed, I couldn't stop smiling.

I'd met the One.

And he was tall.

I was so tired-slash-euphoric that I could barely string the sentences together in the email I wrote to Polly telling her about what had happened,[2] but I knew she'd never forgive me if I didn't send one. As it was, I fell asleep almost as soon as my head hit the pillow.

Still, there is nothing like the sound of someone trying to break into your hotel room to jolt you out of even the deepest sleep.

[2]Polly: Do "Stole car. Got arrested. Met man of dreams. Must go die now. Miss you," count as sentences? Because that is what the email said.
Roxy: Well, they have periods. And verbs in them.
Polly: Yes, verbs like "arrested" and "die."
Roxy: Those aren't my favorites either—I like "eat" and "order dessert" best, I think. Or maybe "slurp milkshake." It was nice of her to say she misses us.
Polly: Um, Rox? That's not the point.
Roxy: Oh. Do you think we should do something? Wait—DOES THIS CALL FOR AN INTERVENTION? INTERVENTION! I love interventions! What should we confront Jas about first? Her increasing drug use? Her slipping grades?
Polly: Jas doesn't use drugs, and she's, like, number two in our class. I was thinking more about her freakish behavior today. Clearly, repressing her interest in Fiona Bristol is leading to all kinds of acting out.

Roxy: It's not that unusual for Jas to find herself in the hands of a security team.

Polly: But auto theft?

Roxy: Hmm, good point.

Tom: Hi, Polly. Wait a sec, what are you two doing down here?

Roxy: Nothing. Move along young Tom.

Tom: Your eye is twitching, Rox. You are up to something.

Roxy: Girl talk. We were discussing whether big granny underwear was In or Out this season.

Tom: How funny, that happens to be a topic on which I'm an expert. Pray, continue.

Polly: Actually, we were discussing what to do about Jas. I'm really worried. But I have an idea. Here, I've made a list of what we need. I think we should —

Roxy: Whisper! In case THEY are listening.

Polly: Roxy, you are being —

Roxy: They have ears EVERYWHERE.

Polly: Fine. Here's what I think we should do. We take six to eight . . . and then . . . which we can easily do with a regular D-cell battery, after which . . . and *voilà*! Jas, good as new.

Roxy: Wow, that sounds great! An excellent plan!

Tom: Are you sure it's not a little extreme? Someone could get hurt.

Roxy: You're either with us or against us, my brother. Which is it? And don't think I won't use this thing, because I will.

Tom: Are you threatening me with a hairbrush, Roxy?

Roxy: Styling attachment. It's Mom's. I think it may be the source of her terrifying power.

Polly: We have no time to lose. Are you in or out, Tom?

Tom: If you're in, I'm in.

Polly: Excellent. I'll pick you guys up tomorrow early so we can stop You-Know-Where before we head out.

Roxy: And I'll go put the You-Know-Whats by the front door so I don't forget them. Next to the Oh-Yes-We-Dids. And the Funyuns.

Tom: Funyuns?

Roxy: For strength. You know, in case Jas gets balky.

Polly: Good thinking. Wow, Jas is so lucky to have us.

Tom: Yes, your devotion really brings a tear to the eye. Hey, get that demonic hairbrush away from me.

Roxy: It's a styling attachment!

Polly: We'd better go to sleep. We'll need our wits about us to complete our mission.

Roxy: Good point. Agents Roxy and Tom of Team Rescue Jas signing off, captain.

Polly: Over and out.

Eight

At first I thought the scraping was a sound in my dream, but since my dream was about Jack and me on a deserted Caribbean beach eating ice cream sundaes, it didn't quite fit.

Neither did the distinctive sound of the door handle turning on the outside door of my room.

I needed something to use as a weapon to protect myself. Polly always keeps a pair of stiletto heels by the bed for emergencies, but I can't wear them because they make me too tall, and anyway, I'd probably hurt myself in the middle of the night. I knew there was a Bible in the night table and that seemed like the kind of weapon a penitent Model Daughter would use to protect her virtue.

I took it and I crept out of bed. The way the room was laid out, there was a little entryway between the sleeping area and the front door. Off of that was the bathroom. I couldn't hear anything over the sound of my breathing, so I held my breath as I pressed my back to the wall and peered around the corner toward the door.

Nothing.

With the Bible in one hand, I slid toward the bathroom, kicked the door open, hit the switch, and yelled, "Ha!"

No one.

I looked in the little separate room with the toilet in it. I looked in the closet. I even bent down and looked under the sink, even though I could see standing up that no one was there.

I was alone in my room. The bolt on the door was locked. The security chain was still in place.

I must have dreamed the noises.

Then I looked at the floor. There, lying on the carpet, was a piece of paper. It was an envelope with the hotel name on it, the kind that came in the stationery set in the desk.

JASMINE CALLIHAN
ROOM 35017

was written on the outside, so there was no question it was for me.

I admit it, as I carried it and my trusty Bible to the desk near the windows, my hands were shaking, partially from being scared and partially because I kept thinking: What if it was a note from Jack?

The curtains had been closed the night before by the hotel staff, and when I opened them, I was surprised to see it was already daytime. The clock on the desk read 7:19 as I took the piece of notepaper out of the envelope. It was mostly blank, except across the center where someone had written:

STAY OUT OF IT,
FOR YOUR OWN GOOD.
A FRIEND

How nice, I thought. I have a friend interested in my well-being. Not.

What I thought was, "Stay out of what?" and then, "Someone is threatening me." So when I heard footsteps behind me, I picked up the Bible and hurled it at the intruder.

Who happened, unfortunately, to be my dad. Coming in through the door that connected our two rooms.

"Bloody hell, Jasmine, what are you doing?" he said, catching the Bible. Before I could commend him on his outstanding reflexes (and I wasn't even going to add "for an older gentleman"), he said, "Never mind. I don't care what you are doing now. I only care what you did last night. Blast all, can't you stay out of trouble for two hours together?"

Which did not seem to mark this as the right time to tell him that I had a mystery correspondent concerned about my longevity. Or lack thereof.

Pretending to stretch, I shoved the note in the elastic waistband of my pajamas. "Sorry, Dad, you scared me."

He was flipping the Bible over in his hands. "Were you reading this?"

"Yes," I said. "I was. To repent. For last night. Sometimes I like to do that."

"I've never seen you reading the Bible before."

"Well, you know, I like to think my literary tastes are a bit eclectic."

"I thought your literary tastes were limited to books like *Introduction to Crime Scene Investigation* and *The Detective's Handbook*."

If my dad had ever wanted to try knocking me over with a feather, that would have been a good time to choose. I had no idea he even knew about those books. They were strictly on the No Read list, which the Thwarter uses to crush my dreams. I'd had to save my allowance for three months for each of them. And pull up a corner of the carpet to make a hiding place. This meant serious trouble.

But then I remembered what Roxy and Tom's older brother said when their parents caught him with pot in his sock drawer right out of rehab, and I saw a ray of hope. I looked my dad in the eye and said, "I'm just holding them for a friend."

Only after I said it did I recall that Mr. and Mrs. Hernandez hadn't bought it.

"Humpf," my father said, or snorted. "We'll talk about that later. Now, about the limo—"

"I was bringing it back. I just got a little lost. I had to take it because these guys were chasing us after Al—"

"Jasmine?"

"Yes?"

"Stop talking. I do not want to hear another excuse about how something else 'happened' to you. About how you accidentally punched a man in the nose. I—"

"What? I didn't—"

"I know all about it. Alyson told her parents. And we will deal with that at a future time. For now, your uncle thinks the entire situation is hilarious. He says he's thrilled Alyson got out and had some fun."

My poor, poor misguided uncle. But what was bad news for the world—Alyson out sharpening her claws on the world's collective couch leg—was good news for me. Because my father adored his younger brother. And if his younger brother wasn't mad and wasn't punishing Alyson, then I was in the clear. Although the fact that Alyson fobbed that right hook off on me smarted.

"Not that I am happy about it, mind you," my father felt forced to conclude. In case I suddenly thought that he had grown a new limb and filled it with Pop Rocks and kindness.

"Don't worry, I'm sure you'll have a chance to ground me again soon," I said.

(But I was joking. Do you hear that, Fates? JUST JOKING.)

(Little Life Lesson 14: The Fates have *no* sense of humor.)

My dad looked at me for a looooooong time, one of those searching looks that make you want to start hopping around on one leg and flapping like a bird to make them stop. He said, "I sincerely hope not, Jas. And to see to it that there is at least a moment of peace around here, I would like you to stay close to Sherri! and me for the rest of the day."

"Sure, okay," I said, and even my dad was surprised by how enthusiastic I sounded. He didn't realize that I was figuring whoever had threatened me would keep their distance so long as I was near my parents.

Or that I needed to get him out of the room for what I had in mind.

I dialed Polly's number as I changed into my swimsuit.[3] When I got her voice mail, I whispered, "Polly, I need to talk to you urgently. Call me as soon as you get this."

Then I put the note carefully into my underwear drawer to deal with later. It was my first piece of evidence.

Good-bye, Model Daughter, we hardly knew ye.

---

[3] Tom: Polly, it's your phone. The caller ID says the Venetian Hotel. It must be Jas. Should we answer it?

Roxy: No way. We are radio silent. From here on in, Team Operation Jas goes black ops code super stealth.

Polly: All cell phones to their OFF positions.

Roxy: And traitors will be shot.

Tom: Put the glue gun down, Roxy.

nine

Despite wearing my lucky bikini with the padded top and my lucky Urban Decay lip gloss and my lucky black cowboy boots with the red broken hearts stitched on them (a precautionary measure; I did not want to have to run in flip-flops again), things were not going my way. Polly didn't call back, and Tom and Roxy's cell phone bounced straight to voice mail, and I hadn't had time to get online before the Thwarter dragged me out of my room, so my major sources of information were out. I would even have been happy to see the Evil Hench Trolls, since if I was right about what "it" was that I was supposed to stay out of, they knew something about it, but apparently recovering from the ordeal of the previous night required them to spend the day at the spa.

Which left me stuck with the Thwarter and Sherri!. I have never been stranded on a desert island by myself with no sign of another soul in sight, but I would imagine it is much more pleasant than being trapped on a lounge chair next to Sherri! and my dad. Sherri! says she loves my dad because he is the funniest, most charming, and most thoughtful man she's ever met, and while I suspect this is a sign of intense mental illness on her part, I think it's great. And Sherri! makes my dad smile and laugh in a way I didn't even know he was capable of. I am thrilled that they have found bliss with each other. Honestly. I wish them all the best. But sometimes I wish they would bliss themselves a little farther away from me. For one thing, they feed each other.

For another, they finish each other's sentences.

And they coo.

But that's not the worst part. Sometimes they giggle to each other in this conspiratorial way like they're remembering fabulous sex acts they performed the night before.

And really? I do not want to think of them performing sex acts. Especially not fabulous ones. I have a very active and delicate imagination and I think it would be only fair of them to respect it, rather than contribute to its downfall. I could become a degenerate with the things I was thinking because they made me.

When we first sat down, they mostly were whispering, and I could ignore them by concentrating on saying the alphabet backward in my head and making myself remember irregular verbs from French class and writing haikus like:

Jack, my one true love,
Where are you hiding yourself?
My eyes must have lunch

And

Ms. Bristol, is your
Cabana as oh-la-la
As it looks from here?

But time passes. Concentration wanes. Hunger sets in. My investigation called to me. And also, Sherri! and the Thwarter started getting louder.

After we'd been outside for an hour, my father began to make audible growling noises. Not the kind he makes at me when he is mad. No, these were some other kind. A kind that made Sherri! go, "Oooh, Mr. Tiger. Are you feeling frisky?"

That was it. That is an image no daughter should ever, ever have.

No no no no no
No no no no no no no
Mr. Tiger no!

Think of my tender ears! I could have died of cardiac arrest right then and there.

But, unfortunately, I did not. What I did do was get up from my lounge chair, which immediately put a stop to the growling. My father returned to his human form to snap, "Where are you going, Jasmine?"

Ah, this must be a sign of his *thoughtfulness*. I said, "I was just going to hop in my personal spaceship and go orbit the moon." It sounded like a good idea. There was no noise—and therefore no MR. TIGER—in space.

My father put on his Frown of Great Menace. "If I were a young lady in your position, Jasmine, I would not be so blithe."

I hadn't even known I was being blithe! "If you were a young lady, Dad, *a lot* of things would be different," I said. Blithely.

"I am being serious."

"Me too. Think of the advantages—with me off in space, you won't have to buy me any new clothes. Or pay college tuition."

"Jasmine," he said in what he thinks of as his Warning Tone. "We had an agreement. You are to stay—"

"I know, Mr. Tiger, I mean, Dad. But truthfully?" I was interested to hear what came out of my mouth next. I hadn't really had any destination in mind when I stood up, so I tried to come up with the most innocent thing I could think of. "Truthfully, I was going to go see if Fred Bristol, who I just saw go into his mom's cabana, wanted to go get an ice cream with me." Only after I spoke the words did I see what a genius idea it was.

Not only did ice cream suggest innocence more than any other food ever, and not only did I actually want some, and not only would an eight-year-old understand eating ice cream before you've had lunch, but buying a child ice cream seemed like a sure way to get him to tell you his life story. And his mother's.

Because there was little question that the "It" the threatening note wanted me to stay out of was connected to Fiona Bristol.

It also meant I had to be careful. But whoever had warned me to stay out of "It" could not possibly think I was in "It" if I was just buying a young boy ice cream. Could they? Ice cream was above such petty things as "It." Ice cream was like saying, "Move along, friend, no 'It' to see here." But in creamy goodness form.

In fact, I reasoned, I was probably even safer taking Fred for ice cream than with my dad and Sherri!. How much danger could Fred and I get into just getting ice cream?

And even as I thought that, a part of my brain—a part which I have to say is really too small. I mean, hello, Part, couldn't you have spoken up?—whispered, "You know, in books, anytime a heroine thinks, 'How much danger could I be in if I just went for a short swim in the pretty blue ocean,' she always ends up being mauled to death by hungry sharks. Just FYI."

But as I said, it whispered all that information, so pretty much all I was aware of was the fleeting thought "hungry sharks." And since there are no sharks at the Venetian, and since I was feeling the need for speed away from Coo, and since the Thwarter actually agreed to let me go, I pulled my black terry-cloth dress over my bathing suit, slid into my cowboy boots, and went off to invite Fred for ice cream— well, blithely.

Little Life Lesson 15: Blithe is bad. Blithe is really, really bad.

Little Life Lesson 16: If you're looking for a good time, don't call an eight-year-old boy for a date.

After a brief consultation with the Fabinator and strict instructions on the use of Kleenex, Fiona agreed to let Fred go with me. I am sorry to say, however, my pleasure in this privilege was short-lived.

Maybe because I am an only child, I haven't really developed my "take an eight-year-old for ice cream" skills. It was okay while we were walking from the pool area into the hotel and then riding the elevator down to the lobby where the ice cream store was, because we could talk about what our room numbers were and how hard they were to remember because there were five digits and what kind of view we had and whether we'd been on a gondola yet, but when Fred and I sat down with our sundaes at a table next to the casino floor, one of those kind of long and awkward silences came up, the kind that make you convinced everyone can hear you digesting. Strained is what it was.

Until Fred paused in the middle of a bite and stared at me and said, "What is wrong with you?"

Which was sort of a relief because it put my fears to rest that Fred's superpower involved small talk. Nope, he wasn't going to be stiff competition for me in the Tact and Small Talk event at the Charm Olympics.

"What do you mean?" I asked, hoping he'd narrow the field. I mean, there are A LOT of things wrong with me. My boobs, for example, and their inability to grow. And the fact that my father treats me like I'm six years old. And that I am taller than almost all the boys I know. But I didn't especially feel like sharing any of that with an eight-year-old. Even one who was apparently as conversationally inept as I was.

He said, "Well, for one thing, your dad is white and you aren't."

Whoa, that was MasterCard! Eight-year-olds are neat! Giving Fred my most cool "don't worry, I forgive you for your grave social gaffe" smile, I explained patiently, "My mother had dark skin. She was from Jamaica." And waited for him to apologize.

Instead he sat up and said, "Is she dead? Your mom? Did she die?" like he was all excited to feast off her corpse or something.

So I said, "Fred, could I give you a tip? That kind of question can be sort of sensitive."

"Oh. It's just that I saw a dead body once." He completely deflated in the chair and wiped his nose on his arm. "I thought maybe you did too."

Boy, did I feel awful. I said, "My mom did die. In an accident. I didn't see her body because I wasn't allowed to go to her funeral. Whose body did you see?"

"Mr. Phillips's. But not at a funeral. In the bedroom."

This was the kind of thing I had wanted to know, but I suddenly felt really bad. It wasn't fair to make a little guy remember stuff like that. Even if he was wearing Spider-Man sneaks and was sort of crusty around the nose. Fred had stopped eating his sundae and was staring at the table.

I started to say, "Why don't we talk about something else?" but he went on.

"I was looking for Mother to show her how Mad Joe could dance if you held a treat over his head, and I thought I heard her voice in the bedroom, so I went in there and someone hit me on the back of my head."

What kind of eight-year-old called his mom "Mother"? Fred was a strange kid. Plus, his voice was calm, like he was telling me about his ant farm, not about seeing a dead body. I said, "Did it hurt when you got hit?"

"A little. And it made me fall down and forget everything. And I let go of Mad Joe, which I wasn't supposed to do. He ran out of the window and got in an accident with a car. That's why he only has three legs."

"Oh."

"And after a little while I woke up and that was when I saw Mr. Phillips lying on his stomach. There was blood all around him, and Father was leaning over him holding a knife."

Oh. My. God.

I was just staring at him, but he didn't really notice. He went on in his little boy voice that had no emotion in it, saying, "For a long time I didn't tell anyone about that because I didn't want to get Father in trouble. But they said he was the one who hit me in the head. So it was his fault that Mad Joe got in the accident, not mine. Because the window was supposed to be closed all the time but he opened it. So I told."

I searched for something to say. "That must have been very hard."

"It was okay. Mad Joe had to go to the hospital and they took off his leg. And for a long time he was sick and wouldn't eat his food. Even if I got down on the ground with him and showed him how. Like this." At which point he leaned down and started licking his ice cream with his tongue. It was probably the most pathetic thing I'd ever seen.

I couldn't stop myself. I got up and went around the table and gave him a big hug and said, "Don't worry, Fred. Everything will be okay."

His little body was rigid in my arms but when he turned his serious little face up to mine I thought I saw a glimmer of feeling. He sniffled and said, "Promise? I don't want anything bad to happen to Mad Joe."

"I promise," I said.

Yes, I know that what waits for people who say stuff like that is way worse than the swimming-in-the-ocean-with-sharks stuff. And now I know why. But did I really have a choice? No.

Besides, it was good that I was there because I felt it right away when Fred flinched like he was startled. Looking down, I saw that he had dropped his spoon and his face had gone completely white and his mouth was open but no words were coming out.

"Fred? Are you okay?"

He tilted his little head up and whispered, "Don't let him come over here! Don't let him get any closer!" and started to shake. I turned my head to see whatever he had been looking at, but all I saw were normal-looking people playing slot machines. Still, there was no question that the boy who could sit calmly talking about witnessing a murder was now terrified.

Or having some kind of fit. Because at that moment he jumped out of his chair, grabbed my wrist, and dragged me into the casino. Maybe you're thinking, how could an eight-year-old drag a six-foot-tall girl into a casino, and all I can say is, he had the strength of ten men.

At least.

He didn't stop until we were in front of a slot machine, at which point he climbed up into the chair, held out his hand to me, and said, "Give me a quarter."

"Fred, how long have you had a gambling problem?" I asked. "You know as well as I do that it's illegal for us to be—"

"You PROMISED," he reminded me. "Put a quarter in the machine. *Please.*"

Suddenly everything that I'd overheard Fiona Bristol saying the night before about someone being after her and Fred, about being scared for her life, came back to me. I didn't know who or what Fred was afraid of, only that he was, and he seemed to think a quarter would help.

Also, I am a complete sucker.

I put a quarter in the slot machine. Fred's little arm shot out like lightning and he pulled the lever. The wheels spun and the machine started making dinging noises and lights flashed before my eyes—

And we were surrounded on all sides by Venetian security guards.

Little Life Lesson 17: Even when you're gambling illegally, standing behind a slot machine yelling, "Big money oh yeah, big money oh yeah" totally does help you win.

It turns out that the Venetian Gulag is more extensive than I thought. For one thing, there is more than one holding cell. The one I was shown into this time was nicer, or maybe it was the consciousness that this time I hadn't done anything wrong. How could I be blamed for Fred's little gaming addiction? Although that wasn't going to play well with the Thwarter. The fact that I was clothed this time probably helped too.

Plus, I only stayed for a little while. I barely had time to ask myself if maybe old-beyond-his-years Fred had actually been aiming for this outcome, aiming to attract the attention of Venetian security, when two members of that elite squad came in. Security Officer Kim and Security Officer Reese stood on either side of me as I got up from my chair, like they thought I might make some kind of getaway. Officer Kim said, "Come this way," and Officer Reese said, "Wait here," and before I knew it I'd been led down a corridor, pushed through a door, and locked in an office. I felt like we had really spent some quality time together.

The office I was locked in was large and impressive, with wood paneling on the walls and a desk in the middle and a bunch of television screens on one side that showed different views of the casino. On the desk was a plate that read, L. A. CURTIS, CHIEF.

But I was more interested in the things on the wall. One side was totally taken up with plaques. The earliest ones were from the navy and then there were several honoring Leonard Curtis for distinguished service in the San Francisco Police Department. So L. A. Curtis's first name was Leonard. And he'd been both a sailor and a cop.

Interesting.

Another wall had two big stuffed fish on it and a bunch of photos of Mr. Curtis and other men on boats. There were also some pictures of him that could have been taken from a "Man on the Go" calendar: one with an old restored car, several in a wetsuit and scuba tank, and one of him wearing a ripped shirt and soiled pants, standing surrounded by a big group of people and gesturing manfully at a sign that said LAS VEGAS THEATER CLUB PROUDLY PRESENTS—*LES MISÉRABLES*. No wonder he kept his veneers up-to-date. I was just thinking that he certainly had a lot of energy when the door opened and that star of stage and security bounced in. Today he was wearing a beige linen suit and looking more than ever like he should be meeting private jets at a tropical resort.

He really didn't seem like a Leonard, even if he did walk kind of strangely.

He settled into his chair, picked a dark thread off his cuff, and then said, "Miss Callihan. Another exciting surprise."

"Yes, sir," I said. "I'm sorry, sir. I did not mean to cause trouble." I also hadn't really meant to apologize. I didn't do anything wrong. But for some reason Mr. Curtis was the kind of person who could almost make me feel guilty for having arm hair. Probably his police training.

"Let me ask you a question," he said. There was something about his tone and the long pause that followed that made me pretty sure it was going to be "Will we have to handcuff you, or will you go quietly?" So I was surprised when he said, "Why did you have Fred pull the lever on the slot machine instead of pulling it yourself?"

"Uh, I didn't. It was Fred's idea."

Mr. Curtis looked at me without saying anything and I started to feel itchy. This was a taste of what I was going to be in for with my dad, I knew, which made itchy turn to desperate.

"Really. I know it was wrong of me to let him," I heard myself blustering on. "I did not mean to do anything illegal. He—"

Mr. Curtis put up a hand. "Actually, I've got to hand it to you. Your quick thinking may be the only thing that stopped a serious crime."

Time for my second visit to Mr. Curtis's parallel universe. "I beg your pardon? A crime? What crime?"

Mr. Curtis flashed me a BriteSmile. "You know, I like your inquisitiveness."

"Um, thank you?"

"You've got a lot going on up here." He tapped his head. "What made you think you needed Security so quickly? Why didn't you just go find one of my people on the casino floor?"

"I didn't," I insisted. Mr. Curtis looked at—or rather, through—

me like it was clear he was not buying what I was selling, even though it was true. "Fred had some kind of fit."

"A fit?"

Only the way he said it, it was like he said, "Ms. Callihan, I can read your mind and I know you are lying." What if Mr. Curtis were telepathic?

"A fit or a hallucination. Or maybe he really did see someone. He said something, something like, 'Don't let him come any closer.' And then he ran off like he was terrified."

"He didn't tell you who he saw?"

"You think he really did see someone?"

"Fred Bristol is very mature for his age and not prone to fits." He found another dark thread on his cuff and pulled it off, turning it between his fingers pensively, like he was trying to make up his mind about something. He leaned forward and said, "Would you like to see how your adventure with Fred looked to our cameras?"

"Yes!" I said, probably too enthusiastically because Mr. Curtis leaned away fast as if he were afraid I might kiss him.

Sorry, Leonard. Not today.

But seriously, the chance to see real surveillance footage? Of myself? Committing a crime (by accident)? Without having to fast-forward through the bad commercials on the Discovery Channel? Who would not think that was the coolest thing ever? I mean, provided you weren't on trial for murder or anything.

Mr. Curtis pushed some buttons and all four of the television monitors started to cycle through different shots. There was the pool and the spa and the Grand Canal Shoppes and the lobby and the parking lot and the room corridors and the casino. There were even cameras behind the hotel, on the loading docks, and in the kitchens and service corridors. It was incredible.

"Are there cameras everywhere?" I asked.

"Everywhere but the bathrooms."

Was that why Ms. Bristol had taken her teary phone call in the ladies' room the night before? Did everyone but me know this about the cameras? "Is that true in all the casinos?"

"Unfortunately, yes. It's the law." I got the feeling that what he thought was unfortunate was that there weren't allowed to be cameras in the bathrooms, not that people required so much surveillance. But would you really want to see people going to the bathroom? If you answered yes to that question, SEEK HELP NOW.

Mr. Curtis had been concentrating on the changing images on the screens and he sat forward now, like he'd found what he was looking for. He pushed a button and three of the monitors went black. On the fourth we were looking at the casino floor and several of the tables adjacent to the ice cream counter.

"I want you to tell me when you see the moment that Fred became afraid. We'll be tightening his security, of course, but if we can narrow down who we're looking for, it will be a big help."

I tried to ask again about why Fred needed security, but Mr. Curtis said, "This is very important, Miss Callihan. Please keep your full attention on the video."

Little Life Lesson 18: If you have to watch yourself on a surveillance video, do not be alarmed: It is not just you; no one looks good when filmed from above.

Probably not everyone looks like their hair could eat them for dinner like mine did, though.

I didn't see myself and Fred enter, but then suddenly there we were, sitting at our table, Fred and my hair, both staring hard at our ice creams. Then Fred looked up and spoke and I saw my hair try to grab him as I leaned forward to give him that etiquette pointer about discussing dead bodies on the first date. Soon my hair was getting up from the table and going around to hug him.

"It's coming up," I told Mr. Curtis. I saw Fred drop his spoon and I said, "There. That's when he had his fit. I mean, got scared."

Mr. Curtis hit PAUSE, and the other three monitors flickered on. They were showing different parts of the casino floor around the table where we were sitting.

"Which way was Fred facing?" he asked me.

I tried to remember. "Toward the slots with the big wheel on the top. Away from the Haywire Hoedown slots."

One of the monitors went blank, leaving the one of us at our table and two with views out into the casino in the direction Fred had been looking. "I want you to watch these," Mr. Curtis said, "and tell me if you see anyone familiar."

I can't say I am proud of what happened next. I had always hoped I'd be a natural at police work, but it turns out that after spotting myself, I was kind of useless at spotting others. I did see the two women with the pink and blue Mohawks that I'd noticed at the pool the previous day, but Fred had been afraid of a man. Mr. Curtis was very patient and rewound the tapes three times for me to try again. I kept feeling like there was something there, but I didn't know what. It was only when he slowed them down that I saw it.

Or rather him.

"That man," I said, pointing to the center of one of the screens. "I think I ran into him last night at the Voodoo Lounge. When I was coming out of the bathroom."

"Do you remember everyone you meet?"

"No, but he was drunk and distinctive—I mean, he's wearing a caftan—and I was sort of in a rush." Caftan Man? Was that who Fred was afraid of? Was he—

"Did he look suspicious in any way?"

"Not apart from his outfit. Why, is he after Fred? What is going on?"

"I just need you to make this identification."

"Could you zoom in?"

Mr. Curtis hit a button and the center of the screen, where the man's face was, got bigger. As did a face in the crowd behind him. My toes and arms and legs started to get tingly and I had a strong urge to get out of Mr. Curtis's office.

"Are you all right, Miss Callihan?" he asked.

"Yes. Fine. I just feel—tired."

"I see. Is that the man?"

"The man? Yes, it is. The man from last night. It's probably just a coincidence."

"Don't you worry about that. Are you sure you didn't see anyone else?"

I almost jumped out of my skin. "Nope. No one else. Not another person."

I was so eager to get out of there I almost missed the part where Mr. Curtis told me that since I'd been so helpful, he didn't think my dad needed to know what had happened, although I did tune in for the part when he said, "These people are very dangerous. They will stop at nothing to get what they want. If you think of anything else, I am counting on you to call. Anything."

I'm sure I was just making it up that he looked at me with special emphasis when he repeated, "Anything." And I really hoped mind reading was *not* L. A. Curtis's superpower. Because if it were, he would have known what I was thinking.

Which was: Little Life Lesson 18 was wrong. Some people looked fine when captured on surveillance video from above. Some people who you could only see when the image was enlarged. Some people looked like dreamboats in green Adidas. Just like they had the night before when they had been surreptitiously questioning me about Fred.

Little Life Lesson 18, REPLACEMENT VERSION: If you meet a guy who is six feet three inches of perfect manly splendor with green eyes and a British accent and warm soft hands and a nice-smelling chest who laughs at your jokes and has lovely manners and is named Jack, keep your distance. Then call security.

Fred *had* been afraid. But not of Caftan Man. No, the man he'd been afraid of was Jack. I was positive.

Just positive enough to want to find out more. Not quite positive enough to tell Mr. Curtis.

Eleven

Little Life Lesson 19: If you drift from the head of Venetian Security's office and make a left turn and walk across the casino and go out the front doors of the hotel in a total daze, having just discovered that the man of your dreams might be at worst a killer and at best a terrorizer of boys, try to keep your wits about you anyway, because you don't know when someone is going to yell, "Here she is," and an arm is going to poke out of a group of people, and you will find yourself being bundled into a gondola as it moves away from land and you will look up and see that you're sitting across from the dream man/boy terrorizer himself.

This really can happen.

(Little Life Lesson 20: You might also want to have applied lip gloss.)

When I finally realized what was going on, I looked around for an escape route. The gondolier, who was perched behind me, was pushing us out into the middle of the canal that runs in front of the hotel. I didn't know how deep the water was, but I did know that my lucky (ha!) cowboy boots would not benefit from a dip in it. Which meant I was trapped. In a gondola.

With Jack. Who was wearing a button-down shirt with different-colored green stripes on it, rolled up at the cuffs so I could see his supple, manly wrists.

And the gondolier. Who was not much comfort because she started singing that song "Memory" from *Cats* really loud. You know the song. The one that makes you want to claw something?

I decided to get right to the point. "Why did you kidnap me like that?" I asked.

Jack looked pleased with himself. "I wanted to see you again."

"That's so nice," I heard my mouth say, and felt myself melt, as he smiled at me with Super Smile and reached out one of his soft firm hands to take one of my—

I said, "No way, buster," and pulled away from him.

He frowned. When he frowned he got these crinkles by his eyes that made my heart *vroom* like I'd just eaten an entire package of mini marshmallows.

"What's wrong?" he asked.

"You. You're a—" I was stumped. "I don't know what you are. But you aren't what you say you are."

Good one, Jas. Monkeys, you couldn't have stepped in here to at least make me say something clever? Monkeys? Hello?

Total silence from the monkeys.

"Jasmine? What are you talking about?"

"I'm talking about an hour and a half ago, in the casino, with Fred."

All at once, like lightning, his face changed. "So you knew I was there and did it on purpose. I didn't want to believe it."

"I beg your pardon?"

"You're working for them. Damn, I had hoped—" He leaned away from me and crossed his arms.

"Who am I working for?" I wanted to know. And I wanted a raise. This job sucked.

"Fiona and her hench people."

And you see, here was an example of how tragic this whole thing was. Because Jack used the phrase "hench people." I used the phrase "hench people." It was a sign we were meant to be together. If only he weren't evil.

Pure evil, as I was soon to find out.

"Wait, you just called her 'Fiona,'" I said. "Why did you lie to me last night and say that you didn't know who the family at the pool was?"

"I never said that. I didn't lie to you."

Which, when I thought about it, was true. He'd only *implied* it, sneaky-snake style. "Who *are* you?" I asked.

He brushed the question aside like it wasn't important. "If you're not involved, you should stay away. Stay away from all of them. You have no idea who these people are. They will do anything to get what they want."

"That's funny, that is what Mr. Curtis just said about you."

"You told him about me?"

I hesitated. Jack smiled a very cute and yet sort of, well, malicious smile. "You didn't. If you had, your precious security forces would be all over us by now."

"If you're not dangerous, why was Fred terrified when he saw you?"

"You terrified him. You told him to run into the casino, away from me. You're the one who gave him the quarter so the guards would come. You were trying to get me caught."

"No, no, yes, no," I said.

"Don't equivocate."

Equivocate. Was it wrong that at that moment all I could think was, he has such a lovely vocabulary? Yes, it was wrong.

I said, "Look, I don't know what you want with me, but—"

"I want you to tell me where they're staying. What room number. Where they're keeping Fred."

"Fred is not being kept, he is with his mother," I corrected. Jack made a very ungracious noise then, but I wasn't going to be stopped. "And the chances of my giving you their room number are infinitesimally smaller than the chances of you turning into a huge plastic cootie that talks." Oh! I see the monkeys are back! Hello, pals. Thank you so much for NOTHING.

Jack blinked at me. "This is not a joke, Miss Callihan."

Why do people always feel forced to point that out to me? "I realize that. I'm not joking. Hasn't Fred suffered enough? He is terrified of you and I see no reason why I should not be as well. Not to mention, I'm already in enough trouble with my father as it is. I don't need any help from you and your chase-boys-through-the-casino tactics. In fact, I think it's time for me to end this little powwow and summon Security myself."

Jack's voice got low and serious. "Don't."

"I—"

He grabbed my wrist. A piece of one of those plastic things they put price tags on was sticking out of the edge of his rolled-up cuff and scratched my skin. He said, "I'm telling you, don't do it. Not for my sake, I don't care about that. For Fred's sake. If you call them, he will very likely end up dead."

"What?"

"You heard me."

I gaped. "Are you threatening him?"

"I am just telling you the truth."

"So he is right to be terrified of you."

"Stop saying that. Just give me twenty-four hours. At the end of that time, you can tell your friend Mr. Curtis about me. But not until then." He let go of my wrist. "Please."

I said, "Why do you think you can trust me?"

He made some kind of sign to the gondolier over my shoulder, and I felt the boat turn slightly.

Then he leaned very close to me. He was looking deep into my eyes and our noses were almost touching. His lips were less than an inch from my lips and his breath smelled like glazed doughnuts.

Bringing his mouth right next to mine, he whispered, "Because I want to trust you." And then he—

—left. He jumped from the gondola to the brick walkway next to the sidewalk, bounced over the metal railing there, and disappeared into the crowd crossing the Strip.

I was too stunned to follow him. I was too stunned to move. I'm pretty sure I didn't even breathe. When I regained my senses—DID I MENTION HE WAS LOOKING AT ME LIKE HE WAS GOING TO KISS ME AND THEN HE TOOK OFF?—the gondolier was singing about how she remembered a time, now past, when she knew what happiness was.

Boy, she could not have been expressing my own thoughts more clearly. For me, that time had been only about thirty seconds earlier, when I thought Jack was going to plant one on me.

But thirty seconds earlier and right that minute were two very different things. Because when the haze from not getting kissed cleared I was forced to face the facts that:

1. Jack was a very bad guy
2. Jack had threatened Fred
3. Just thinking he was going to kiss me made me tingly everywhere
4. In a way no other guy ever had
5. And that was without our mouths even touching
6. Which meant that
7. If they ever did
8. Woohoo baby!
9. Except that it did not matter
10. At all
11. Because he was plotting against Fred
12. And I was complicit in whatever he'd planned if I didn't tell Mr. Curtis
13. And I was trapped on a boat with a woman singing show tunes

But suddenly I knew what I was going to do. I wasn't going to turn Jack in. Maybe that sounds like a bad idea, or you think I made the decision based solely on the fact that when he was near me my insides felt like a Slurpee, or because he had an astonishingly cute butt. A*ston*ishingly.

That is not, however, why I made my decision. I was not thinking with my hormones. I was thinking, What if he wasn't lying? What if my telling on him really would result in Fred's death?

I decided that was a chance I couldn't take. Plus, he'd only asked for twenty-four hours. Mr. Curtis had told me himself he was stepping up the surveillance on Fred. The boy would be safe for that long.

Jack said he trusted me; I would trust him.

Little Life Lesson 21: Trust means different things to different people.

Twelve

As I went inside and took the elevator up to my room, I had no idea that I was the one who would be needing the round-the-clock surveillance to stay safe. Or that Jack had only asked me to trust him for that much time because he planned to have gotten rid of me long before that.

Nope, I was back to blithe. My guard was completely down. Which is why, when I opened my door and saw that there was someone in my room, I screamed.

And they screamed.

And Sherri!, coming through the connecting door, screamed.

And my father, coming in after her, yelled, "Does anyone know how to work this blasted contraption?" and brandished the television remote control.

Because that is what a genius does, you know. Interact well with others. Stay up on what is going on in his immediate environment. Be down with the scene.

He looked around now. "Hello, Polly, Roxy, and Tom. Good to see you. Do any of you know about these things?"

Many people would have paused to wonder, "What are Jas's best friends doing in her hotel room on a Friday afternoon when they're supposed to be 250 miles away in Los Angeles at their summer jobs?" but not my dad. That's the kind of basic, mundane question that geniuses don't trouble themselves with.

Not being a genius, I was curious.

Before I could ask, though, Polly came over, stood in front of me frowning, and said, "Oh, Jas, I can't believe you did that."

In case you think she was referring to my:

running with the cat
ruining a wedding
getting arrested by casino security
stealing a limo
getting arrested by casino security again
or even just not emailing her coherently the night before,
     you're wrong.

She was mad because I was wearing my bikini with the padded top.

"I told you to get rid of that thing last month," said my best friend since kindergarten.

There's no question that Polly knows what she is talking about fashion-wise—people stop her on the street all the time and try to buy her clothes off of her (including once a stylist from the WB who offered her a job on the spot and was very surprised to learn Polly was still in high school)—but I really wish she'd get over her no-padding rule. I mean, what's wrong with trying to help myself a little? We can't all be B cups like her.

"Hi, Polly, it's great to see you," said I, taking the high road.

I looked at my friends. It had been three days since I'd seen them, and three days in Polly Time could mean a lot of changes, but she was pretty much as I'd left her. At first glance Polly looks like a typical, really pretty California girl, all long blonde hair and blue eyes and skinny tan limbs, the kind you see rollerblading at the beach. Except when Polly goes rollerblading, she wears a huge helmet and Kevlar body pads.[4]

Roxy and Tom's parents had both been *telenovela* stars in their youths, perfect specimens of the human form, and that physical perfection had been passed down to the twins. Tom was like

---

[4] Polly: I am going to choose to assume that is your sweet, sweet way of making clear that I am NOT a "typical" California girl, rather than some immature jibe at my safety consciousness.
Jas: What are you doing down here?
Polly: Don't evade the issue.
Jas: There is no danger, P, of anyone thinking you are typical. Or even normal.
Polly: Be careful that you don't choke yourself with all that cackling, Jas. Or shall I call you Girl Who Considers *Cops* Educational Programming?
Jas: Do as you see fit, Girl Who Sleeps with a Hazmat Suit Next to Her Bed.
Polly: You may laugh now. But who will be laughing—
Roxy: Hey, Jas, when it's my turn to be described, could you say I have some kind of cool scar? Or a single alarming eyebrow? Ooh, or what about a snaggletooth?
Jas: Um, I'll think about it.
Roxy: You are a really bad liar. Anyway, do you know where the room service menu is? My snaggletooth and I are starving.

Antonio Banderas times ten, and Roxy was one of those people who men turn around in their seats to look at—ALL the way around— as they walk by. She'd literally caused a traffic accident last year when we were shopping on Melrose, just by crossing the street. And not, like me, because she tripped and fell running after the guy who stole Mrs. Azaji's purse. Typical of Roxy, she didn't even notice. [5]

Today Roxy was wearing a tank top with a pirate flag on it that said SURRENDER THE BOOTY, jeans, one red and blue Puma sneaker and one blue and yellow one. Tom wore jeans and a dark green Fred Perry shirt that he had clearly chosen to impress Polly. And Polly was, as always, wearing pink. [6]

I said, "It's great to see all of you. But what are you doing here? What about your jobs?"

They were all working for their parents—Roxy and Tom for their dad, the Cadillac King of Southern California, repossessing cars that people were overdue paying for, and Polly as a paralegal in the law firm her mother and father founded before their first divorce—so it wasn't

[5] Polly: Remember the time Roxy came to school wearing one tennis sock and one knee sock with her uniform? And she didn't even realize it.
Jas: Yeah. And the next day all the seventh graders were doing it because they thought she was making a fashion statement.
Roxy: Wow, look at this! You can order an entire hors d'oeuvres party sampler with little baby spring rolls and cut-up vegetables and dip! DIP! It says one is enough for a party of ten. I'll order two. We're going to need to be well fed for what we have planned.
Jas: Planned? What are you talking about?
Polly: Nothing. Hey, Jas, weren't you in the middle of something up there? In your story? Like, shouldn't you be telling what we're wearing today instead of picking on things we wore AGES ago?
Jas: Um, no. What do you have planned? What plan???

[6] Jas: Are you happy now?
Polly: Not. I could get more description from a Do Not Dry Clean label.
Roxy: Look! They have bagel dogs too! I love those!
Jas: You aren't going to tell me your plan, are you?
Sigh.

that hard for them to get a Friday off, but it wasn't exactly normal.

Roxy, with the room service menu in her lap, was busy trying to make my father understand that the ON button also turned the television OFF (geniuses really are not like other people), and Polly had gone over to root through my drawers and see what other forbidden items of clothing I'd brought with me, so I looked to Tom for an answer.

He said, "We needed a road trip."

Tom is many things—a total fox (see above), a complete gentleman, the captain of the Medford Boys School water polo team, the number-one crush for everyone at my all-girls school (except me, because he's too good a friend, and Polly, because she does not believe in love), funny, smart, romantic, and cutely shy around most girls—but he is a sucky liar.

"So you just happened to choose Vegas?" I interrogated.

"Um, yes." He leaned toward me to whisper, "We didn't know Polly would make us listen to country music all the way here. Although we did hear this one good song on the college station called 'I Wanna Whack Your Piñata.'"

"Is that really what the song is called? That is just wrong."

"Only to the perverted. It's about this guy who goes to his younger brother's birthday party. It's good. About nostalgia for lost youth, the yearning to be free. I can sing some of it—"

I was not going to be distracted. "Nice try. What is the real reason you're here?"

"Well, we missed you. Nothing fun happens in LA when you're not there, Jas, you know that. No random riots, no mall brawls."

Sadly, that part sounded like he was telling the truth.

Sherri! came over then. "Isn't it great having everyone here?" she said. "I was so happy when Polly called yesterday and asked if they could come."

"You knew about this? And my dad knew? And it was okay?"

"Yes. I told Cedric that I thought your cousin Alyson was a bad influence on you. That you needed your friends to keep you out of trouble."

Is there a stepmother Hall of Fame? Because Sherri! totally deserves a plaque there. "Thank you so much," I stammered.

"No problem. Listen, I don't know what you're involved in, Jas, but be careful, okay?"

I didn't bother to deny involvement. "I will."

"Oh, one other thing. If it has anything to do with Fiona Bristol, be extra careful."

"Why?" I asked.

She got a serious look on her face. "Her augments." ("Augments" is Sherri! for "fake boobs.")

"What do you mean?"

"They're by Dr. Neiman," she said in a voice that made it sound like it was something profound. When I just looked blankly at her, she said, "Only a particular kind of woman went to Dr. Neiman. He's dead now, but about ten years ago, he was well known all over LA and Hollywood because he did quality work, but he let you pay on an installment plan."

"So Fiona got augmented on layaway? Why is that weird?"

"It means that although she's carrying a $5,000 Hermès Kelly bag—"

"More like $7,500 with the current exchange rate," Polly called from across the room, where she was still poking through my drawers, sighing occasionally. I am such a trial to her.

"A $7,500 purse," Sherri! went on, "at the pool, and wearing at least $300,000 in jewelry, she didn't always have resources. In fact, she worked hard to get where she is. Dr. Neiman was very strict about payment. There were some scary rumors about what he would do if you weren't on time. Only the very determined—the very ambitious— went to him. Which means that there's more to Ms. Bristol than it appears, more strength. More, well, gumption."

"Gumption?" I asked.

"Drive. Something," Sherri! said vaguely. "She would fight to keep what she has. I don't know why I'm telling you this—it's probably stupid, but just . . . be careful, okay, Jas? For my sake? And your dad's?"

"Of course," I said. "I'm always careful."

And it's more evidence of Sherri!'s supreme excellence that, instead of rolling her eyes like my father would have, she said, "I know."

Then she looked toward the television where Roxy and the Thwarter himself were staring mesmerized at a man demonstrating a new concept in pipe unclogging. "I'd better go get Cedric before he makes us buy one of those things. You know how he is about the Home Shopping Network."

Yes, I did. I was still recovering from the meat "solid flavor injector" incident. "Please," I nearly begged.

She glided over to my dad, then glided him off the couch and toward their room. I turned around to shut and lock the door behind them, and when I turned back, Polly was facing me with her hands on her hips.

"I thought you weren't interested in the affairs of others named Fiona Bristol," she said. "Don't tell me we came all this way to rescue you and you're already back to Normal Jas."

I shook myself out of the memory of what I'd forever think of as the Meat Enema Nightmare. "Sorry?"

"Personally, I'm thrilled, sweetie," Roxy said, putting her arm around me. "This saves us the trouble of forcing you to read *People*, *Us Weekly*, *In Touch*, *Entertainment Weekly*, and the *Journal of Forensic Science* for two days straight to deprogram you."

"That's why you came? *That* was the plan?"

"Part of it," Tom said. "You don't want to know the rest. I believe the words 'these dog collars would make excellent restraints' were involved."

"It was a brilliant idea," Roxy said defensively. Roxy and Tom are twins DNA-wise and good-looks-wise, but opposites in almost every other way. "And we only got really cute well-made collars." She pulled a purple leather dog collar with diamond-shaped stones on it out of a bag on the floor. "This is my favorite. We had the tag engraved to say BUBBA."

Is this normal? Do normal people automatically assume a friend of theirs has been brainwashed and then drive 250 miles to "deprogram" her? Using gemstone-covered dog collars? I do not think so.

It was kind of sweet, though. In a severely messed-up way.

But the fact was, it was fantastic to see them. And with the way things were going, I could really use their help.

As if to remind me, Polly held up the envelope that had been pushed under my door that morning, which she'd apparently found while invading the sanctity of my underwear drawer—which is illegal, by the way. Even police cannot do that without some paperwork, so I am pretty sure best friends aren't allowed either. Not that this would stop Polly—and said, "Explain. Now."

Thirteen

"What's that?" Roxy asked, tearing her eyes from Bubba's collar to look at the paper Polly was holding.

"Oh, only a note threatening our sweet Jas if she doesn't stay out of 'it,'" Polly told her, then moved her eyes to me. "You were about to start explaining what you're staying out of."

So I did. I filled them in on everything that had happened during the last two days, right up through the gondola ride with my one true (evil) love. Their comments—

Polly: I can't believe Fiona Bristol would walk around with a smudge on her pedicure.

Roxy: I can't believe Alyson and Veronique consider lip gloss food.

Tom: I can't believe anyone uses lines like that one about love at first sight. And that they work.

(Hello? Anyone hear the part about ALMOST KISSING? Why is it that me not being interested in gossip requires a full-scale intervention, while me falling in love with an evil, evil man gets no mention? Not even the barest notice? WHAT IS WRONG WITH PEOPLE?)

—were not immediately helpful, but when I told them I wanted to start by finding out everything I could about Fiona Bristol, they sprang into action. Polly hoisted a pink backpack with a silver rhinestone P on it—Polly's hobbies are organizing and BeDazzling—onto the coffee table and started pulling magazines out.

"This is the last year of articles on Fiona Bristol from the *LA Times* and all the majors," she told me. "Should be enough to get us started."

The majors, to Polly, are *People*, *Us Weekly*, *TV Guide*, *Weekly World News*, *Vogue*, *Bust*, *Psychology Today*, and *Hot Rod*; everything you need, she says, to understand modern culture. Which, if you think about it, is both true and scary.

"How did you even know I would want these? I didn't even know I would want them. And why do they smell like Funyuns?"

Polly shrugged. "We figured if the situation was at all crazy, it was just a matter of time before you were up to your neck in it."

"What do you mean?"

Roxy said, "Sweetie, you wouldn't be our Jas if you weren't."

Great. I'm a crazy things human magnet.

We ordered room service and then got to work reading all the articles about, as Polly dubbed it, "The Terrible Tragedy of Fiona Bristol and Red Early, Star-Crossed Lovers."

The main characters in the Terrible Tragedy were the world-famous model played by Fiona Bristol; her world-famous photographer husband played by Edgar "Red" Early (so-called because of his red hair); and, in the role of the dead man, Red's business manager, Len Phillips.

It all started when Red came home early from a photo shoot, went into the bedroom he shared with Fiona, and found his business manager lying on the floor in front of the wall safe. In a puddle of blood.

At least that is what he said happened in his call to the police.

Len Phillips's throat had been slit and his thumb cut off, and since the safe was open, the police originally thought it was a robbery gone bad. But as the investigation continued, the robbery idea fell apart: There was no sign that anyone had broken into the house; the safe that was open only held negatives, nothing of any real value; and, it became clear that Red Early had been with the body for more than a little while before calling the police.

Suspicious? Are candy necklaces yummy?

The official police conclusion was no surprise: Red Early was the murderer and staged it to look like a robbery to divert suspicion from himself. There was no sign of the murder weapon, which they guessed he ditched in that long time before he called the police. The motive, officials speculated, was jealousy that Len and Fiona had been having an affair, and by coming home early, Red interrupted a rendezvous.

All of which made perfect sense to me.[7]

In the last act of the Terrible Tragedy, Red Early was arrested. He pled not guilty, but refused to cooperate with his defense attorney, who eventually quit.[8]

I flipped back through the articles, skimming them.

"What's wrong?" Polly asked. "Don't frown like that, you'll wrinkle."

"I was just trying to see if they ever found the thumb. The first

---

[7] Roxy: Not me. I think aliens did it. They could totally have used their advanced technologies to get into the house without being seen.

Tom: Then why didn't they use their advanced technologies to kill him? Why use a regular knife?

Roxy: They like to experiment with our ways.

Jas: Okay, Roxy, but what about this? It says here that police linked Len Phillips's murder to an unsolved murder two months earlier here in Las Vegas. One that looked like it was done with the same weapon, by the same person. And Red Early was supposedly shooting a series on homelessness here in Vegas when that murder happened.

Polly: Correction. He wasn't just here in Las Vegas when the murder happened. His car was, like, a block away from the murder scene at the exact time of the killing. He was *there*, where the murder was going down. And he can't produce any of the negatives of the photos he claimed he was taking.

Roxy: That doesn't mean it wasn't aliens.

Jas: What about the fact that Fred saw his father, Red Early, leaning over Len Phillips's dead body?

Roxy: Duh. Red got there *after* the aliens.

Jas: You win. It was aliens. Here, I award you this beautifully carved lemon garnish.

[8] Roxy: I sense your skepticism. But I accept your carved lemon garnish.

Roxy: Likely because he would not believe it when Red spoke of the aliens.

Polly: Or possibly because HE KNEW RED WAS GUILTY.

Jas: Um, Roxy, why is there a piece of black licorice on your upper lip?

Roxy: It's supposed to be a mustache. I thought it would make me look more distinguished and give my arguments more credibility.

Jas: Oh. It does. Definitely.

article mentioned it, but none of the others do.[9] It's weird for a murderer to take something like that unless he's a real psycho."

"I guess that means Red Early is a real psycho," Polly said. "At least he's locked up."

That was when Tom looked up from the article he'd been reading. "Oh, he's not locked up. He's on the run. In fact, I bet he's here right now, looking for Fiona Bristol."

[9] Roxy: Ahem. This article in *Weekly World News* does.
Tom: Let me guess. The thumb was taken by aliens.
Roxy: Aliens happen to think the human thumb is the seat of the soul.
Tom: And you know that from your long discussions with aliens?
Roxy: You are just jealous because this proves I am right and have been right all along. Admit it!
Jas: Roxy, menacing Tom with your garnish does not make you look distinguished. Thank you for bringing that very interesting article to my attention. Now—
Roxy: You should really read it, Jas. Look, they have proof, too. They found a weird footprint outside the window of the room where the body was found. See? In the photo? Does that look like a normal footprint to you?
Jas: Um, no. But how do we know that the picture was really taken outside that window and not, like, outside a building with a sign saying Weekly World News Headquarters?
Roxy: Fine. If you want to be one of those people who think aliens only murder in the movies, go right ahead. But don't come crying to me when they knock on your door and you don't know the proper way to greet them to avoid having your brain slurped out through your nostrils. It happened five times in California alone last year.
Jas: You made that up.
Roxy: Did I? Can you be sure?
(slurrrrrrrrrrrrrrrrrrrrrrrp)

Fourteen

Apparently I'd been wrong. There was still one act of the Terrible Tragedy left to go. The last, bloody act.

Tom handed me the article he'd been reading. RED EARLY ESCAPES FROM CUSTODY IN LOS ANGELES.

"Before he quit, his lawyer got the judge to grant him bail. The next day Red took off. He's been out for almost eight months and no one knows where to find him," Tom said. "They think he might have had help, but no one knows who it was.[10] He skipped on a million-dollar

10 Polly: Probably aliens.
   Jas: Funny, that is exactly what I was thinking.
   Roxy: Oh, ha ha. Let it be known that while you two were riding the Scoff Express, I was eating the
          last of the cookies. That's right. Who is laughing now?
   Polly: You mean the cookies that fell on the floor?
   Roxy: I hear nothing.

bail bond, so all the best bounty hunters are after him."

I saw what Tom meant about him looking for Fiona. Right after he disappeared, Red sent her a letter with the cheery message: "If you give me Fred, I will leave you alone. Otherwise I will hunt you for a hundred years."

"Ooh, a love note!" Roxy said. "What a romantic."

I decided to assume she was kidding.[11]

There was a kind of bad photograph of the note in *Us Weekly* with the headline RED INK: THE RED EARLY NO ONE KNEW. I couldn't tell from the picture if it had been written by the same person who sent me the "Stay Out of It" message. Some of the letters might have been the same. Or not.

And I hoped not. Because a handwriting expert had been called in by *Us Weekly* to study the note to Fiona and determined from the way the letters were formed and words were spaced that the writer was "organized, calculating, and unscrupulous, the classic criminal.

---

[11] Roxy: For real, though, "I will hunt you for a hundred years" would make a good song title for our band, don't you think?

Polly: It does have a kind of country-meets-punk vibe.

Jas: Yes, where "country" means "serial" and "punk" means "killer."

Polly: Oh, you with your crazy crime-fighting obsession. I bet you even think Little Bunny Foo Foo is a serial killer.

Jas: He *was* known for scooping up the field mice and bopping them on the head.

Polly: Have you considered seeking help for this condition?

Jas: Have you considered that the story is up there? Get back up there! Enough chitchat!

He is usually pragmatic, but occasionally lapses into the dramatic, possibly due to a stunted childhood. He lies easily and without compunction, and probably kills the same way." The article also suggested that the person enjoyed diverse hobbies and most likely drove a nice car.

"A nice car. Well, that helps narrow it down," Tom said.

"I wonder what kind of car Jack drives," I said. "I bet it's not nice."

"Of course you do," Polly said, patting me on the head.

Tom pointed to a photo of Red Early in his prison uniform that accompanied the handwriting article. "Do you recognize him at all? Could he be the man you saw on the surveillance tape? Caftan Man? Like, in disguise?"

"I don't know. I didn't get that good a look at him—it was dark the first time I saw him, and the tape wasn't that clear. There *is* something familiar about Red Early." I put the picture aside. "But Caftan Man wasn't the person Fred was running from."

"Jack," Polly said.

I nodded miserably. "He definitely doesn't seem to like Ms. Bristol, and Fred was really scared of him. Maybe he is the one helping Red Early. Maybe he is working for Red, trying to kidnap Fred." I couldn't help it. I sighed. "I wish I just knew what his connection with them is. Why he is doing it."

No sooner had I said that than there was a knock on the door and I got my answer.

Well, sort of.

The bellman at the door asked me if I was Miss Callihan, and then handed me an envelope.

"Who gave this to you?" I asked.

"No one. It was in a pile of items submitted to the concierge to be delivered."

Untraceable. Of course.

On the outside my name and room number had been typed. But inside there was a ticket to Madame Tussauds wax museum and a handwritten note. My heart started to pound like crazy.

MISS CALLIHAN,
I MUST SEE YOU, ALONE. MEET ME AT
MOHAMMAD ALI AT 5:30 TONIGHT SO I CAN
EXPLAIN EVERYTHING AND APOLOGIZE
FOR MY ABRUPT DEPARTURE TODAY. COME,
IF NOT FOR MY SAKE, FOR FRED'S.
YOURS,
JACK

The writing was the same as on the first letter. The one that told me to stay out of It. And again, there were similarities to the note in the magazine. The one written by a person who "lies easily and without compunction and probably kills the same way."

"What are you doing?" Polly asked.

"Calling Mr. Curtis. This has gone too far."

Polly made a face, but Roxy and Tom nodded. Tom said, "I agree with Jas. She should consult a professional."

"Thank you," I said.

"And put it on speakerphone so we can all hear," Roxy added.

I had to talk to three people before I could get transferred to Mr. Curtis's cell phone. It sounded like he was chewing when he finally answered. "What can I do for you now, young lady?"

"I'm sorry to bother you, but I just got a note that made me nervous."

"A threatening note? What did it say?"

I read it to him. He chuckled. "Do you always consider it a threat when a boy asks you out, Miss Callihan?"

Wow. Mr. Curtis had different ideas about dating etiquette than I did. "No," I said, "but I got a note earlier today that said I should mind my own business, and it was in the same writing."

"Can you read me that one?" Mr. Curtis said. I was pleased to notice he sounded more interested now and less like he was snacking. When I was done sharing my most intimate correspondence with him, he said, "I'll tell you how it sounds to me. There's a boy who spotted you at the pool and liked you. Today he finds you, talks to you, and has to leave for some reason. Now he's trying to make it up to you, romantically. Make it seem exciting."

"You think I am overreacting."

"Miss Callihan, you seem to have a very active imagination. Go and have fun with this young man. You're only young once."

"Thanks for the reminder." Roxy and Tom and Polly and I stared at the phone speaker for a few seconds after I'd hung it up.

"He said you are only young once," Tom repeated, dazed.

Polly looked at me piteously. "You've been punished enough, so I'm not even going to say I told you so. But we have our work—" She interrupted herself when she saw what I was doing. "Wait! Stop it! You can't use a blush brush with eye makeup! Haven't I taught you anything?

And where do you think you're going with that green eye shadow? I haven't even decided what you're wearing yet."

"I'm dusting the letter for prints," I told her. "I tried to do things the responsible way. Now we're doing things my way."

Roxy said, "Does that mean we're investigating?"

"Yes."

"Hurrah! Hot dog! Dyn-o-mite!"[12]

Tom was leaning over the paper on the other side of the desk. "You really think you can find something?"

"It's possible," I said, "but they disappear fast, especially on paper. If there are any, my only chance to find them is to try it now."

"Couldn't you at least use blush? You know, so the brush isn't ruined?" Polly asked.

"This is long-wearing eye shadow. It works by adhering to the oil in the skin. Since fingerprints are oily deposits left on paper, it adheres to them and shows up better than blush does."

"Been practicing behind the Thwarter's back, haven't you?" Tom asked.

"A little."

I dipped the brush in the eye shadow and started twisting it over the paper as lightly as possible. Too hard, and you could see there was a print there, but the ridges would be destroyed. Too soft, and you wouldn't even make them come up.

"I guess you can get another brush at Sephora," Polly said with a sigh after a little while. "But if you do find prints, what will they tell you?"

---

[12] Jas: Was there another one of those *Solid Gold* marathons on VH1 while I was gone?
Tom: I'm afraid so.

Which was a really good question. "I don't know," I admitted. "Maybe they will be useful later. When we have something to match them to."

"You're just trying to stay busy and keep your mind off Jack," Polly told me in a voice that showed she knew she was right. "Which is okay. But make it snappy. We've only got three hours until you're supposed to meet him and you don't have a thing to wear."

"I brought half my wardrobe to Vegas."

"Yes, I see that. Maybe next time you can bring the half that goes together. Jas, can you look at me for a second?"

I turned toward her, expecting a talking-to. Instead I got a Bioré pore strip across the nose. "Don't touch it," Polly said. "You go on about your business, we'll take care of the rest."

Which was comforting until I saw her heading toward my French Kitty T-shirt with her pinking shears.

I knew the sound of my wardrobe screaming out in pain would be a distraction, so I put on my headphones, turned up my iPod, and focused on my work. Two hours later, I had clean pores, two partial prints from the back of the note, and a new outfit. Polly described it as "assignation chic," which meant my transformed (and much cuter, I had to admit) T-shirt with a skirt and a pink ribbon belt. Or so it appeared. "You can use the belt to tie him up if you need to," Polly explained. "And I made a pocket in the shirt for this." She held out a square foil packet that said PIZZA HUT on it.

"What is it?"

"Hot red peppers. Throw them in his eyes if you need to create a diversion. Here's your watch," she went on, handing me an object I'd never seen before, which I knew did not belong to me. "My father brought it back from Japan. Push the top button."

I pushed and the opening bars of that old *NSYNC song "Bye Bye Bye" started to play.

"It stops if you push it again," Polly said, and I did. Fast. "That's so you can attract attention if you need to."

"'Bye Bye Bye' is universally regarded as the most annoying song in history," Roxy explained. "It is bound to get you noticed."

"Plus, it only plays the first twenty seconds," Tom said. "Over and over."

I was moved. And a little frightened. "Thanks, you guys. This is really . . . super."

"That's not all," Roxy said.

"We modified this ring," Polly explained, slipping a big plastic flower on my finger, "so the petals are sharp. If anyone ties your hands up behind you, you can use it to cut through the ropes."

"It's a trick I learned from reading about the Russian Mafia," Roxy explained.

How quaint. "Ouch," I said, cutting myself on one of the handy, sharpened petals. "I think this is dangerous."

"That is the point, precious," Polly said.

"Is there anything else I should know about? Any other way my clothes might try to attack me?"

"Forget it," Polly said. "If you're going to be that way—"

Roxy shook a finger at me, then turned to Polly. "Come on, P, show her the boots."

"Boots? You did something to my cowboy boots?"

"Just a little alteration, calm down," Polly said. "Plus, it was to the blue ones with the birds on them, which aren't even your favorites. Look." She slid her finger to the side of my left boot and reached into an incision between two layers of leather, pulling out a thin tube.

"What is it?" I asked. "Bobby pins dipped in spider venom?"

"Close," Polly said. "Cyanide pills."

"What?"

"Just kidding." Ha ha. "It's lip gloss, for touch-ups. In case Jack turns out to be one of the good guys."

Which was thoughtful and made me feel kind of bad for thinking mean thoughts. "Thank you," I said. I felt around the same place on the other boot and pulled out a different tube. "And this?"

Polly shrugged. "Designer Imposters perfume. In case he's not. It's completely debilitating if sprayed near the face."

"Obsession," Roxy filled in. "The Russian Mafia uses it to disorient their prey."

"It works, too," Tom said. "Roxy sprayed some on me during the drive here and I still can't smell out of one side of my nose."

Roxy nodded. "I can't either. And sometimes I feel my eye twitching."

"That's really super," I said, making a mental note to get rid of it as soon as possible. I just knew I would try to apply it instead of the lip gloss and end up with oozing sores where my lips were supposed to be. And also probably unable to taste food.

Polly looked me over from head to toe to head again, then smiled. "I think you're ready."

I wished I felt ready. On my way out, I stopped at the door and gave the two partial green fingerprints one last glance. They didn't look like a kidnapper's fingerprints. Really.

Little Life Lesson 22: Ha!

Fifteen

In seventh-grade Ancient History, we learned that the Greeks and Romans believed strongly in portents and omens. Like if a blackbird flew overhead, they took that as a bad sign and called off their mission, went home, got cozy by the fire, and settled in to read a good wax tablet or scroll or something.

They had the right idea. We were innocently walking through the lobby on our way to Madame Tussauds when I saw Alyson and Veronique coming toward us. At that moment, I should have turned on my heel and picked up the first wax tablet I could lay my hands on. What worse omen could there be but the Evil Henches? Especially Evil Henches who were wearing bright orange Ultrasuede tops about the size of my palm (not counting the single shoulder strap on Alyson's or the halter ties on Veronique's), miniskirts that were only slightly larger, and matching boots with fringes and beads. Yes, BEADS. Both of them. Because you wouldn't want to be out on the town like that alone.

Although if I'd left, I would have missed Roxy saying, "But what is Pocahontas wearing if they have all her clothes?"

And Tom saying, "No one told me Thing One and Thing Two were going to be here."

And Polly saying, "Ack! I think I just went blind!" Which, all taken together, wasn't just MasterCard. It was MasterCard Platinum.

You see why I love my friends.

Except for this one tiny problem: Tom is like crack cocaine to Alyson and Veronique. They can't get enough of him. One glimpse and they go crazy.

He makes them so high that they almost forget they hate me on general principle, hate Roxy for being prettier than them, and especially hate Polly, because even to the Henched Ones, it's clear that Tom entertains a special tender feeling for her. Almost makes them forget, but not quite. Still, they go out of their way to be nice to Roxy, because they think it will make Tom like them. Polly and me they largely ignore.

Veronique started waving frantically at us, as if we could have missed the love children of Pocahontas and Destiny's Child parading through a casino, and they were breathless when they reached us.

"OmygodTommyTomTom hi!" Veronique screeched, throwing her arms around him.

Alyson took a more sophisticated approach. She blew one of her world-class bubbles—bright orange. Thank God she'd coordinated her gum with her outfit—and said, "Hi, Tomás. When did you blow in?" Alyson believes that since Tom and Roxy's parents are from Mexico, his name must have some kind of accent in it, which she alone, of all people on the planet, pronounces correctly. This, it turns out, is totally not true. But it is fun to watch her do it, so none of us corrects her.

Then she turned her bubble prowess on Roxy. "Hi, Roxána," she said, massacring yet another name. "Wow, I really like your necklace-slash-choker."

"Thanks," Roxy said, fingering the purple dog collar. "My mother brought it back from Paris-slash-France. Everyone there is wearing them this year."

"For real?" Veronique asked. "What does that tag mean? Bubba?"

"It's the brand. The best kind." Roxy likes to lie and, unlike Tom, is super good at it. Some might think this is a vice, but I think it's a real talent when used on the right people.

"Hi, Allie. Hi, Vera," Polly said, calling them by their least favorite nicknames.

Alyson turned toward Polly and squinted. "Oh, um, Polly. Hi. I didn't notice you there. You just, like, blend in with the decor."

Little Life Lesson 23: Before making a snide comment about someone else's outfit, check to see if you're wearing knee boots with fringe. If you answer yes, drop it. Just do.

Unaware of this important lesson, Alyson felt she'd scored big and refocused her attention on her main man. "How long are you hanging around, Tomás?"

"Yeah, do you need a room?" Veronique asked. "We've got some extra space in our bed. It'd be totally Visa," she added with a wink.[13]

Tom swallowed hard, thanked the Evil Henches, and quickly explained that he and Roxy had gotten a suite, and also that we were on our way to Madame Tussauds, but he'd look out for them later.

Ah, what a dreamer, that Tom. Veronique said, "Right on! See you later, TomTomgator." But Alyson jumped all over going to Madame Tussauds as if it were an extra-credit paper she could use to raise her grade point average above mine (never happen, short girl), saying, "Check it: Veronique and I were just saying we wanted to go there! We'll slide along!"

"Totally!" Veronique said, and they flanked Tom on either side and dragged him up the escalator.

"Check it?" Roxy repeated as we followed behind them.

"Totally," Polly said. "Let's slide."

I think the Evil Hench Trolls must have been pummeling Tom's shapely calves with their fringe beads all the way to Madame Tussauds, because when we caught up with them at the entrance, his face was looking pained. Or maybe it was just their company.

It was five o'clock, half an hour before my assignation. Our plan was for everyone else to go in ahead of me, scout the place, and assume reconnaissance positions. Then I would enter as though I was alone, and head to Mohammad Ali.

Saying "I'll see you inside," I turned toward the moving walkway that led to Sephora. I needed a new blush brush, obviously, and Polly had given me a list of things to buy that *might* compensate for my

---

[13]Tom: I don't want to know what that means, do I? "Totally Visa"?
Jas: Everywhere you want to be, hot stuff.
Tom: I feel so unclean now. I mean, thanks.

"absurd packing notions."[14]

"Aren't you coming in with us, Jas?" Veronique wanted to know.

Polly said, "She's meeting someone."

Alyson frowned in the middle of the bubble she was blowing. "You have a date? With *what*?"

Ooh, good one. Too bad about the FRINGE BOOTS.

Polly answered for me. "Jas has an admirer."

"Probably some geek." Alyson reasserted her grasp on Tom's arm, said, "Well, we don't have to wait," and clickity-clacked on her Hench claws into the museum. Okay, she didn't, because she was wearing boots, but she could have.

"Check y'all later, homies," I said to Roxy and Polly, and then bolted down the moving walkway before they could make faces at me. I could hear Polly saying, "Oh no you di-in't just say that, girlfriend," behind me as I went.

Sephora is a really good place to kill time, but it is more fun when Polly is there bossing me around, so I got back to the museum early, went through the Rat Pack room and the Hollywood Celebrity room and was standing in front of Mohammad Ali by 5:20. I know it's not right to show up for a date too early and look all eager, but I couldn't stop myself. And it wasn't just that I missed Polly's shopping assistance.

It was that I wanted to know exactly what part Jack played in all of this. Badly. Because I was really hoping it wasn't the villain.

That's what I was thinking about when all the lights went off and the shooting started.

---

[14] Little Life Lesson 24, generously and out of the kindness of her heart provided by Polly Prentis, ~~fascist~~ fashion guru: Sometimes you can save a mismatched or hideously unflattering outfit that you have no idea why anyone would buy—that means you, Jas. What have I told you about wearing olive green? That's right, hang your head in shame—with the right shade of lip gloss and eye shadow.

sixteen

I guess I had always known it would happen but now it was official: I had died and gone to hell. I knew I was dead because as I threw myself to the floor to escape the shots, my life flashed before my eyes. (Little Life/Death Lesson 25: Live large or else you, like me, will be forced to fall back on second-rate memories like kissing Jimmy Drabber on the floor of the Beverly Center Cineplex in eighth grade.) And I knew I was in hell because I could smell two distinct odors: sulfur, which, according to *Paradise Lost*, is what hell smells like; and Bubble Yum, the signature scent of evil in my world.

After my mom died, I listened in on a lot of conversations between grown-ups I wasn't supposed to understand, and what I remembered the most was my mom's sister, Aunt Jean, saying that when you died, you walked toward a bright light and God was waiting for you there to mete out your punishment. Which is why I wasn't that surprised when, opening my eyes, I found myself blinded by a light.

I was a little surprised when the first thing God said to me was, "Get your ass out from under there. How many times do I have to tell you kids—no messing around in the Sports Stars room?" because I hadn't expected that God would use words like "ass."

Or, for that matter, that God would be a middle-aged woman with big platinum-blonde hair dressed in a museum security uniform. If I were God, I'm not sure that is what I would choose to wear. I think I'd go for one of Cher's old show costumes or at least some cool platform boots. But maybe those are too hard to maneuver in. Because God had some moves. For example, the Grab-Jas-by-the-Hair-from-Under-the-Fighting-Ring-Where-She'd-Thrown-Herself-to-Avoid-Being-Shot-and-Drag-Her-Out-Toward-You move. Which was a doozy. And came with its own backup band singing "Bye Bye Bye."

Which got me started thinking that maybe I wasn't dead.

The fact that God was sporting a name tag that said SGT. DARLEEN SMITH, PATROL, also helped. Oh, and that the lights had come back on.

Sgt. Darleen gave me a powerfully disapproving eye as I stood up. "Can you make that thing stop?" she said, glaring at the watch.

"Sorry."

I pushed the button and Sgt. Darleen studied me in silence for a moment. "You should have run away like your friend did. Now I will have to make a report."

"What friend?"

"Your little boyfriend. Don't play stupid with me. You were up to hanky-panky. Oh, yes, I know why you kids all come in here—"

"What? Hanky-panky?" I interrupted. "In case you didn't notice, someone SHOT at me."

But Sgt. Darleen kept right on like I hadn't said a word. "—you girls like to do the necking under the ring. Disgusting, that's what it is. I know you all think Vegas is a playground, but we are decent, family-loving people here, and we don't look kindly—"

Wow. I'd never been mistaken for a slut before, especially one who liked to do the necking. It was kind of . . . novel. But I didn't have time to enjoy it. I was still registering the fact that Jack had tried to kill me.

I had been so stupid. A guy like him would never go for a girl like me for real. Never in a million years.

I felt my eyes get hot, and it was suddenly hard to swallow. I guess I must have looked pretty bad, because Sgt. Darleen's expression softened. "Are you all right, honey? He didn't hurt you, did he?"

"No," I said, not managing to keep the quaver out of my voice. "And I promise you I didn't come here to do the necking. I just wanted—"

Her walkie-talkie crackled, and she put up a hand. I heard something through the static about a "Code 6 in progress at American Idol." Sgt. Darleen said, "Not another one. I have to go take this call. Guess I'll just have to let you go without writing a report. You be careful now and stay out of trouble."

"I will. Thanks."

"I mean it."

I nodded, but only like a robot. I was a mere shell of my former self. I'd never realized it was possible to feel fine and not fine at the same time. I was completely alive. But I felt dead inside. The only time I remembered feeling anything close to this was after my mom died, when my dad threw away all her fingerprints.

It was so stupid, too, because it was not like I even knew Jack.

He was just a guy I had a crush on, right? I'd had crushes before. Crushes that ended, well, badly. But nothing that made me feel like this.

Because I felt totally betrayed. Jack had made my body tingle. He'd looked at me with those eyes in a way I thought only a guy who liked me could. I would fully have done the necking with him if the opportunity arose. But he didn't care about me. He was only using me.

When he wasn't trying to kill me.

I should have known he was evil. Only someone who had made a pact with the devil could make my body do the things he made it do without even touching me.

And, on the up side, he hadn't killed me. Because by now it was clear that I was alive, whether I liked it or not. This led to other interesting questions like: What had stopped him from finishing me off?

And: Did the Thwarter need to find out that something else had "happened" to me?

If he did, would *he* kill me? Would it go better for him if I wrote a letter to the police explaining that it wasn't his fault? That I was a trial as a daughter? Or would Sherri!'s testimony be adequate?

And finally, where was my crack reconnaissance team? My I-got-your-back squad?

Committing a Code 6 Statue Violation on *American Idol* judges, I soon learned. Which, translated, meant putting their fingers up Simon Cowell's wax nose. Or rather, one of their fingers. And getting it stuck there.

Who could resist a temptation like that? Apparently not Alyson.

"We're really sorry we were late, Jas," Veronique said from the corner where she and Alyson were consulting over what repairs would be necessary to Alyson's newly replaced acrylic nail tips. "But Polly told us we didn't need to be here until five thirty. We would totally have been on time. It wasn't Alyson's fault."

"Yes," Roxy agreed solemnly. "Nostrils on the statues may be smaller than they appear."

Alyson, never one to have dampened spirits for too long, said, "Did you have Mexican food for lunch, Jas? It stinks in here."

"Gee, Allie, thanks so much for caring," I said. "As a matter of fact, I *am* feeling a bit queasy. The reason it smells like this is because while you were busy picking Simon's nose, I was getting shot at."

"Exaggerate much?" Alyson sneered. "I'm sure this isn't the first time a guy stood you up, Jas. If there even was a guy."

But Polly, Roxy, and Tom knew better. *Now* they crowded around me, all concerned for my welfare. I shrugged the whole thing off, playing down how bad I felt inside, because even with your closest friends, you still do not want to look like the idiot who fell for the cute but EVIL boy. With the British accent. And the Adidas that matched his eyes.

Polly gave me an up-and-down look. "There's no blood on your outfit, anyway," she assured me, getting her priorities SO straight. "But you did snag the hem of the skirt."

"I'm sorry, next time someone SHOOTS at me in the dark, I'll be certain to look before I dive for cover to make sure there are no nails protruding."

"How could you do that if it was dark?" Veronique asked.

It was a sad, sad day when the only person tracking was Veronique. I gave Polly a pointed look to indicate this fact, but she and Roxy were leaning against the boxing ring, completely ignoring me and talking intently. Most likely about how my brush with death scarred them and how they were trying to put on a brave face for me, but they were trembling deep inside.[15]

I should explain that you get into the Sports Stars room by going down some metal steps from a catwalk. In the middle of the room is a boxing ring, and it's in there that Mohammad Ali is standing (and there that I took refuge when the shoot-out started). Roxy was now walking around the ring like she was searching for aliens (which she probably was), but Polly was just sitting there frowning. I looked to see what she was frowning at and saw Tom who, no doubt savoring the freedom from the Henches that Alyson's broken nail tip was giving him, had wandered up to the catwalk. He had been leaning down, but now he stood up and his expression was not cheery.

He said, "Jas, I think you should get up here."

Veronique was on her befringed feet heading for the stairs. "What is it, TommySalami?"

"News flash for Veronique: He asked for Jas, not you," Alyson hissed. Oooh, trouble in Evil Hench Paradise over a boy. Of course

[15] Polly: No, I think, "I got shot at Madam Tussauds" is a better song title than "Mohammad Ali saved my life."
Roxy: Although that one is kind of inspirational. Sort of gospel.
Polly: We're an angry girl band.
Roxy: You're right. What about "Simon Cowell's Boogers"? That sounds angry.
Polly: THAT is a—
Jas: Hello? What are you doing?
Polly: You said we were whispering among ourselves. So we're whispering.
Jas: I said you were talking about how you had to Wear the Mask to cover your heart-wrenching reaction to my near death.
Polly: We did that already. You don't want us to get maudlin, do you? Plus, we're working on the band. Don't you have evidence to find or something? We'll be there when you need us.

that had to happen right then, when I didn't have time to enjoy it.

Instead of staying to watch the carnage, I clomped up the metal stairs and went to where Tom was standing. The smell of sulfur was stronger there. He pointed to a pile of ash and red paper. A long piece of wire was coiled around it.

"I thought it might be evidence," he said. "Do you have any idea what it is?"

"Yes." I did. It *was* evidence. Evidence of what a dorkus maximus Jack was. And me, too, for ever liking him, and even being a little scared. King and Queen of the Dorki people is what we were. "They're firecrackers," I said. "Like from a joke store." The popping noises I'd heard weren't shots at all. Jack hadn't been trying to kill me—he'd only been trying to terrify me.

But I had news for him. He'd picked the wrong girl. I'd been terrified when I thought someone was aiming a gun at me. But now? Now I was pissed. Pissed at Jack for toying with me. Pissed at L. A. "You Are Only Young Once" Curtis for not taking me seriously. And really, really pissed at myself.

I wanted answers. Only I had no idea what questions to ask.

And then I heard Roxy saying, "Hello, clues! Come to Auntie. Jas, I think I've got something else over here."

seventeen

"When I didn't see any bullets or bullet holes downstairs, I came up here to look around," Roxy explained. "And I found this."

She was standing in front of a light switch and pointing at the floor. I bent down to look and saw two matches ripped out of a matchbook.

"You said it was dark, so I figured he must have turned out the lights. It looks like there was a fuse that ran from here, at the light switch, to the firecrackers."

"And he lit it right here," I said, picking up the two matches and putting them into my Sephora bag.

"What are you going to do with those?" Roxy asked.

"If we're lucky, he'll still have the matchbook when we find him, and we can show these matches were taken from it and prove he was the one who was here. So we can confront him and make him tell the truth. Of course, first we'll have to find him."

Polly had come to join us. She said, "You probably want that too, then," and pointed to a cellophane mint wrapper partially crushed on the catwalk. "Hang on, I have tweezers in my bag to lift it with so we don't destroy any evidence."

"I doubt there is any to find now," I said, but I emptied out the box one of my eye shadows came in and slipped the mint wrapper into it.

"I think I saw mints like those at the taquería inside the mall," Polly said. "Maybe he had a snack before coming to meet you and paid with his credit card or told his life story to the waitress. We can go check."

"And have dinner?" Roxy asked brightly. "Because it would be bad to investigate on an empty stomach."

"Yes," Veronique agreed. "I'm starving."

Which meant that she and Alyson ate an order of salsa with forks while the rest of us had tacos like normal people. None of the waitstaff or the hostesses remembered seeing anyone like Jack, but the place was really big, they pointed out, and he could have taken a mint without them noticing.

"So," Polly asked, trying unsuccessfully to wrangle some salsa from the Evil Hench Hogs, "are you going to call Mr. Curtis and tell him what happened?"

"Let me see," I said. "Hmm. No, that does not seem to be on the menu this evening. I think he's already had enough belly laughs at my expense."

"Yes, you don't want to tax his heart," Roxy agreed.

"Besides," I said, "I doubt he can help me. I mean, all I know is the guy's name is Jack."

Polly shuddered. "I can't believe you almost shared germs with a guy who's last name you don't even know. That's so gross. Of course, discernment has never been your strong suit with guys."

"I resent that."

"Remember that last one? The one who wore his cell phone on a hand strap? And those cargo pants that were so tight you could see—"

"EATING HERE," I said, gesturing wildly to the plates of food.

Polly raised an eyebrow. "Oh, *now* you're squeamish. Anyway, you know who I mean."[16]

"He was Italian!" I complained. "They were high-fashion trousers. Giacomo was making a fashion statement."

Polly frowned. "I don't think those words mean what you think they mean."

I looked at Roxy, but instead of coming to my aid she said, "Polly has a point. I mean, you are the only person I know who

---

[16] Roxy: Is that the guy that Jas picked up at the UCLA library the day she'd had that eye test that messed up her vision?

Polly: Exactly.

Roxy: The one who wore that metallic rainbow Speedo bathing suit when we went to the beach?

Polly: Sometimes I wake up screaming in the night, and I think it's because I'm remembering how that looked.

Roxy: That could be a sign of an alien mental probe as well.

Polly: You always give me such comfort, Rox.

Jas: Hello? The book is up there. You two, zip it. And it was not metallic.

dated a guy on probation."[17]

"Two guys," Tom corrected her. "There was that one with—what did you call it, Jas? The clunky bracelet."

Okay. So he'd been under house arrest. How was I supposed to know he was only allowed out to go to his job at the library? He had the sweetest smile and was so knowledgeable about the latest developments in law enforcement technology. "He said he got it at the Renaissance Faire."

"Never date guys who wear jewelry," Veronique looked up from the salsa long enough to say. "It's a sign of vanity."

"Thanks." It was hopeless. I was surrounded on all sides by enemies. I looked down at my hands in my lap, figuring that at least they would not start cracking wise about my love life, but I was wrong there too. Because I was looking at the wrist He had touched.

> *Your hand, my wrist: Why*
> *do I still burn from your touch?*
> *I think you scratched me.*

---

[17] Jas: Um, Roxy? I am not sure you should be saddling up your high horse here. Do the words "I have fallen in love with the sad clown at the state fair and I am leaving all of you to follow him wherever carny life leads" ring any bells?

Polly: Downtrodden Dan! That was his name.

Jas: Yes, except that he turned out to be a sixty-five-year-old grandmother named Selma.

Roxy: How was I supposed to know what was under the makeup? I fell in love with his heartache!

Jas: People in glass stables shouldn't throw stones, that is all I am saying.

Polly: Gee, that is so profound. I can't believe no one has put that on an inspirational poster yet.

Jas: Your negativity flows off of me like burbling water over a smooth rock.

Polly: Jas, you have outdone yourself. That was truly Pepto-abysmol.

Jas: Thank you, I try.

"I think he scratched me," I said aloud. That was it! I turned to Polly. "If I describe a shirt to you, could you figure out where it came from?"

She shrugged. "Of course. How will that help?"

"Today, in the gondola. The shirt he was wearing still had that plastic thing attached, the kind that holds a price tag. Maybe it was new. And maybe if he bought it here in Vegas . . ."

Before I'd even finished talking, Polly pulled a napkin toward her, grabbed my new purple eyeliner out of my bag, and said, "Button-down collar or flap? Channel buttonholes or exposed? French cuffs or regular?"

It only took five minutes for her to get it right. When it was done, she looked down, then nodded with a little smile. "Maybe your luck is changing, Jas. For once you've chosen a guy with taste. This shirt is from John Varvatos's fall line. Brand-new, and for now available only in his stores."

Say there's one in Vegas say there's one in Vegas say there's one in Vegas, I prayed silently.

"And," Polly went on, "I'm pretty sure there's one at the Forum Shoppes at Caesars Palace."

Gotcha, sweet lips, I thought. *You can run but you can't hide.*

"How are you going to find out where a guy is by knowing where he buys his clothes?" Veronique asked.

"I have an idea," Polly said, looking intently at Alyson and Veronique. "But I need the two of you to help me."

"Us?" Veronique gasped. "For real? Cool!"

"Stop sign, Veronique," Alyson said, holding up her palm. She looked around the table. "You guys are so gullible-slash-stupid. You know there probably wasn't even a guy. Jas makes things up all the time."

Polly's eyes lit up in a way they almost never did, and I saw her kind of enlarge herself to come to my defense, but I didn't need it. In fact, for once Alyson's skepticism did not bum me out at all.

"Maybe Alyson is right," I said. "Maybe it wasn't Jack at all. The security guard didn't see anyone specific."

"Jas, sweetie—" Roxy began.

"No, I'm serious. We have no proof it was Jack."

"We have no proof it was human," Alyson snorted.

"Proof?" Veronique said. "Like on *CSI*?"

And then, all at once, I figured out how to get it. I grabbed another napkin and the eyeliner from Polly and started making a shopping list.

When Polly saw what I'd written, she gave me an approving smile. "You get to work here. I'll take the Children of the Squaw over to Caesars to see what I can find out."

"Tommy, are you coming?" Veronique asked, holding out her arm.

"No, I, um, have to stay and help out Jas," Tom answered quickly.

"Do we need to change?" Alyson asked Polly. "Because I am not changing."

"Are you kidding?" Polly said. "Your outfits are the key to my plan. They're totally front row."

Veronique gave a little clap. "For real? I designed them myself! I got the pattern from *Sewing for Dummies*."

"You used a pattern? Wow," Polly said, and led them away.

As we watched them get lost in the crowd, Roxy frowned. "They won't hurt her, will they? Push her in front of a bus or anything?"

I tried to look confident. "Probably not."

"I'm not worried," Tom said. "Polly can do anything."

And I thought, not for the first time, that one day I would like to have someone look at me the way he looks at Polly. For even, like, just half a second.

But that day was not this day. This day we had shopping to do.

Roxy picked the list up from the table and read it over as we waited for the bill. "Superglue, shoe box, Diet Coke, coffee warmer, mug, paper clips." She looked up. "The only thing I could build with those is a shortwave radio. Am I hot or cold?"

"Brrr, freezing."

Eighteen

Roxy was a little depressed that none of her guesses about what we
were making (lie detector, mousetrap, diorama) were right, but she got
over it when I bought her a churro and let her choose which shoes we'd
buy to get the box. By 7:30 we were back in my suite with everything
we needed to make an at-home latent fingerprint fumer, and we hadn't
even had to leave the Venetian.

Little Life Lesson 26: Las Vegas is an EXCELLENT place to
engage in amateur crime fighting.

We spread everything out on the desk. I handed Roxy the Diet
Coke and said, "Drink this."

"I thought it was for our project."

"Drink. I need the can."

Tom came over and frowned at everything on the desk. "Okay, I get what the shoe box is for, but how does it work?"

I got a piece of thread from Polly's sewing kit, put Roxy's new clear plastic four-inch-heel mules on the floor, and centered the box on the desk. "We run the thread across the middle of the box and hang the mint wrapper from it using the paper clip. This second mint I'm doing has my prints on it, so I'll be able to see if the fuming worked."

Roxy handed me the empty Diet Coke can. "What's this for?"

Using the sharp edge of my flower ring, I cut the bottom half-inch off the can and flipped it over. "We drop a little of the superglue here, into this indentation, then place it on the coffee warmer in the box. The coffee warmer heats the glue and makes it fume, and the fumes make hidden fingerprints come up."

"Cool," Roxy said.

"Totally Visa," Tom agreed. "But if we're putting glue on the coffee warmer, what is the mug for?"

"We need a container of hot water in the box because humidity makes the prints come up better." I put the mug in, made sure everything was in place, plugged the coffee warmer in, then put the lid on the shoe box.

"How long does it take?" Roxy asked.

"Ten minutes."

"Can we peek?"

"No, the lid has to stay on." But in my mind I pictured what happened, the way I'd seen it demonstrated in glass tanks. It was amazing—one minute there's nothing there, the next you can see all the prints of the people who touched something.

I wished you could do the same thing with people. Fume them

and find out who had touched them to make them what they were. Like Jack. If he was evil, probably someone had done something to make him feel bad about himself. Or even Polly. Every guy she dated was like a less cute, less cool version of Tom. It was so clear to everyone but her that she and Tom were made for each other, but she refused to even think of him that way. There were some people, though, like the Thwarter and Alyson, who weren't influenced by anyone and who just did what they wanted and lived in their own worlds. They would not be so interesting to fume.

But Jack . . .

Stop thinking about him, I told myself. Bad Jas. But even if I had wanted to, I couldn't. Because our do-it-yourself fuming chamber worked great, raising a beautiful print on the mint wrapper. It looked like a thumbprint and had a tented arch, which is rare. And it matched the larger of the two partial prints on the note signed by him telling me to meet him at Madame Tussauds. So there was no question that it was his.

HATE HIM, I told myself. Make like the characters in a Fox show and Do It.

I was working really hard on that when Polly and the Evil Fringed Henches returned.

"Fingerprint?" Polly asked right away.

Roxy was beaming. "It's so cool!"

I, however, was not beaming. I was barely even being. I could have modeled for a porcelain sculpture with the title "I Hate to Love Him." I was lying on my back on my bed with an arm over my eyes, the internationally recognized position of extreme mental anguish. "The print matches," I announced, struggling against the dark heaviness trying to engulf my soul. Which really is a lot of work, and possibly harder when you're lying down.

"So?" Polly asked in a voice not at all sympathetic to my suffering.[18]

I moved my arm just enough so I could glare at her with one eye. "That means Jack was the one at Madame Tussauds. The one who tried to kill me."

"Scare you," she corrected. "And that is all the more reason for us to go and find him. But we have a lot of work to do."

I propped myself up on my elbows to look with both eyes. "What are you talking about? Do you know where he is?"

"No, but I know where he'll be in four hours."

"You should have seen it, Jas," Veronique said. "Polly told the man in the store that Alyson and I were foreign exchange students who met Jack at a casino and were supposed to go to his room but forgot where it was and did they know who he was and where he was staying and the man was so helpful."

"Foreign exchange students?" I asked.

"From Belgium," Veronique said. "Did you know french fries are really from Belgium?"

---

[18] Polly: That is because, precious, you just looked like you had indigestion. You should work on those poses. Just FYI.

Roxy: Or maybe you could put a sign next to yourself. Like wall text at a museum. "Girl, depressed. Materials: teenage girl, angst, lip gloss."

Polly: That would completely have helped. And it would make a good song title.

"She wouldn't let us talk," Alyson said.

"I just wanted him to focus on how great you looked," Polly told her with a smile that frightened me.[19]

Alyson nodded. "I guess it worked. I mean, he fully believed Jack would want to see us again."

"Of course he did! We're bacon," Veronique said. "That's why he told us Jack had mentioned going to this party tonight."

"The Play Nice winter line private launch party," Polly said. "Invitation only, tight guest list."

"And my dad is on an airplane so he can't help," Veronique said sadly.

I was glad to know that Jack could take time out of his busy Reign of Terror and Kidnapping schedule for something important like an invitation-only VIP fashion show. He was a man with his priorities straight, that was clear.

"I have an idea." I sat up. "We could sneak in as caterers."

Polly looked at me pityingly. "You've been watching *Hogan's Heroes* late at night again, haven't you? Your television habits frighten me."

"Okay, then what if we wait outside and waylay him? In the parking lot?"

"That would be one way to do it," Polly said in a tone that implied, "if we'd all had operations where our brains had been removed and replaced with Peeps marshmallow snacks."

While she was mentally comparing me to a marshmallow, she'd set two full-looking Walgreen's bags on the bed and was now digging around in her backpack. Using as little of my precious energy reserves

---

[19] Jas: Did you suffer horribly?
Polly: It wasn't that bad. I just pretended I was the spokesmodel for the I'm With Stupid world tour.
Roxy: You know, that would make a sweet title for a song.

as possible, I slithered on my stomach toward one of the Walgreen's bags and tilted it toward me. I glimpsed something that looked alive, but before I could get a better view, Polly's hand came down like a barrier.

"Get back," she hissed.

I got back. Polly can be scary when she's planning. And she was definitely planning.

Any doubts about that were extinguished when she stood up from her backpack, held up not one but two BeDazzlers in different sizes, and said, "Here's what we're going to do."

Little Life Lesson 27: When picking a best friend, make sure she is not insane. One good warning sign to look for: if she says, "We have everything we need to get into that VIP party right here," while pointing at a BeDazzler, a cell phone earpiece, six stuffed bunnies left over from Easter, two Blow Pops, and a large canister of Aqua Net.[20]

Little Life Lesson 28: Actually, traveling with a BeDazzler is a good warning sign all by itself.

[20] Polly: Oh, you want to play that way, do you? Okay, homegirl, here you go. Polly's Life Lesson 1: When choosing a best friend, look her over for scars. If she has any that go with stories featuring such gems as: ". . . and then I got cut trying to get the girl's flute out of the shark tank" or "I didn't know monkeys could throw a punch either!" or "No, it's all healed. My hair hasn't caught fire for at least three weeks," steer clear. You know what I am talking about, Jas.

Little Life Lesson 29: And/or anything having to do with remain-dered stuffed animals.

"You're going to get us into a private party with this?" Alyson asked, sneering at the items on the bed. "No-slash-way."

Polly laughed. "Never underestimate the power of the BeDazzler. It's totally American Express."

"American Express?" Veronique said.

"Don't leave home without it," Polly explained.

Score one for the Braille-speaking crowd. "That," I told my insane friend, "was way MasterCard."

"We do our best," Polly said humbly. Then she reached for the hem of the dress I was wearing and started cutting. "This is about two years out of date and three inches too long. But we'll have it fixed in no time."

Little Life Lesson 30: Insane people should not have scissors.

(Little Life Lesson 30!!! Halfway there!)

By eleven thirty that night, we were all ready to go. The Henches were still in their Little Big Boobs outfits, but the rest of us had been restyled. Roxy was wearing the purple cat collar, a fur vest made out of the Easter bunnies, and an astonishingly short version of one of my skirts which now had INTEL INSIDE BeDazzled across the butt. Tom had on a pair of dark pants and a white T-shirt that made it really clear that he'd spent a lot of time at the gym this summer working out his love for Polly. Polly herself was wearing a pink fringed bustier that made her ta-tas very TA, jeans, and a dragonfly-shaped choker that I think was made from bunny innards. I couldn't even see what I was wearing, partially because Polly had made my emerald green Betsey Johnson dress so short it was nearly invisible, and partially because she'd made my hair so large it was impossible to see through. It was like a hair nest, with a green flower over my ear courtesy of the former hem of my dress and the BeDazzler.

Nor was my vision helped by the fact that it was night and I was wearing sunglasses. We all were. It was part of the plan.

As we got out of the elevators and walked through the lobby of the hotel, people stopped to stare at us in what I sincerely hoped was a good way. Most people anyway. Polly had been in front, leading us, but she turned around to see how we looked as a group and did a double take when she got to me.

"I swear you're not wearing Ray-Ban Wayfarers, Jas. You aren't, are you? And don't say they're so out they're in."

Ha! I had her. "These sunglasses? They're the beef." I looked over the top of the glasses to wink at her. "They're what's for dinner."

"Oh, no no no," she said. "They are not the beef."

I nodded. "Prime rib."

"Not even Grade-D ground chuck."

"Beef stroganoff. Man-size."

"Precious, they couldn't get near Lean Cuisine Salisbury steak. In fact—what's that I hear?—they just failed their audition for the other white meat."

I decided to try reason. "Look, fashion tyrant, a famous person would wear them. Famous people like taking fashion risks."

"There's a difference between a fashion risk and a toxic fashion disaster," she said as we reached the door to the valet area. "But I guess unique taste is in your DNA. Speaking of which, where *are* Pocahontas's Muggers? Oh, there you two are. Coming?"

Veronique and Alyson came up behind us, looking confused. "What are we doing here in the parking lot? Aren't we going in the limo again?" Veronique asked.

Had she had a lobotomy? I looked at the Henches over the top of my 2-kool-4-school Wayfarers. "Uh, no. I don't think that would be advisable."

Alyson put her hands on her hips. "Then how are we getting there?"

It got sort of quiet then in the valet area like it always did when the Pink Pearl pulled up.

The Pink Pearl is Polly's van and it makes quite an impression. The exterior is painted in hot-pink glitter paint and the windows are framed with big fake diamonds. Inside, it's like what *I Dream of Jeannie*'s van would have been like if she'd had one. The dashboard is pink metallic leather, and the whole rest of the interior except the floor is done in pink satin with big cushions and cool lanterns hanging from the ceiling. The floor has a puffy white carpet, and off to one side is a table that is made of Lucite and filled with Barbie shoes. Polly did the entire interior herself, except the table, which Roxy, Tom, and I made and gave her for her birthday. I still had the scars from the glue gun to prove it.

No one has ever seen a car like the Pink Pearl.

"I am so not riding in that thing," Alyson declared. "No-slash-way."

"Bye-slash-bye!" Polly said, climbing into the driver's seat and waving happily.

Roxy is always the navigator and gets to sit in the passenger seat, so Tom and I got into the back through the sliding door. "Catch you later, squaws," I said, but before the valet parker could put away the zebra carpet–covered retractable steps and slam the door shut, Alyson was climbing in with Veronique behind her.

"Fine," she pouted. "But drop us off a block before the party entrance."

I'm pretty sure it wasn't just because she was talking to some of her good buddies on the CB—her handle is Princess P—that Polly acted like she hadn't heard what Alyson said. Instead, Polly not only pulled up right in front of the place but came in so fast the brakes screeched in order to ensure we'd get the most attention possible. She looked at Roxy and said, "How are we on time?"

"Thirty seconds and counting."

"Are you ready, cupcakes?" Polly called into the back of the van. "Costumes in place? Sunglasses on?"

"Ten-four," Tom answered.

"Let's go. Places, everyone."

We'd worked out the choreography at the hotel, but I was still really ambivalent.

I crawled toward the front of the van and tapped Polly on the shoulder. "There is no way this is going to work. I think we should drop it. No one is going to believe I'm a famous person."

"Want to bet?"

"Yes."

"If they do, if it works, I can drive over those sunglasses, and you will never replace them."

"And if I win?"

"You won't."

Ha ha ha. Funny.

What happened after that was kind of a blur. Polly got out of the driver's seat and pushed open the van door all sexy-girl chauffeur, and I saw that the sidewalk was jammed with people. There had to be at least a hundred of them there, all facing the van expectantly.

I decided my job should be to concentrate on not letting my stomach come out of my body. It was harder than it looked.

152

Tom got out and stood next to the van with one hand on his telephone earpiece, legs apart, like he was a bodyguard. Roxy came around the other side and, clutching her cell phone, marched through the line to the three doormen standing by the velvet rope. Alyson and Veronique walked out next, holding hands and sucking on the Blow Pops, and paused to do what I swear was a move from a *Sweatin' to the Oldies* video. Then Roxy waved at me, which was my cue.

All I could think about as I stepped to the ground was I must not trip and fall because then Polly will say it was because of my sunglasses.

Suddenly there were shouts and cheering and flashbulbs flashing like I was a real celebrity and we were being moved through the crowd and *boom!* like that! we were inside the party with the chic and beautiful of Las Vegas.

At least, I assumed we were.

Little Life Lesson 31: Ray-Bans are not the best glasses to wear when you're doing the sunglasses-at-night thing. Not if you want to be able to see where you're going.[21]

[21]Polly: I told you so.

nineteen

"How did you get all those people there doing that?" I asked Roxy as
we were walked in.

"Flash mob. I just told everyone to be at this address at eleven
thirty-eight and cheer when they got a happy-face text message. It
worked great, didn't it?" She'd been smiling, but as we got farther into
the place her face changed. "Oh. Oh, no. Polly didn't tell us this was
at a roller rink."

"She probably figured we would back out," I said. And she might
have been right. There were tables all around the edge and platforms
for go-go dancers, but there was no disguising the essential fact that
we were at a roller rink. For example, the women modeling the clothes

were rolling through the crowds on skates.

Tom, Polly, Alyson, and Veronique joined us at the side of the rink. Tom looked at Roxy and laughed. "You're all pale. What is it, still a little gun-shy after your last time on skates? When you and Jas and Polly did that—"

"Thanks, Tom," I said, cutting him off. "That will be all."

"What?" Alyson demanded. "What did they do? I bet it was stupid."

"No way. It was great. What was it, in, like, eighth grade?"

"Sixth," I said through clenched teeth. "The beginning of sixth. A VERY long time ago."

"Ancient history," Polly said, giving Tom a warning glance.

Tom ignored that, addressing himself to the rapt Evil Henches. "Roxy, Jas, and Polly decided they were going to be roller skate queens. So they put together this routine to some really cheesy song. What was the song?"

"Do you hear something?" Polly asked.

"I don't. No one is talking," Roxy confirmed

Tom went on undaunted. "That's right, it was 'Macho Man' by the Village People. Anyway, they choreographed the whole thing in the living room, thinking that practicing in their socks on the wood floor would be just like roller skating. It had a lot of turns and fancy jumps in it."

"Well, we had to show we were macho," Roxy said defensively. "So we did macho things."

"Yes, and we were wrong, and it didn't go that well," I said, trying to wrap it up.

Tom was having no part of it. "Jas, you're cutting out the best part."

"No. I'm not."

"Yeah. The part where Polly swan dived into the audience and knocked that man unconscious."[22]

"Who besides me hears the sound of Tom shutting up?" Roxy asked.

"Mmmm, I do," Polly said. "Sounds nice."

"What?" he said. "It was great. Everyone loved it."

"Not as much as they loved your break-dance show," Roxy said. "Remember that, M.C. Hernandez?"

"You can break dance?" Veronique squealed. "Show us!"

"Aren't we here to do something?" Tom asked. He sounded a little desperate. "Something important. Find someone?"

"Don't worry, you go show Veronique your smooth moves. I'm on it," I said. And I was. I was scanning the crowd looking for Jack. Or trying to.

Little Life Lesson 32: Ray-Ban Wayfarers? Also not so good for trying to spot someone across a dark roller rink so you can question him about being a kidnapper.

---

[22] Jas: I don't know what Tom is talking about. What happened was Polly was supposed to jump up and land on my back, only we didn't take into account how much more momentum there would be in that move with WHEELS involved.

Roxy: Or that Polly would put her hands over your eyes.

Jas: So I couldn't see where I was going and vroomed straight into the side of the rink so hard that I flipped over it, and Polly flew through the air.

Roxy: And landed in that man's lap.

Polly: He was very nice. He dropped the lawsuit right away when he heard who my parents were. And he can walk just fine now.

Roxy: Tom is such an exaggerator. Still, it's a good thing Polly was wearing a hard hat.

Fortunately, that didn't matter, because as I squinted into the crowd in front of me, a knee-melting voice behind me said, "I would have liked to see your skate performance. I bet you were quite macho."

He was standing so close to me when I turned around that I almost couldn't breathe. He was wearing dark jeans, a T-shirt, and a light-weight caramel-colored blazer that hung on his body in a way that did things to *my* body and made it hard for me to swallow. Or think.[23]

He's a kidnapper and worse, I reminded myself. But he's so . . .

EVIL.

"Hello, Jasmine," he said in that voice. His voice. With his accent. "You look especially stunning tonight."

CUTE!!

EVIL!!!

CU—EVIL. And I was mad at him. Steaming mad.

"You've got a lot of nerve coming up to me like this," I said. Well, look at that. The monkeys were back and channeling Noir films of the 40s. A lot of nerve? Thanks, guys.

He looked at me with those eyes for a moment before saying, "I have to admit, I was surprised to see you here."

I moved my eyes from his eyes to regain control of my brain, but they settled on his chest, which wasn't much better. I decided to focus on the buttons of his coat. They were square. How interesting. Not as interesting as his pecs, which—

I pulled myself together. "I bet you were, after what you did today."

"What I did? Oh, the gondola. I'm sorry I left like that."

"That's not what I was talking about and you know it."

---

[23] Polly: I have to say, Jack surprised me. I mean, Jas was obviously smitten, but given her track record, I expected to be underwhelmed. Instead, here was this guy who was unquestionably Front Row material.

Roxy: I know. He was so cute, my first thought was that he had been genetically engineered.

Polly: And well dressed. And he looked great with Jas.

Roxy: Yes. Oh, well. I still can't believe—

Jas: Nothing to see here, folks. Eyes up on the story. Just ignore this space. Blah blah blah.

"I beg your pardon?"

"Madame Tussauds? You, me, and a bunch of cheap fireworks?"

"Fireworks," he said, pronouncing it like I'd said, "Alien love children."

"Small incendiary devices," I elaborated. "Pop pop pop?"

"Don't take this the wrong way, but were you dropped on the head as a child?"

"Oh, good one, Mr. I-Was-Raised-by-Wolves-to-Prey-on-the-Defenseless," I said.

He did a very convincing imitation of someone who was bewildered. "What? Wolves?"

"That's the only explanation I can think of for the kind of job you're doing here. When you're not taking in fashion shows, anyway."

"Job? What job?"

"Trying to hurt Fred and Fiona. Working for Red Early."

That got him. He dropped the bewildered act. "I thought you said you weren't involved. What do you know about that? About Red Early?"

"That he's a murderer and a fugitive. And that you're his hired hand. His lackey."

"His lackey," he repeated to himself. He shook his head. "I can assure you I am most definitely not being paid by Red Early. But you have no idea what you have gotten yourself involved in, Miss Callihan. I tried to warn you with my note, but you didn't listen."

"So you admit you sent the notes! Finally we are getting somewhere."

"That doesn't matter. Take my advice: Leave here right now and stay as far away from Fiona and Fred as you can. "

"Okay, I will. If you tell me why." Which I thought was a request any mature and reasonable person would honor.

So of course he said, "No."

I tried again. "What about this: If you're not Red Early's paid lackey, what are you? Who are you working for?"

"I'm not going to tell you that either. The less you know, the safer you are. Trust me."

"You know, I think I used up all my *trusting you* this afternoon. Yep, fresh out. And fresh out of promises."

"You did keep the promise you made to me before, though, didn't you?" he said, sounding concerned. "Not to tell your friends in the security office about seeing me in the casino?"

I crossed my arms and said, "I'll take 'It's Jack's turn to answer some questions' for two hundred, please."

He stared at me very, very hard for like twenty seconds, which is a light-year in silent time. Then he said, "Pity."

Pity? Deafening silence and then . . . PITY? What does that mean?????

"What does that mean?" I asked.

"It means—" he started to say, and then—because I have the worst luck in the world and am destined never to fall in love, or at least never to fall in love with anyone who is not headed for probation/on probation/breaking probation—he said, "Excuse me," and turned to go.

This time, however, I was ready for him.

"Not so fast, hot stuff," I said, grabbing his arm. "From now on, you and I are going everywhere together."

He stopped walking, looked down, and unleashed his secret weapon: Super Smile. The one that displaces time and location so that there are only the two of you, together, alone in a world made exclusively for your bliss. As soon as he hit me with Super Smile I stopped hearing the noise of the party around us, and I couldn't see anyone but him, and I felt like I was flying.

Until I realized, I *was* flying. He'd picked me up, turned, and put me on top of a go-go dancing stage.

"I'm afraid I'll have to take a rain check on your company," he said. I felt something click and looked down.

He had handcuffed one of my wrists. To a stage. In front of hundreds of people.

I HAD BEEN DISABLED BY SUPER SMILE! SUPER SMILE WAS KRYPTONITE TO ME! I HAD A KRYPTONITE BUT I DIDN'T EVEN HAVE A SUPERPOWER!

Which was bad, but what was worse was why he'd done it. It had to mean that he wasn't just here because he took a keen interest in women's clothing. No, he must have been up to something super bad to want to get rid of me that much. Plus, only someone really bad carried restraints with them.

Okay, or friends of mine.[24]

But mostly really bad people. He was probably on his way right now to hurt Fiona and Fred. I'd set out to get information about him and hopefully follow him, and I'd completely failed.

Calm down, I told myself. I took a deep, mind-clearing breath, and got a big whiff of something really sugary. Accompanied by the *click-clack* of FRINGE BEADS. Which could only mean one thing.

Little Life Lesson 33: Just when you think things can't get any worse, they can.

Not only was I handcuffed to a go-go platform with no means of escape in sight, but I was handcuffed to the go-go platform currently occupied by THE EVIL HENCH TWINS.

"Jas! Isn't it cool up here with everyone watching?" Veronique

[24] Polly: THAT WAS A SPECIAL CIRCUMSTANCE AND YOU KNOW IT, JAS. We were coming to help you. Sheesh.
Roxy: Yeah. And ours were super cute.

shouted in my ear over the sound of Def Leppard's "Pour Some Sugar on Me," then pulled my uncuffed arm in the air and started doing the bump with me.

Little Life Lesson 34: They can ALWAYS get worse.

A guy standing below started bopping his head in time to our bumps and gave us two enthusiastic thumbs-up. Then he pointed at me, cupped his hands around his mouth, and shouted, "I dig your Kermit the Frog underwear!"

Little Life Lesson 35: I mean, *always.*

Just as the music went off.[25]

---

[25] Roxy: Do you remember the look on Jas's face when this happened?

Polly: I will remember that forever. I don't think I've ever seen anyone's eyes get that big.

Roxy: HER eyes. What about the eyes of everyone around her when they got a glimpse of Kermit?

Polly: And Jack's expression. He —

Jas: What? Jack saw this? You never told me that Jack saw my Kermit underpants.

Hello?

Okay, you two. You can't just mention something like that and disappear.

Come back here!

Hello?

Drat. Please do not let him have seen my underpants.

Twenty

Four things were immediately clear to me:

1. I was going to die of embarrassment.
2. After I did that, I was going to have to find Polly and
   kill her for making my dress so short.
3. Twice.
4. And I was never buying Muppet underwear again.

But all that was in the future. Because in the present I was still HANDCUFFED to a stage, with, courtesy of my friend and Kermit, several hundred people looking at me. Including Alyson. Although I guess you'd call what she was doing more like Death Ray Eyes than regular looking.

Especially up close, which they were when she scooted over, put her hench talon fingernail against my throat, and said to me, "Don't you dare tell anyone we are related or you'll regret it," before swinging off the go-go dance platform, followed by Veronique.

"Okay, cuz," I shouted after her. I was going to be dead of mortification LONG before she could make me regret it.[26]

The music started back up again and more models went skating out onto the rink so the attention kind of drifted, but I was still stuck up there. And where were my friends? Maybe this was my superpower, to shed people! Maybe I was Repellent Girl, able to avoid emotional entanglements, destined to spend my life as a crime-fighting mercenary wandering the plains, saving babies—or maybe baby horses since babies don't really like me—from marauders, and then, forever the mysterious stranger, riding off alone into the sunset. In my totally hopped-up cherry red pickup truck. With silver leather seats. And red Lucite dice as the gearshift.

And broken hearts on the mud flaps, the only visible sign of my secret, soul-wrenching pain.

Yeah, that would be pretty cool.

Especially if Polly would help me with the interior. Which got me back to needing friends.

I decided to take advantage of my scenic view spot above the crowd to see if I could locate any. The entire place was packed, but if there is one thing that being almost six feet tall and on a stage is

[26]Polly: Where were we? Oh, right, Jack and the underwear. I've never seen anyone gape like that.
Roxy: I know. It was like a movie. His mouth open wide. And then he—oops, here she comes.
Jas: I see you guys down here. Hello? Cut it out. This is MY book. He didn't really see my panties, did he?

good for, it's showing the world your underwear. I mean, it's looking for people.

Because clearly he is my mortal enemy in this epic battle between good and evil, the first person I saw was Jack. I could not help noticing that everywhere he went, women stopped talking and turned to stare at him, no doubt enchanted, like me, by his immense-slash-treacherous hotness. He was threading his way along the edge of the skating rink at the far side of the room, not quickly, but like he had a purpose. And I thought I knew what that purpose was. Just beyond him I saw the Fabinator♥ talking on a cell phone. Which could only mean one thing:

Fiona Bristol was here. Fiona was here and Jack was going to—

Well, given the way he had talked about her in the gondola—the words "hench people" were used, after all—I was concerned.

Very concerned.

"Stay away from her!" I shouted, but I might as well have been whispering, because no one, not even me, could hear it over the 80s rock they were blasting. And there was zero comfort in the fact that I had been right, that Jack had cuffed me up here so that he could go do something devious and evil.

At least, I thought, as I followed him hopelessly with my eyes, the Fabinator♥[27] was on the spot to watch out for Fiona. But of course, no sooner did I think that than a cocktail waitress on roller skates with a tray full of drinks careened right into him. It looked like an accident, but part of me would not have been surprised to learn Jack had paid the waitress to do it because if he'd choreographed the move, it could

[27] Jas: Who put this heart next to the Fabinator? Cut it out.
(DID HE SEE KERMIT? ANSWER ME!)

not have worked better to distract the Fab one.[28]

These things happened at the same time: The Fabinator♥ started yelling at the waitress, who appeared to be apologizing while trying to dry him off with cocktail napkins. Fiona came walking around from behind him. And Jack walked right toward her. I braced for it to happen, whatever it was. A gunshot, a knife fight, a scream. Here it came. They were practically face-to-face. I tensed, ready to shout and point.

Jack walked right by her. Without even looking at her. THEY PASSED EACH OTHER LIKE TWO COMPLETE STRANGERS. No knives. No blood. Nothing. NOT EVEN EYE CONTACT.

Which made me suspicious. Iper iper suspicious. I mean, it wasn't natural. Every woman in the club had checked Jack out as he walked by EXCEPT Fiona.

And I was right to suspect! Because as I watched, for a split second, I thought I saw their hands touch.

Were they passing something? Or had I just made the whole thing up?

---

[28] Polly: I would not be surprised either, because I saw her advanced speed skating like an Olympian one minute, and then the next she was pretending she wasn't a very good skater and careening into that guy.

Roxy: She had her hands all over his chest.

Polly: She was drying him off. I liked her outfit though. I hope she didn't get fired for spilling. I bet it was her first night and she wasn't used to skating with a whole tray of drinks.

Roxy: I bet she wasn't even a waitress at all but A MEMBER OF THE RUSSIAN MAFIA. Seriously, did you see that black lace-up corset and leather pants she was wearing? And the studded leather choker? Very Russian Mafia. She could have even been a hired assassin.

Polly: But her wrist cuff was very Fox network teen drama. And I don't think they get those in Russia.

Roxy: Should we tell Jas?

Polly: That the cocktail waitress was wearing out-of-date accessories? Or about Jack seeing her—

Jas: Did he? Are you saying he did???

And what did it mean if I hadn't? Were they working together? Had something changed since that afternoon in the gondola? If they were working together, maybe Fred was safe. Maybe everything was okay.

But where was Jack going? He'd kept walking after he passed Fiona and had now reached a door with a big red EXIT sign over it. As though he could read my thoughts, he turned, looked right at me across the floor, pointed to his wrist, and left.

Jack: Exit, stage left, with obscure gesture.

Jas: Stuck, stage center, with Kermit panties.

Friends:

Friends?

"Anyone?"

I didn't realize I'd spoken aloud until someone below me said, "Talking to yourself again, Jas?" in the sweet tone that could only belong to the Evil Hench Mistress herself.

"Yes," I said through clenched teeth, "it beats talking to you."

"Oh, time machine back to first grade much?"

"Only to visit with your brain," I heard myself say.

"You're not the brain trust in this family!" Alyson shouted.

"Shhh. I don't want people to know we're related," I told her. Her hand came up and I swear she was going to claw my ankle, but she stopped midway.

I turned around and saw why. Tom was coming up behind me, accompanied by Roxy and Polly.

"Finally!" I said. "Where have you been?"

"Not having as much fun as you were, Kermit pants," Polly said.

"I am not speaking to you," I told her.

She shrugged. "As you wish. We were following your piece of all right. Roxy thought he looked familiar."

"He is not my piece of all right. I hate him."

"What a cute bedtime story for you to tell yourself, precious," Polly said.

Roxy changed the subject. "Jas, what do you know about the man with Fiona Bristol? The one who looks like her bodyguard?"

"That's the Fabinator♥[29]," I told her. "He carries a gun and wears bows in his hair. At least he did last night."

"He had one again tonight. It was blue. And really sexy."

Little Life Lesson 36: What I said about things getting worse? Always.

"Oh, no," I said. "You're not suggesting what I think you're suggesting. That was a joke, right? RIGHT?" I looked at Tom and Polly. "Did you know about this?"

Tom nodded, and Polly said, "Rapid onset. I've never seen it happen like this. And I think it might be too advanced for conventional treatment."

That was bad.

Because that time Roxy fell for the Sad Clown, Downtrodden Dan aka Grandma Selma at the circus? Unfortunately, not an isolated incident. Oh, no. Although every guy at Tom's school would have sold his soul to a zombie cult to go out with her, Roxy didn't date. At least not anyone normal. Not for Roxy the fresh-faced, young-man-about-town-with-100-percent-human-DNA type. She was the mistress of the Freak Crush. And it looked like she'd done it again.

"Do you know what his real name is, Jas?" Roxy asked, oblivious to our horror.

[29] Jas: Please ignore the heart.

"Um, no. You don't either. Do you?"

"Ivan ♥30," she said with a smile. "Isn't that perfect? So Russian Mafia."

"How do you know that?" I asked. I was filled with fear. Unless I was very mistaken, this could only mean—

"I looked in his wallet."

"You picked his pocket," I said, trying to sound calm. Roxy is a really good pocket picker, but a very bad judge of people. I took a deep breath. "He carries A GUN, Roxy. He could have killed you."

"A gun, and a knife under his arm," she corrected me, like that was supposed to make me feel better. "In fact, I'd be surprised if he didn't have at least two of each. Stop looking at me like that, you know I always put the wallets back. I just wanted to know what his name was." Then she added, with some pride, "It wasn't easy. He has extraordinary reflexes. You don't think he and Fiona Bristol are a couple, do you?"

There was no right answer to that question but I said, "The man Fiona called 'Darling' on the phone was named 'Alex,' so I doubt it."

Roxy's eyes lit up in a truly alarming way. "Good."

"I will deal with you later," I told her, and turned to Tom and rattled my handcuffs. "Can you pick the lock on these things?"

"You sure you are ready to come down off your pedestal, goddess?" he asked.

"Off. Now."

"Your wish is my command." He looked at the handcuffs for about a second, pushed a button on the side, and they flipped open.

---

30 Jas: Please also ignore this one. [I SAID STOP IT!!!]

I gaped. "You mean I could have just—?"

"They're novelty restraints," he said. "You can get them at a magic store or joke shop. They don't really lock."

They don't really lock, I repeated to myself. He'd been joking with me again. I wasn't sure whether I was more humiliated or infuriated. But I did know one thing:

♥♥Jack♥♥ [31] and his little bag of tricky tricks was going to get it. I wasn't sure what it was, but it was going to be bad. And the fact that he pointed to his wrist like he was trying to tell me as he left did NOT make it better.

"Where are you going, Jas?" Polly called as I took off through the crowds toward the door Jack had used. Chances were he was long gone, but I was still going to look. I was not going to sleep until I got my hands on him and he gave me some answers.

Complete ones.

I pushed open the door with the EXIT sign over it so hard it slammed against the wall. I was standing outside, in a deserted area at

---

[31] Jas: This is not funny. You think you're funny but you're not.

Polly: I think it's funny.

Roxy: Me too.

Polly: You know, Jas, I think you should take a more Zen approach to this.

Roxy: Give in to the power. Ask yourself, What Would Bambi Do?

Jas: What?

Roxy: WWBD? You know, from the famous line in the movie *Bambi*, "If you can't say anything nice, don't say anything at all."

Polly: It's the craze that's sweeping the nation.

Jas: You two are insane, you—

Roxy: Uh-uh-uh. WWBD? Bambi would not use ouchy words like "insane."

Jas: I surrender. I give up.

Polly: Really?

Roxy: Does that mean we can put hearts wherever we want?

Jas: Yes.

Roxy: Oh. Well, that takes all the fun out of it.

Jas: I'm sure you'll think of something. (Can someone please tell me if Jack saw my Kermit panties?)

the back of the roller rink. There were three Dumpsters against a wall, a set of metal stairs that went to a metal door, and two beat-up parked cars. But there was no Jack or sign of Jack. There was an alley that ran along the back, giving access to the street, but there was no sign of him there either.

I was walking back to the exit door when something on the ground caught my eye. As I bent to get a better look at it, I heard a screech of tires and the sound of an engine being gunned and someone, somewhere, yelling my name.

I was turning around to see what was happening when it hit me. I felt myself get pushed through the air, felt a powerful impact with the ground, felt a sharp pain. And then felt nothing at all.

Twenty-one

When I opened my eyes I was terrified something awful had happened because Polly was crying. Polly never cried. She was crying and holding my head and saying, "Jas, Jas, make a sound."

"Any sound?" I asked. I realized I was lying on my back on the ground. "Or did you have a specific one in—"

I didn't get to finish because she was hugging me. HUGGING ME. Polly, who opposed touching except while dancing, whose idea of close intimacy was air kissing. She was hugging me.[32]

[32] Polly: For the record, I was not crying, I was not hugging, and I was not making "you're my hero" eyes at anyone or doing any of the other sappy things Jas said I was doing. I believe her head injury made her a little overemotional.

Jas: You're so cute when you lie, Polly.

Only for a second. As soon as she realized I was okay, she stopped. Still, I was touched.

"What happened?" I asked, sitting up next to her.

She dried her eyes on her pant leg. "Someone tried to kill you, and Tom saved your life."

"Hardly," Tom said from behind Polly. "I just gave Jas a little tap. If I'd done a better job, she wouldn't have hit her head."

It came back to me then. The sound of an engine revving, a car coming at me, Tom yelling my name. And then leaping on me and pushing me out of the way just before the car hit.

"You did save my life, Tom," I said. "You're a hero."

"A superhero," Polly said.

I swear Tom lit up from the inside. "It was nothing. I was just in the right place at the right time."

"And you threw yourself in front of a speeding car," I pointed out.

"You would have done the same for me, Jas," he said, but he was looking at Polly. He smiled at her. She smiled at him. I smiled at both of them but they didn't notice.

Tom tore his eyes from Polly to look at me. "I don't want to scare you, Jas, but I don't think whoever did this was joking this time."

I'd just been thinking the same thing. "Did anyone see what kind of car it was? Or the license number?"

"The windows were tinted and there was a fleur-de-lis sticker on the window," Veronique said. We all turned to stare at her. "I learned about fleurs-de-lis in *Stenciling for Dummies*.[33] They are an easy accent to an elegant room. They're from France. Not like french fries."

[33] Polly: This is not true! I looked it up! There is no *Stenciling for Dummies*! She was just trying to get next to Tom.

Jas: So? You don't care about Tom. You said. Tra la tra la.
La la la.
La.

"Thanks, Veronique," I said, causing her to beam and go plaster herself to Tom's arm.

Alyson, sensing that she was missing an opportunity, grabbed Tom's other arm and said, "Um, I saw that the driver had dark hair."

"Veronique said the windows were tinted."

"Are you calling me a liar, Jas?" Alyson asked. "I know what I saw. I saw a man with a beard. Through the *windshield*."[34]

"I thought you said he had dark hair."

"He did. Dark hair and a beard. Like one of those freaky religious ones."

"Did he have a mustache too? A hat? A caftan?"

"You know what? I was trying to help because Tomás almost bit it for you, but forget it. I don't need this attitude-slash-annoyance." She turned to Tom, grabbing his other arm. "I was just doing it for you."

"I was serious about the caftan," I told her.

"Is someone speaking?" Alyson said. "Because I don't hear anything."

I sighed. "Did anyone notice, for example, the color of the car? Or the shape?"

Roxy said, "Four-door sedan, midsize, Japanese, with aftermarket headlights and brake lights. A souped-up Toyota, Honda, something like that. I'm not that good at imports since the Cadillac King is strictly all-American. Oh, and it was white. It left some paint behind." She pointed at the side of the building where I had been standing. There was a gash in the cement blocks, and a swath of white paint. I did not want to think of what I would have looked like if Tom hadn't

---

[34] Polly: She's a liar, too.

Jas: Now now, P. That's not a very Bambi sentence.

Hey, by the way, did Jack see my Kermit underpants?

Hello?

Sigh.

pushed me out of the way.

Polly said, "As soon as we get into the Pink Pearl I'll get on the CB and put out an alert for a white import with a scrape on one side and a, um, sticker on the window."

Veronique, who had been trying to hug herself as close as possible to Tom, looked up now and said, "The back window."

"And the driver has a beard," Alyson said, clinging to Tom's other side like a lamprey.

Polly smiled at the Henches in her new dangerous way. "Thanks." She looked at me. "I was thinking you'd want to get out of here before anyone inside knows what happened and calls the police."

"Or my dad," I said. "No reason not dying just to have to face him."

"Exactly."

I went and stood in front of Alyson, closer than I normally would. "I have a deal for you," I told her. "If you don't tell my father about this, I won't tell your parents that you were the one who punched that guy last night at the Voodoo Lounge."

"Not much of a bargain, Calamity. My dad thought it was cool when I told him you did it. So I don't think he'll mind if he hears I'm actually the cool one."

Not working. Like a lightning bolt, I remembered another moment from our special time at the Voodoo Lounge the previous evening.

"I will also tell your parents about Miles."

I saw a flicker of fear—yes!—on her face, but then it was gone and she went, "You don't even know about Miles."

"You're seeing Miles Malone?" Tom asked, pulling his arm away from her. "I didn't know he was out of prison yet. Or is he on probation?"

Merry Xmas, Jas, is what I thought. I wanted to dance and play and kiss Tom on the lips. Instead I kept my cool. I turned a steely gaze on Alyson. "So, do we have a deal?"

She could barely whisper her reply. "Yes."

And it was a good thing I sealed it up right then because Polly's phone started to ring. She answered it, frowned, said a few words, and handed it to me. "It's the Thwarter."

"Dad? Is everything okay?" My father hated to use the phone— another genius thing—which meant there was a real problem.

"Is that you, Jas? Is it really you? Talking?"

"I think that's what I'm doing. What's going on? Did something happen to Sherri!? Are Uncle Andy and Aunt Liz all right?"

"Don't change the subject," he barked.

"Um, okay. To what do I owe the pleasure of this call?"

"A man just called on Sherri!'s mobile apparatus and told us you'd been in a car wreck and were badly injured. Is this true?"

"No."

"You haven't been in an accident? You aren't unconscious?"

"Not that I am aware of."

But I almost did faint into unconsciousness when he said, "Oh, thank God. I was so—thank God," in a voice that sounded like he was having trouble breathing.

That couldn't be good. He might be the Thwarter but I didn't want him to die or anything. I mean, he's the only dad I have. And Sherri! would be really sad. I said, "Dad, I assure you that I am speaking to you right now. Unless you think I've been possessed by aliens, I am obviously fine." I was trying to exhibit the wit and verve he loved so well to put his mind at ease and help him get his respiration back on track. It seemed to work.

He sort of snorted and said, "That does sound like you. Still, I would prefer to see you. Come back to the hotel now."

"We were just planning to do that when you called. We'll be there really soon unless—wait, Dad, what if the man who called you was psychic? And the accident just hasn't happened yet?"

"That is not amusing, Jasmine. Although it does prove that you are fine. Tell Polly to drive adequately on the way back. And be sure to strap yourself in."

That's right, geniuses don't use seat belts, they use straps. It's like a whole parallel universe.

"Polly, drive adequately," I instructed her as we got into the Pink Pearl. "I'd love to stay up front here with you kids but I must go strap myself in."

"Do you know what she is talking about?" Polly asked Roxy.

"I think maybe she hit her head harder than we thought."

Little Life Lesson 37: One man's madness is another man's genius.[35]

---

[35] Polly: Jas, I've been wondering. Are you making these things up by just, like, combining words together? Because a lot of your little life lessons don't make any sense.

Jas: Fie.

Polly: Not exactly unproving my point.

Jas: What's wrong with them?

Roxy: I think they're very helpful. That one about fringe boots especially. I never would have thought of that.

Jas: Why, thank you. You were saying, Polly?

Polly: Fine. You can leave them as they are. But you miss some good opportunities.

Jas: For example?

Polly: A good time for a little life lesson might have been when Tom saved your life.

Jas: You mean something like, "Life is short, eat out more often"?

Polly: Um, no, I did not mean something you got off a paper straw wrapper.

Roxy: But it's very good advice. Now I'm hungry. Are you guys hungry?

I could hear Polly up front on the CB spreading the word that Princess P was desperately seeking a white car and asking anyone who saw it to call her cell phone.

Stuck in the back, I ignored Alyson's pouting and Veronique's attempts to probe Tom for bruises and thought about my father's call. Why would someone phone my dad and report that I had been in an accident? Exaggerating what had happened even? Was it the person who had driven the car, anticipating I'd be hurt more than I was?

Or was the point simply to get me in trouble?

I had to admit, it was kind of a tidy idea. One call to my father and I would most likely be grounded. Which would get me out of whoever's hair I seemed to be tangled in. There was an elegance to it that I respected . . . even as I recognized Jack the Immature Jokester's slimy fingerprints all over it.

Little Life Lesson 38: If you find yourself thinking, "His soul may be black as pitch but his logic is sound," do this: Stop, Drop, and Roll. Stop what you're thinking. Drop the pretense. And Roll right on to the admission that what you are admiring—still—is his cute butt and his eyes and his glazed doughnut–flavored lips, which have nothing to do with the quality of his brain.

And DO NOT think that maybe this means you can just have a physical relationship with him and without his shirt.

Polly exhibited admirable adequate driving on the way back to the hotel, and after my father had hugged me (!!!), he inspected every inch of me and, finding them all wanting in all the same ways he always did—"Stop fidgeting, Jasmine. Why are you making that face? Stand up straight"—he decided I was fine.

Little did he know.

When we parted in the lobby we had made sure Tom would escort

Roxy directly to their room, without any stops to look for ♥I♥ᵥ♥ₐ♥ₙ♥. The Evil Henches had gone to hang upside down by their talons or read aloud from *Ritual Sacrifice for Dummies* or do whatever they did for fun, so Polly and I were now on our own in my room. I decided to take a bath because not only had it been the longest day of my life involving one arrest, two near-death experiences, two makeovers, one underwear exposure, and a hug from the Thwarter, but I also felt a little grimy from my tumble behind the roller rink.

I stayed there for a long time, asking myself any questions I could think of that did not lead to thinking about Jack. This limited the possibilities pretty much to questions from ninth-grade earth science like, "Define igneous rock."

When I got out and finished flossing my teeth, Polly was scanning the sheets of one of the queen-size beds for germs with her black light. She looked at me with horror as I pulled back the bedspread and got into the other bed.

"I haven't checked that yet!" she said. "You don't know what you're sleeping on."

"And I don't care. It is bound to be less deadly than a speeding car."

"But there could be microbes," she complained. "Or hairs."

"Oh, look, Howard Hughes is alive and well and living inside my best friend. I can't tell you how much your company cheers me at times like these." I turned off my bedside light. "Goodnight, P. Sweet dreams."

"Are you going to sleep? Now?"

"I was giving it very thorough consideration. It's after three AM."

"Don't you want to talk?"

"About what?" I asked into my pillow.

But as soon as the words were out of my mouth, I knew. She

wanted to talk about Tom.[36]

Ha! I had waited YEARS for this and she sprang it on me now, at three in the morning, when I was exhausted. No. She could wait for one night. In fact, it would be good for her.

Little Life Lesson 39: Never put off until tomorrow what you could do the night before because tomorrow you might have bigger problems. Like a madman pointing a gun at you.

[36]Polly: That is not true! I wanted to talk about you. To make sure you were —
Jas: Do you hear that?
Polly: What? I don't hear anything.
Jas: Exactly. Silence. Mmmmmm.
Polly: I hope bedbugs bite you.

Twenty-two

I dreamed about my mom that night. That's not completely weird; I dream about her at least once a month, but this dream was sort of different from the normal ones.

Usually in my dreams she and I are taking walks somewhere and she's giving me advice. But since our relationship ended when I was six, most of her advice is sort of basic like, "Don't forget to brush your teeth, sweetie," and "Wouldn't you like to wear a barrette to keep your hair out of your eyes?" Polly says it's not my mom talking to me from beyond the grave but my memories of her, grafted onto things in my own head I know but have forgotten or buried. Like one time in a dream she said, "Look for the car keys your father lost in his tennis shoes, which he hid in the back of his closet after Sherri! made him take a lesson last week." And once I heard that, I remembered seeing him put them there.

But sometimes she says things that I don't think can possibly be in my head. Like, "French fries are not a food group." Or like the dream I had that night. Because at the end of the dream, she turned to me and said, "Look at the whole picture. Pay attention to what is there, not what you see."

Um, sure, okay, Mom. Just as soon as I figure out WHAT THAT MEANS. Could you have thoughts in your head, even buried ones, that you did not understand?

Doubtful.

After the dream, I couldn't get back to sleep. Polly was still paying a visit to Snoresville, USA,[37] and I didn't want to wake her by turning on the TV, so I decided to make a few notes and surf the Web.

I was surprised, when I logged on, to see that I had email. Everyone I usually emailed was with me in Vegas, and probably asleep. But even more of a surprise was the message.

[37] Jas: By this I did not mean that Polly snores. In fact, Polly looks adorable at all times, including while she is sleeping. This was simply an unfortunate turn of phrase that I regretted almost immed—

REAL Jas: Polly, what are you doing? You're supposed to be asleep. I just wrote up there that you were sleeping.

Polly: You wrote I was snoring. I don't snore. You made it sound like I snore.

Jas: You do. It's like sleeping with a human popcorn popper.

Polly: TAKE THAT BACK.

Jas: Or a car without a muffler. Oh, and P.S.—THIS IS MY SPACE AND MY STORY. Get back up there where you belong.

Polly: You, Jas, are not the boss of me. And I do not snore.

Jas: Is it nice on your cruise? On the river called DENIAL?

Polly: You lie like a rug.

Jas: You lie on your back. Maybe if you lay on your side you wouldn't snore so—don't even think about it. There are two BeDazzlers here, my friend, and I have the larger one. That's right, step AWAY. Oh, yes. Farther. Good. Victory is mine!

Polly: I'm not done with you.

Jas: Oooh, shaking.

To: Jasmine Callihan <Drumgrrrl@hotmail.com>
From: J.R. <JR_211@hotmail.com>
Subject:

Miss Callihan—
Are you Winnie Callihan's daughter?
A friend

That, coming on top of my dream, was kind of freaky. If the past day had taught me nothing else, it was to be skeptical of "friends" sending notes. The right thing to do, probably, was not to write back at all, but this person knew my mom's name, so I decided on something non-committal.

To: J.R. <JR_211@hotmail.com>
From: Jasmine Callihan <Drumgrrrl@hotmail.com>
Subject: ?

Dear Friend,
Who are you? Why should I answer your question?
JC

A minute after I sent it, my email chirped and I found this:

> To: Jasmine Callihan <Drumgrrrl@hotmail.com>
> From: J.R. <JR_211@hotmail.com>
> Subject: You already have

And that was all. No text, nothing.

I was looking back at the email I'd sent to see how I could possibly have answered a question when Polly's cell phone rang. Princess P went from snoring to answering it in two seconds flat.

"Princess P speaking," she said, reaching for a pad and pen. She laughed. "No, I'm not a man," she said, then got serious and listened. "Thank you so much, Captain. Yes, that would be great. I can't tell you how much you've helped. I'll leave right away."

"You have a date?" I said. "I never figured you for the Captain in Every Port type."

"Shut up. It's about the car. The white car? The one that tried to kill you? One of my CB pals, Captain Doom, saw it when he was delivering flowers this morning, remembered my alert, and called."

"No way. Where is it?"

"The Venetian parking lot, level eight. He said he wished he could stay but he was already behind schedule. He said he left a red carnation on the trunk so we'd be able to identify it."

"How . . . nice of him," I said. Where nice equals B-Movie Stalkerish. But this nuance was lost on Polly.

"He said he's been wanting to meet me. He said he might stop by later if we're around. Apparently there's a pool going about who the driver of the Pink Pearl is, a hot chick or a gay man. Fifty percent think I'm a guy."

"How'd they find out?"

"Funny."

We got dressed, me once again wondering how on earth I ever manage to clothe myself when Polly isn't breathing down my neck.[38] I mean, helping me.

Polly looked me up and down. My final outfit was a blue T-shirt with puffy sleeves, the only skirt of mine she hadn't shortened beyond decency, and my blue cowboy boots with the birds on them she'd altered for my date the day before.

"Is this okay?" I asked. "Or do I have to change some more times before going to the *parking lot*?"

"Haven't I taught you anything? What you wear always matters. You should dress every moment like it could be your last.[39] Now put

[38] Polly: No, Jas, you canNOT wear glitter eye shadow before noon. And just step away from that shirt. Is that—gasp—a CARE BEAR on the front?

Jas: He has poofy ears. Look. Cute!

Polly: I'm going to close my eyes and count to ten, and when I'm done, this will all have been a terrifying mirage. Okay, here we go. One, two, three—are you changing? I don't hear the sounds of changing.

[39] Jas: I am fully making that a Little Life Lesson.

Polly: Too late. It's one of mine.

Jas: Can I use the one about no glitter eye shadow in the morning?

Polly: Only if you recant what you said about me snoring.

Jas: I will not sacrifice my journalistic integrity.

Polly: Way to take a stand. I'm moved. But I'm still not giving in. (Or telling you if Jack was looking in your direction when you—never mind.)

Jas: That's okay, I'm totally over that. (Polly snores so loud, cows think it's a mating call.)

on some mascara, pick a lip gloss, and we're outtie."

I wanted to call Roxy and Tom for reinforcements before we left, but Polly said, "Jas, it's only ten AM on a Saturday. Let them sleep."

"We are going to a place on the instructions of a man named Captain Doom."

"So?"

"If I were planning to abduct someone, calling and telling them to go to the top floor of a free parking structure at ten AM on a Saturday morning and look for a red carnation would be just the thing I'd think of," I pointed out.

"His license plate is 'Puppy Luv.'"

"Oh, look who just got on the express elevator from marginally suspicious to EXTRA CREEPY."

"Do the words just come out, or do you think about them first?"

"Sarcasm doesn't go with your lip gloss, lovie."

Polly dialed Tom and Roxy's room. "Can you two come to the top floor of the parking structure right away? Otherwise I might have to strangle Jas."

"You just try it. I have Designer Imposters perfume in my boots," I told her.

"Come QUICK," she said into the phone before hanging up.

Captain Doom wasn't hanging around to serial-kill us, but the red carnation was there, and it certainly looked like he'd led us to the right white car. It had a scrape on the driver's side in the front that had some cement block dust in it, and a fleur-de-lis sticker on the back window. It also had, unfortunately, tinted windows, which made it really hard to peer in to. I was doing yoga-style contortion moves to try to get a good look through the windshield when Roxy walked over and said, "It's unlocked. Just try the door."

"Is that legal?" I asked.

"From what I saw last night, it was supposed to be *you* scraped on the front of that car, not the wall," Polly said. "I'd say that gives you legal standing. Besides, what crime could you be committing just by opening an unlocked door and looking inside?"

When I hesitated, Roxy took off the star-shaped pin she was wearing that said SHERIFF on the top and BUFFALO BILL'S WILD WEST SHOW! beneath it, and pinned it to my shirt. "There. Now you're official."

I took a deep breath and opened the door.

What I saw inside was truly shocking.

Twenty-three

Polly was the first one of us to regain speech. What she said was: "Jas, stand behind me. I think I'm going to faint."

Followed by Roxy saying, "It—it's everywhere. The entire interior is covered with it. Floor, seats, even the ceiling. I know this is Las Vegas and things get out of hand here, but it's just so—"

"Purple," Tom said now, shaking his head over his breakfast menu. "It was so incredibly purple."

It was true. Every surface on the interior of the car had been covered in purple shag carpeting. Which was both hideous to behold and extra inconvenient. Shag carpeting meant no fingerprints. And since there was nothing in the car, no custom-made shirts or business card cases, at first I'd thought there was nothing to help us.

Look at the whole picture. Pay attention to what is there, not what you see, my mother's voice in my head reminded me. And just as I was about to get snarky with it—PURPLE SHAG, MOM. THAT'S WHAT I SEE—I got what she was saying. Because I'd been so busy looking *for* something, I hadn't realized what I was looking *at.* Which was a supreme environment for trapping tiny pieces of evidence.

After that, I spent fifteen minutes quickly going over the car while Tom, Roxy, and Polly stood guard, and then we moved to the hotel coffee shop to eat brunch and plan our next move.

At least, everyone else was going to eat brunch. Delicious griddle cakes, savory bacon, fluffy omelets—these were not for the likes of Jas. No, although I hid it behind a Brave Face, a carefree laugh, a winning smile, and of course my normal *savoir faire,* I was in pain. Soul-searing pain.[40]

---

[40] Polly: Why are you making that face, Jas? Are you growling?

Jas: Ha! Can't you recognize the carefree laugh, the winning smile, a bit of *savoir faire,* when you encounter them?

Polly: Have you begun taking some kind of medication I should know about?

Jas: Oh, my funny little friend. I may bleed inside, but never fear, I will continue to display a Brave Face.

Polly: Is that what you were doing? I thought it was some kind of vampire impression.

Roxy: That little girl in the corner just started to cry.

Because there could no longer be any doubt. The night before, when Alyson blurted that she'd seen a man with a beard driving, I had started to hope that maybe she was telling the truth. Maybe it had been a man with a beard, like Caftan Man. Maybe someone other than Jack had it in for me. Maybe Jack had no part in this at all.

I know. There's a table for one waiting for me at the Fantasyland Diner.

Little Life Lesson 40: If you're lucky enough to visit the Fantasyland Diner, try to stay as long as possible because their desserts are all no-calorie, and also, the real world sucks.

Naturally, the first thing I saw in the Purple People Maimer, trapped between the cushions and the seat belt of the backseat, was a square brown button. Just like the one on Jack's blazer.[41] And as if that weren't enough, I found dark hairs like Jack's on the headrest of the driver's seat.

Little Life Lesson 41: Pinning any hope on Alyson is like wearing leg warmers (Even cute ones.[42] With unicorns on them.[43] Or

---

[41] Polly: I would have expected better quality from John Varvatos. Buttons should not come off like that.

Jas: Well, cross him off the list of designers to wear WHILE COMMITTING MURDER.

Polly: Exactly.

Jas: I meant that to sting.

Polly: How nice for you.

Roxy: Maybe the button was sewn on fine, but got caught on something.

Polly: Good point. That would be better.

Jas: I'm so pleased we got that settled.

[42] Polly: It is not possible to use the word "cute" to modify "leg warmers."

[43] Polly: Ack! Unicorns! Make it stop! What did I ever do to you, Jas? WHAT???

Jas: Ho ho ho, look who's stinging now. Sting-y sting-y! Ouch ouch!

Polly: I never thought of it before, but with your height and build, you are going to look SO CUTE in your straitjacket.

frolicsome dolphins.[44]) around Polly: a Very Bad Idea.

I'd collected the hairs up, along with similar ones we found on the steering wheel. I wasn't sure what I was going to do with them, but it was great to know that if I did need evidence of Jack's corrupt soul, I had plenty of it.[45]

Roxy was finishing my breakfast as Tom said, "You know, Jas, I don't think those were Jack's wheels. It seems like if you were going to try to kill someone, you wouldn't use your own car. Plus, purple shag seems kind of feminine. Like maybe it's a woman's car. I just don't see Jack cruising in that on a regular basis. Do you?"

"I wouldn't even know. We haven't really gotten past the whole 'You're evil,' 'Perhaps,' patch of dialogue," I told him. Bitterly. And yet with a hint of great inner fortitude. Because that is the kind of woman I am.[46] "Do you think he stole the car?"

"It doesn't look messed with. I'm thinking he borrowed it. Did you notice all the cars around us also had that sticker Veronique mentioned? I think we were in the employee parking section. Maybe we can use that

---

[44] Polly: They don't even make leg warmers with dolphins on them.
Jas: Oh, how you are going to WUV your birthday present.

[45] Tom: The button was in the backseat, right? Why was Jack back there?
Roxy: Maybe he just took the jacket off for driving, to have more flexibility.
Jas: You mean, like, for TRYING TO KILL ME?
Roxy: Exactly. That means he's a pro. Or at least someone who plans ahead.
Jas: Ah, delightful. I'm so pleased. I wouldn't want to be killed by a bad planner.
Roxy: Good point. Jas, what is that shape you're cutting your pancakes into?
Jas: A coffin. For my hopes and dreams.
Roxy: Oh. Well, are you going to eat it?

[46] Polly: Jas, you're making that face again. Can you cool it until we get up to the room?
Roxy: I think the boy at the next table just wet his pants.

to find out who owns the car and get a line on your magic man."

"He is not my—never mind."

"You mean like Jack got close to someone who works here to find out where Fred and Fiona were?" Polly asked. "But how do we find out whose car it is?"

Roxy swallowed the last of my pancakes and said, "That's easy. We just have the head of hotel security make a few calls." She looked at Tom. "Right, *Mr. Curtis?*"

"You're only young once," Tom said, doing a perfect imitation of L. A. Curtis's voice. "Nothing happens in my hotel I don't know about."

We decided that it would be better to impersonate the head of security on the phone from a more private location than the hotel coffee shop, and I wanted to put the evidence we'd collected into envelopes, so we went back to my room. In case I was worried my day couldn't get any better, when we got there we found the Thwarter snooping around. Fortunately I'd decided to store all the magazine articles and the evidence we'd collected so far in Polly's backpack, so it was safe from his patented ThwartVision. The shoe box fuming chamber was poking out slightly from under the bed, but from his relatively pain-free expression I deduced he hadn't found it yet. When we came in he scowled at me for a moment, then launched into one of his loving father-daughter chats:

Thwarter: Where have you been?

Jas: Breaking into cars in the parking lot.

Thwarter: Is everything a joke to you, Jasmine?

Jas: Actually right now I am suffering from a secret sorrow so heavy my organs are being smashed by it.

Thwarter: (snorting) Sherri! and I are having brunch with your aunt and uncle. Don't forget that our final family dinner is tonight at eight o'clock.

Jas: I'll be there if I'm not dead by then.

Thwarter: You'll be there. Period.

Which left me with the cheery knowledge that my father would want to spend time with me even if I were a cold, stiff corpse. Not every daughter can say that, I bet!

Once he and Sherri! were safely out of the room, Tom, who was our sherpa because his carpenter pants had the largest pockets, dumped the hairs and button we'd collected on the desk and went to the phone to make his call.

"Hey, Jas, your message light is blinking," he said.

"I bet it's the Hench Twins looking for you, Tomás," I said. "Could you play it on the speakerphone?"

I'd just finished writing EVIL BOY HAIRS FROM DEATHMOBILE on the outside of an envelope when the sound of the voice leaving the message stopped me cold. It wasn't Alyson's voice. It was a little boy's voice. Fred's.

And he was scared to death.

He was whispering and sniffling at the same time so it was hard to hear him, but it sounded like he said, "Jas, you said everything would be okay, that you would keep him away but now he's here. Mad Joe is scared, Jas. He's trembling and he wants you to come help him. Jas, you promised . . . I'm so scar—"

Click. Dial tone.

It had happened. Red Early had come for Fiona and Fred.

"Should we call back?" Roxy asked.

But I didn't stay to answer. "I'm taking the stairs, you take the elevator, meet me at room 40215."

Twenty-four

Fred had told me his room number the day we went to get ice cream, but when we got to room 40215 the DO NOT DISTURB sign was up and there was no answer to our knocking.

"There's a house phone just down the corridor. I'll go call security," Polly said, and took off.

I put my ear against the door. There was no sound. Nothing. "I don't think there's anyone inside."

Polly came running back, panting a little. "Security says they're sending someone up to investigate the situation and we should go back to our room."

Hmmm, or NOT. Roxy and Tom did in fact go back to my room, but only to grab the evidence we'd found in case we needed it, while Polly and I waited in front of Fred and Fiona's door. If they were in trouble, I wanted to be there to help.

Little Life Lesson 42: Security officers have very good, if selective, memories.

The first thing Security Officer Kim and Security Officer Reese said when they saw me at the end of the corridor was, "Miss Callihan." They recognized me! Even though our time together the day before when they escorted me to Mr. Curtis's office had been brief, it obviously left an impression on them. I would have been flattered if Security Officer Kim hadn't immediately clicked on his walkie-talkie and said, "Cancel that emergency status on floor forty. It's a prank."

"It's not a prank. That boy, the one I was in the casino with yesterday?"

"The minor you were willfully corrupting? Yes?"

There was so much wrong with that statement I didn't even know where to start. And I had more important things to get to. "This is his room. He called me and left a message that he was in trouble and we came right down here but now there's no answer when we knock. I think something is really wrong."

Officer Reese reached out and flicked the DO NOT DISTURB sign with his finger. "You *can* read, can't you, Miss Callihan? Or do you need me to tell you what this says?"

Okay, now, that was just unnecessarily mean. Maybe I was a repeat offender in the eyes of the law, but that didn't mean I was lying. Or illiterate. I felt like I'd been punched in the stomach. I looked down and saw three things at the same time.

1. My hands were trembling.
2. I had run to Fred's room still holding the envelope marked EVIL
   BOY HAIRS FROM DEATHMOBILE.
3. There was a dark brown drop on the carpet just outside the
   door, and another, smaller one, a little farther down the
   corridor.

I also saw Tom and Roxy coming toward us, with Tom's pockets bulging with our evidence. I put up my hand to stop them, looked back up, and said to Security Officers Kim and Reese, "You're right. I'm making a big deal about nothing. I'm sorry for the inconvenience. We'll go back to my room." I nodded to Polly. "Come on. We've caused enough trouble already."

We caught up with Roxy and Tom. "Don't say anything, just come with me," I whispered to them and kept walking, head down, toward the elevators.

"Where are—" Polly started to say when we got in, but changed course when I nodded toward the security camera, and finished with, "—Mr. and Mrs. Pac-Man, would make a good song title, don't you think, Rox?"

When we got out, I made a sharp left. Polly said, "Jas, our room is the other way."

"But the closest staircase to Fred's room is this way," Roxy said, figuring out what I was doing.

We reached the staircase and started going up.

"Okay," Polly said as we climbed, "I saw that you had your fingers crossed when you were talking up there and knew that meant you were lying, but why did you do it?"

"Because if we stayed, they would never have left." I stopped at the landing of the fortieth floor. "There were what looked distinctly like blood drops going from the door down the corridor. They got smaller, meaning they were leading away from Fiona and Fred's suite. The way they looked, I think someone was injured and removed from that room. And Officers Kim and Reese weren't going to do anything about it."

"So the sooner the security guards go away—" Roxy said.

"—the sooner I can bypass the electric lock and get us in there," Tom finished.

"You can do that?" I asked.

"I think so. One of the guys from work this summer is an ace locksmith and told me all about them, but I've never tried it before."

Polly carefully opened the stairwell door a crack, said, "All clear," and stepped into the corridor. When we were back in front of the Bristols' room, Tom studied the lock for a moment and turned to me. "Could you lend me your Sheriff's badge?"

I handed it to him, and from where I was standing it looked like all he did was touch the lock, say, "Abracadabra," and the door opened.[47]

[47] Tom: Um, Jas? I did not say "Abracadabra."
Jas: You said something like it.
Tom: I said "ouch."
Jas: Poetic license. How did you get the lock open, anyway?
Tom: It was totally simple. All I did was ███████████████████████████████████
███
Jas: Cool. So anyone could do it?
Tom: Yes. Anyone with a ███████████████.

Little Life Lesson 43: If you find yourself in a room you're not sup-posed to be in, via a means you're not supposed to use, doing some-thing you're not supposed to be doing, remember to lock the door. Putting on the safety chain might not be a bad idea either.

Twenty-five

We walked in, paying no attention at all to whether the door locked behind us.

(Little Life Lesson 44: One of those portable motion detectors with an alarm on them could also come in handy in a situation like this.)

I thought my room was nice, but Fiona and Fred's made it look like a coat closet.

(Little Life Lesson 45: Or a chair jammed under the door handle.)

Their suite was easily four times the size of mine and very deluxe. You walked into a marble foyer, with a door on one side to a guest bathroom. If you kept going, there was a dining area with a table, and then, farther in down some steps, two sitting areas, one with a TV and chairs and one with a couch. There was a door on either side of the foyer that led to two bedrooms, each with their own bathroom, one of them with a folding bed against the wall.

"Is it only me, or are you guys getting a totally creepy vibe?" Roxy said as we stood in the entry way.

"Creepy," Polly agreed. "But I don't know why."

At first glance it seemed like your regular morning in the Bristol household, right down to the breakfast dishes on the dining table and the chairs pushed back casually, as though Fred and Fiona had just gotten up to go in the other room for a sec and would be right back. It all looked totally normal.

Except for the line of dried blood drops that went from the door to the table. Or rather, the other way: The drops got closer together near the table, which meant the line started there. The ones I'd seen in the hallway were a continuation of it.

"Someone was hurt right here," I said, pointing to the place where the drops started. "Polly, is your Howard Hughes freaky germ light in the backpack?"

"Would you be referring to my black light? Yes. Why? You want to use it now, Miss Mocky-Mock?"

"Yes, please. I have an idea."

Polly found the black light while Tom closed the curtains and Roxy turned off the overhead lights. When it was dark, I flipped the black light on and pointed it at the area with the most blood.

Polly said, "Wait, I think there's something on the arm of the chair." I moved the light to where she was pointing, and a long thin object lit up. A hair.

"Can you shine the light into the sitting area more?" Tom asked from down there. "On the floor. Yeah—wow. Check it out."

The black light was picking up traces of dirt left by someone walking around. It looked like a treasure map on the floor, glowing footprints marking all the places the person had gone—from the dining table down the stairs to the couch, then to each of the two chairs, standing in front of them, over to the armoire with the television, back to the couch, and finally back up the stairs to where we were standing.

"Someone has ADD," Polly said. "They were going in circles."

"Or maybe they were searching for something," I said.

"The cushions on the couch and the chairs do look sort of sloppy," Tom agreed. "Maybe that's why the place feels so creepy."

I went to flip on the light. "That and the blood on the floor."

Polly said, "Do you think it's Fiona's or Fred's?"

"I don't know, but judging from this"—I held up the hair we'd found on the chair arm, which was a distinctive shade of bright red—"I'm willing to bet that Red Early is the one who is holding them. The hair still has its root attached, which means it got pulled out. They didn't go without a fight."

"But Red Early told Fiona he was going to hunt her down," Tom said. "Why would she agree to see him?"

"I don't know. Maybe she agreed to see Jack and he snuck Red in."

"But we were right behind Jack at the roller rink last night, and he didn't even talk to Fiona," Polly said.

"No, but I thought I saw their hands touch, like they were passing notes."

"So what happened?" Polly said. "Fiona and Fred are having breakfast, Red Early comes in, they fight, he wins. Then he ties them up or something while he searches the room?"

"I guess," I told her. "I wonder what he was looking for. Given the places he searched, like under the couch cushions, it can't be very bulky. But there's no question something bad happened here." I sighed. "We should call the police, shouldn't we?"

"Oh, yes. I think telling them we broke into Fiona Bristol's room against the orders of Venetian security and tampered with a crime scene to search it is a great idea," Polly said. "Should we vote?"

"No." I picked up the phone and started dialing.

Little Life Lesson 46 (from Polly): Naïveté goes beautifully with prison orange.

The 911 operator put me on hold, so I hung up, got the main police number from information, and when someone answered I explained that I was at the Venetian and I thought a crime had been committed.

"What's your name, Miss?"

"That doesn't matter, what matters—"

"Name?"

"Jasmine Callihan. And—"

"Callihan with two Ls? And you say you are at the Venetian?"

"Exactly. We called—"

"Are you the Jasmine Callihan who stole the Venetian limo two nights ago and had to be chased down?"

"Um. Not exactly."

"Miss Callihan, I don't think you realize how lucky you are not to have been arrested the other night. Now I suggest you stop playing games and start counting your lucky stars. If you must play pranks, call Venetian Security. Falsely filing a police report is a felony and if you call here again, I will do my best to see to it that you are arrested."

"Okay, thanks a lot, bye," I said, trying to sound cheery so Polly would not know what had happened.

"They hung up on you. I heard it," Polly said.

Roxy frowned. "That means the only people who know Fred and Fiona have disappeared are us."

"And that we're the only ones who can find them before anything bad happens," I said.

"I think you mean something worse," Polly said, pointing to the blood trail.

I gave her my most nice smile. "Oh, you with your tidings of comfort and joy. Less talking, more looking for evidence."

Tom, still standing in the living room area, said, "They might have found what they were looking for. Someone burned something in an ashtray here. Whatever got burned is gone, but they left the matchbook."

"Tom, do you have the envelope labeled Madame Tussauds Matches in your pocket?" I asked. "If the matches Jack used the other night came from the matchbook here—"

"—it means he's working with Red Early," Tom finished, handing me the envelope from his pocket. "Undoubtedly."

Of course the ripped edges fit against two of the stubs in the matchbook perfectly. No wonder Jack had acted so weird when I said he was Red's lackey. He was no lackey. He was more like an accomplice. Part of the big show.

As I put the matchbook in its own envelope and gave it to Tom to hold, I reflected that it was good to know I hadn't set my sights on a mere errand boy, but a real hard-core gangster type. Yes, my taste in men was outstanding. What I wanted to do then was go and quietly hang myself. But I decided the right thing to do was put that off until after we helped Fiona and Fred.

Roxy squealing from inside of one of the bedrooms broke into my deep and important thoughts. "This is Ivan's room," she said. "The closet is filled with specially made clothing. The pants have been specially altered to accommodate his extra large—"

Polly put her hands over her ears. "I DON'T WANT TO HEAR THIS."

"—guns," Roxy finished. "Hey, Jas, can I have that black light to use in here?"

I turned to Tom. "You go in there and make sure she doesn't transition from obsessed girl to stalker. Polly, you take Fiona's room. I'll stay out here and finish looking around."

Tom followed Polly with his eyes but said to me, "Your wish, my command, Sheriff."

"Are you sure we should humor her this way?" Polly asked, from the door of Fiona's room. "I mean, if she's checking his sheets for—"

"I am trying not to hear that," I told her. "Don't forget to check the folding bed. I think Fred was sleeping there with his mother."

While Polly looked through Fiona's room, occasionally making disapproving noises about her wardrobe, I checked out the fax machine, the notepad by the phone, all the drawers, the phone book, and even flipped through the Bible to see if any clues had been stuck there.

Nope.

I dumped out the garbage can. The largest items were three local newspapers from the past week, each open to an article where Fiona was mentioned as having been spotted in different places around Las Vegas. There was also an empty prescription pill bottle in Fiona's name, two Oreos with the top cookie broken the same way on both, some pinkish white powder, and a chewed piece of gum.

Polly joined me then. "Fiona Bristol's shopping habits show signs of deep torment," she announced, slumping into one of the chairs at the breakfast table. "The poor woman needs help badly."

"Just because you don't like her clothes?"

"It's not a taste thing, although she is a bit frumpy. It's more her approach. Half the clothes are like two years old, while the other half were practically purchased yesterday. They still have the tags on them and everything. If they were different sizes, like she'd gained weight or something, I would understand, but they aren't. Absent extenuating circumstances, that kind of binge shopping is a warning sign, a cry for help. It makes it impossible to establish a singular style. People think that bad dressing is a sign of inner unrest, but so often it goes the other way. Style dysfunction leads to lifestyle dysfunction."

"That is very deep. Tell me, Professor Prentis, did you happen to look in the garbage can in her bathroom?"

"Yes, Madam Sarcastico, I did. There was nothing in it. It was bare. Empty. Devoid of contents. Why?"

"I don't know. I kind of hoped there would have been some pills. Look at this," I said, using the pen from the hotel stationery set to lift the empty prescription bottle toward her so I wouldn't mess up any fingerprints on it. "It is made out to Fiona and says to take for sleeping. The recommended dose is only two tablets a day, but it was filled two days ago and it's empty."

"It's no surprise Fiona was having trouble sleeping," Polly said, holding open one of the hotel envelopes so I could slip the bottle into it for safekeeping. "If I had to share a room with that fuchsia Zandra Rhodes dress she's got in the closet, I'd have nightmares too."

Before I could say something about how I was sure Polly was right, that it was a dress that was freaking Ms. Bristol out, and not, oh, her murderous husband on the loose, Tom staggered toward us, looking sort of dazed.

"Are you okay?" I asked.

"Oh, yeah. I just wanted to come out here to see if I could help. Roxy's in there looking for, um, evidence." He lowered his voice. "In Ivan's underwear drawer. It's hopeless, Jas."

"Is there any sign of a struggle in the Fabinator's room?" I asked him.

"No, why?"

"It looked like there was only one set of footprints doing the searching, so I'm wondering, where was he during all this? He seemed to be protecting Fiona when I saw him, but it would take a strong man to overpower him."

Tom nodded. "Maybe he was actually working for Red Early all along. Another conspirator."

"Poor Fiona," Polly said. "Are we the only ones on her side?"

"It looks that way," I said.

"Then we'd better bust a move," she said. "None of what we've found gets us any closer to figuring out where Fred and Fiona are."

Roxy came into the dining room then, holding up a sheet of paper. "This might. Look familiar, Jas?"

It did. It was a note in handwriting I recognized. And not just handwriting. Even the wording was familiar. The note Roxy had found said:

FIONA,

I MUST SEE YOU, ALONE. MEET ME SOON—
TODAY? TONIGHT? SO I CAN EXPLAIN
EVERYTHING. I KNOW MY ARRIVING SO

ABRUPTLY LIKE THAT FRIGHTENED YOU AND I APOLOGIZE. I PROMISE TO LEAVE YOU IN PEACE AFTER WE TALK, IF YOU WANT ME TO. CALL ME AT 555-2437. IF NOT FOR MY SAKE, OR YOURS, FOR FRED'S. PLEASE.

JACK

"Where did you find it?" I asked Roxy.

"Ivan had it. But check this out. This is the best part." She flipped on the black light and parts of the note started to look almost three-dimensional.

"What is that?" I asked.

"It looks to me like someone traced over some of the letters."

I am embarrassed to admit it, but my heart started to beat very, very fast. Before I'd even asked, Tom pulled the two notes I'd received earlier out of his pocket and handed them to me. I said, "Thanks," to him, and to Roxy, "Shine the black light on these too."

Different inks show up as different colors under fluorescent light. The ink on the first note I'd gotten, the one from "A Friend," and the ink on the note to Fiona looked the same. But the ink on the note telling me to go to Madame Tussauds was definitely different. The pen strokes looked different too.

And that wasn't all. Under the fluorescent light, another message showed up on the Madame Tussauds note. It was an indentation of a note that had been written on a piece of paper above the one that the letter to me was written on. The writing was unfamiliar, but the message wasn't. It said:

MISS CALLIHAN,

I MUST SEE YOU, ALONE. MEET ME AT ~~GEORGE FORMAN~~ MOHAMMAD ALI AT 5:30 PM TONIGHT SO I CAN EXPLAIN EVERYTHING. ~~I KNOW MY ABRUPT ARRIVAL DEPARTURE FRIGHTENED YOU AND I AND~~ APOLOGIZE FOR MY ABRUPT DEPARTURE. ~~I PROMISE TO LEAVE YOU IN PEACE AFTER IF YOU WANT ME TO.~~ COME, IF NOT FOR MY SAKE, ~~OR YOURS,~~ FOR FRED'S.

YOURS,

JACK

TAC. CANION. 2:15

It was like someone had written a rough draft of the letter I got, carefully selecting the words and then—

"They traced the letters from the note to Fiona, to make it look like Jack's writing," Tom said. "The first note you got, from 'A Friend,' looks like it was real. But the second one you got was a forgery."

"What does that part at the bottom mean, 'Tac. Canion'?" Polly asked.

"It looks like someone made a note to themselves on the same page they were using to write the draft of the letter," I said.

"Canion could be Taqueria Cañonita," Roxy suggested. "The taco place with the mints where we had dinner after the wax museum."

"So whoever was trying to scare me met someone there for a late lunch, and grabbed a mint then."

"By 'whoever' you mean Jack, right?" Polly said.

"No. Someone forged the note to make it look like Jack wrote it, but he didn't. Someone was trying to frame him and scare me at the same time. Last night at the roller rink Jack said he'd sent me a note and I assumed he was talking about both notes. But maybe he just meant the first one. Warning me to stay out of all of this."

Roxy said, "Does that mean Jack didn't lure you to Madame Tussauds?"

"I think it does." Jack's not evil! I wanted to scream. But I had to play it—He's good! He's innocent! He's the man of my dreams!—cool.

Polly was frowning. "Then whose fingerprints are those on the note and the mint wrapper?"

"I have no idea. They could be the Fabinator's since he had the note they were traced from."

"He is just holding it for a friend," Roxy said positively.

"Of course he is, Rox," I told her. I could afford to be charitable. "But if someone was trying to convince me that Jack was evil—"

"Then he could be good," Polly said.

"He *is* good," I corrected.

"But he could be in trouble," Tom said.

Polly nodded. "We have his digits. Why don't we give him a call and see?" She dialed and handed me the phone.

I willingly took it[48] and listened through three rings.

"No one is answering," I said. "He's—"

Roxy interrupted me to say, "Shhh."

---

[48] Polly: I'm sorry, did that say "willingly"? As in, adverb, English, meaning "to do something in a voluntary or agreeable manner"? I have let you slide on a lot of things, Jasmine "My friend Polly snores" Callihan, but I'm not going to let you lie about this.

Jas: What? I totally did.

Polly: My recollection is that you started screaming, "Eek, the phone! Get it away from me! I can't talk to him. What will I say to him? Eek!"

"What?" The phone bounced into voice mail. I hung up.

"Dial again," Roxy said.

"There was no answer."

"Just do it."

Since Roxy almost never gives orders, I did what she said. The phone started to ring again.

"Do you hear something?" she said. "It sounds like—"

Polly's eyes got huge. "The music to the arcade game Centipede."

Roxy said, "I think it's coming from Ivan's room."

She was right. Jack's phone was in Ivan's room. Under the bed.

Along with Jack's unconscious body.

Roxy: You're forgetting the part where Jas leaped backwards and tangoed a little with the wastebasket.

Polly: Quite right. Thank you, Roxy.

Jas: Yeah, thanks. The atmosphere is quite thin over there on Planet Polly and Roxy, isn't it? Is that why you two are so delusional?

Roxy: You're also leaving out the part where Jas tried to hide under the table. And kept repeating to herself, "I am invisible. I am invisible. If I keep my eyes closed, I am INVISIBLE."

Polly: Indeed. "Cowering," I think is the word that describes what she was doing.

Roxy: That's an advanced SAT prep word, isn't it? Very nice.

Polly: Thanks. Who would have guessed that our sweet Jas, who one time *willingly* jumped into the wild boar pit at the zoo during feeding time to retrieve a child's balloon, would be afraid to talk to some boy?

Jas: They were wildebeests. Their tusks are shorter. And I was just worried he wouldn't remember who I was. I didn't want it to be awkward for him.

Polly: There's no danger of that, precious. No one who saw you dancing on that stage in your Kermit panties will soon forget who you are. That I promise.

Roxy: Snicker.

Jas: Sometimes I really hate you guys.

Twenty-six

I would like to say that I reacted like a pillar of strength and clear-headedness to seeing Jack unconscious, but that would be, well, a total lie.

Fortunately, due to their older brother's occasional "bad trips," Roxy and Tom had experience finding passed-out bodies on the floor and knew exactly what to do.

Tom and I dragged Jack out from under the Fabinator's love arena,[49] then Tom bent down to inspect him. "His pulse is steady and he's breathing, but his pupils are dilated. That means someone drugged him. He'll be fine once he sleeps it off."

---

[49] Roxy: IS NOT ONE EITHER. I went over every inch of his sheets with the black light and I didn't find one single piece of evidence that anyone besides Ivan slept there. Take it back, Jas. My Ivan is no slut. He is a chaste and true warrior.

"So then we don't need an ambulance," I said, recradling the phone I hadn't even realized I had picked up. I looked down and saw my hands were trembling.

"It's too bad Alyson isn't here to stick her finger up his nose," Roxy said. "That would wake him right up."

"Don't invoke the name of the Evil Henches," I said. "They'll hear you."

"He looks peaceful," Polly said.

"As peaceful as a guy with a cut on his forehead and his hands tied behind his back can look," I said. He was still wearing the clothes he'd worn to the roller rink. I fingered the place on his jacket that was missing the button. There was some purple fuzz like the carpeting from the car that tried to hit me on the front of the jacket, and a little in his hair.

Hair that, I learned by comparing them, did not match the dark hair we'd found on the driver's seat of the car. But there was one of those, too, on his shoulder. "I think whoever tried to run me over last night must have conked Jack on the head first and put him in the backseat of the car."

"But who was it?" Tom asked as I handed him the envelope with the hairs back.

I thought about that. "Alyson said it was a man with a beard and at the time I decided to ignore her, but what if she was telling the truth?"

"You mean like your Caftan Man. I guess we just have to wait until

Jas: You're scaring me, Roxy.
Roxy: Are you going to take it back?
Polly: (I'd do what she says, Jas. You know what happens when Roxy gets crossed. Remember that time at the mall when that woman said there were no such things as extraterrestrials, and Roxy decided to fashion a hand grenade out of a hot dog on a stick and an Orange Julius and we had to—)
Jas: I take it back.

Jack wakes up to figure out what is going on," Tom said. And then he said, "Jas, why are you undoing his belt?"

"I'm looking for evidence," I explained. "There may be something on his person that will tell us who did this and where to find them."

"Something in his underwear?" Tom asked.

"You never know where you will find evidence."

"Why don't we start with untying his hands and looking through his pockets?" Polly said, stopping me before I could undo the top button of his jeans.

"I can't take off his pants? He saw my underpants. It seems only fair. And a lot of evidence could be trapped there."

"Maybe you could start with his shirt," Polly said gently.

"Oh, fine." I put his belt back on (while surreptitiously using my fine detective skills to ascertain that he was wearing boxers with what looked like Snoopy on them. Snoopy! How could I ever have thought he was a bad guy?).

Little Life Lesson 47: If everyone just went around in their underwear all the time, there would be less crime because it would be easy to tell who was nice—people wearing Snoopy boxers!—and who wasn't—people wearing satin jock straps with holster attachments.[50] Also, there would be a lot less stealing because people wouldn't be able to hide things in their, ahem, pockets.

We rolled Jack onto his side so we could free his hands. "We should cut the cords but keep the knot intact," I said, "in case we need it later for evidence."

---

[50] Roxy: I just know you weren't thinking about anyone in particular there, Jas.

Jas: How would I know that the Fabinator had blue satin jock-strap-plus-gun-holder undergarments? Unless, of course, I saw one sticking out of your pocket.

Roxy: Nice try. It's not in my pocket, it's in my bra. Close to my heart.

Jas: MY BRAIN! MY BRAIN IS BLEEDING. MAKE IT STOP.

"What kind of evidence can you get from a knot?" Roxy asked.

"Maybe there's something special about the way it's tied," I said. "It looks kind of complicated. I think it might be a sailor's knot."

"How do you know?" Polly asked. "You've never been sailing."

"No, but I have watched *Horatio Hornblower* every time it's on TV," I told her. "I am a storehouse of nautical facts."

Polly muttered something about my only being interested in the parts where Horatio had his shirt off, while I used the scissors from her pocket-size auxiliary sewing kit to cut the knot off. Even with his hands freed, Jack didn't wake up. It was sort of weird, like having a Jack doll you could do whatever you wanted with.

Unless of course you were with my friends. In which case the possibilities were severely limited. I will admit, however, that given how things turned out, their caution was all for the best.

When Jack's arms were loose it was easier to check the pockets of his jacket. What we found was a little strange. There was an invitation to the party the night before, a Velcro wallet with $31.64 in cash and no ID of any kind, and an unopened bag of Pounce kitty treats.

"He could have been on a diet," Polly said. "My father's third-to-last girlfriend said cat food is the best diet she knows."

"You made that up," I said.

"I wish. You should have seen what she was like at restaurants."

"I don't think Jack is dieting. If I had to guess, I'd say these were for Mad Joe. Fred's cat." I started patting down Jack's jeans pockets. "I am not being perverted," I told the room at large. "I am just trying to be thorough.[51] Tom, stop looking at me like that."

[51] Polly: Methinks she doth protest too much.
Roxy: Methinks so also.

"Touchy touchy," Tom said.

Little Life Lesson 48: cf. Little Life Lessons 43–45.

"Well, isn't this a cozy scene," a familiar voice said from the doorway behind us.

I turned around slowly and saw my good friend L. A. Curtis standing just outside the bathroom, staring at us. He had one hand on his hip.

And his other hand on his gun.

Twenty-seven

"I heard about your call to hotel security," Mr. Curtis said, bounce-walking toward us. "I have to admit, I didn't expect to see you *inside* the Bristols' room. May I ask, how did you get in?"

"Door was open," Roxy said, thinking quick.

"I see," Mr. Curtis said, not buying it for a second.

It was time to change the subject, and fast. "I'm so glad you're here," I said, which was true. "I know that you have been protecting Fiona and Fred from Red Early."

Mr. Curtis nodded. "I have, but—is that guy on the floor okay? Does he need an ambulance?"

"No," I said, trying to look like I had not just been undressing him. "He's just tired and his clothes were, um, binding. But we have no time to lose."

"What are you talking about?"

"I think Red Early has kidnapped Fred and Fiona and taken them somewhere. We've found a lot of evidence," I said. "Including some blood. I tried to call the police but they laughed at me."

He nodded toward Passed Out Jack. "Where does he fit in? You sure he's okay? I could—"

"He's fine," Tom assured him. "He'll start snoring in a second."

I said, "I'm guessing that Red Early brought him here to show Fiona what he thought of her go-between. And then he left him because he was a liability. He was tied up with this"—I held out the rope—"I think it's a sailor's knot."

Mr. Curtis fingered it and nodded. "You're right. And from what my connections on the police force have told me, Red's always been partial to the water. It was a filleting knife, a fisherman's tool, he used to kill his victims. This could definitely be his handiwork. Nicely spotted."

"Will Red hurt Fred and Fiona? Now that he has them?"

"It's hard to know. A man who's fallen that far, on the run, he's pretty much capable of anything." He looked back at the piece of rope. "Thank you for showing me this. I've got to go."

"Then you know where he is? Where he's keeping Fred and Fiona? We'll come with you."

"I have a general idea, thanks to you, but you've got to leave this to me and the professionals now. It could be very dangerous." And he made for the door.

I ran to intercept him. "What is dangerous is leaving Fred and Fiona in Red's hands."

"You are a persistent little lady, aren't you?" he said.

For the sake of efficiency, I decided not to point out that he was slightly shorter than I am. "I'm just worried. Look, the police are going to have to organize a rescue team, right? If you give us directions, where you think they are, we could go there now and just keep an eye on things until the police come. We won't do anything, just make sure that Fiona and Fred are safe."

Mr. Curtis stared at me. "You think I am going to send a group of inexperienced kids to find a murderer? No, Miss Callihan."

"Then come with us. Let us drive you wherever it is. Polly is an excellent driver. Even my dad thinks she's adequate. We won't get in the way."

"No one would suspect us of working with the police if we're in the Pink Pearl," Roxy pointed out. "It will be the perfect surveillance vehicle."

"And we're going to follow you when you leave here anyway," Polly said.

I wanted to kick her but, incredibly, that seemed to be the argument Mr. Curtis responded to best. He gave her a bemused half-BriteSmile, then looked down at his watch, absently twisting a brown thread caught in the metal band and shaking his head. "I don't have time to argue with you, or to take any measures to make sure you don't follow, so I think you've got me. I don't like it"—he shook his head again—"not one bit. I'm going to notify the local cops. I'll ride with you so I can keep an eye on you and make sure you stay safe. As soon as the police get there, though, you leave. And until then you have to promise to do whatever I say. Got that?"

"Yes, sir," I said, so giddy with wonder that I almost saluted. As Mr. Curtis went to use the phone I said to Polly, "I can't believe that worked."

She shrugged modestly. "I picked up a few pointers about finding your opponent's weak spots while working in my parents' law firm this summer."

Mr. Curtis had been on the phone with his back to us but now I overheard him saying, "We can fight about that when I get there. Just get your gear in place and be ready. We've both been outdone by a group of teenagers. The important thing now is for each of us to do our parts right. Yes, I'll see you there." Outdone by a group of teenagers! Way to go us!

"What do we do with Jack?" Tom asked me.

"Bring him," I said. "I'm not done undressing him."

"Jas—"

"I was kidding!" I was. I WAS.

(Mostly.)

(Come on, I'm human. And he was F-I-N-E. And he smelled ever so slightly like Oreos.)

"Seriously, we can't leave him here. What if THEY come back to finish him off?" I asked Tom, who had to agree with my outstanding and mature logic.

I was so excited that Mr. Curtis agreed to let us go that I was practically skipping and felt like I was brimming with superhuman strength. Tom and I hoisted Jack between us and drag-carried him to the elevator and through the lobby to the valet.[52] No one even gave us a second glance.[53]

---

[52] Tom: What I still don't understand, Jas, is why you had to carry him with your hand in the back pocket of his jeans. Is that an approved Girl Scout carry or something?
Jas: I wanted it to look natural, like we were just strolling along. Him and me. And you, his conjoined twin.
Tom: Oh. I'm sure we fooled everyone, then.

[53] Jas: See? It worked.
Tom: I am not sure you count as an objective observer.
Polly: (Did he have a nice butt?)
Jas: (I believe they have just dedicated a wing of the National Gallery to it, representing, as it does, complete artistic perfection in every way.)
Tom: Is there a suggestion box? Because I don't think you should be allowed to say things like that without warning people first. I mean, some people have weak stomachs.

When the Pink Pearl pulled up, we stashed Jack in a cozy corner. Mr. Curtis succumbed to Polly's Look of Don't Even Think About It when he offered to drive, so instead he sat up in the navigator's seat, while Tom, Roxy, and I stayed in back.

"Where are we going?" I asked as we pulled out of the parking lot.

"Lake Mead. The marina. I think Red Early might be hiding out on a boat there."

The drive turned out to be kind of long, and seemed longer because Polly will only drive the EXACT speed limit, and Mr. Curtis kept looking at his watch and fidgeting nervously with the thread caught there in a way that showed how anxious he was, which was making me that anxious as well. He did spend some of the time filling in a few things about the Red Early/Fiona Bristol case we hadn't known. Like how until recently, Fiona had been in hiding, not even using credit cards, afraid for her life if Red Early had any idea where she was.

He said, "She became the prisoner while her husband was out roaming around."

"I wonder what made her come out now," I said.

"Maybe she decided she couldn't stand all those old clothes," Polly said.

Mr. Curtis chuckled. "I think that's close. That she felt like she couldn't live that way anymore."

"She made a pretty radical change," I said. "I mean, from living like a recluse straight to celebrity parties and gossip columns. And it was a risk—it seems obvious that her husband would come after her as soon as she resurfaced."

"I guess it was a chance she felt like she had to take," Mr. Curtis said. "And there are certainly enough professionals looking for him.

Police in both California and Nevada have been trying to track him since he skipped out of custody, not to mention the bounty hunters."

"Who did he kill in Las Vegas, anyway?" Tom asked. "None of the papers were very clear about that."

"Young man, Adam Nightshade. Adam worked casino security at one of the other hotels. A real up-and-comer, wouldn't have been surprised if he had my job someday."

"Why would Red Early want to kill someone who worked casino security?" I asked.

"Rumor has it Adam used his position to collect dirt on people, then blackmail them. I don't believe it. Adam was a good boy, and no one's been able to find any trace of it. The best anyone can figure is, he had something on Red Early, and Red got tired of paying."

I'd moved up and was sitting toward the front of the van, between Polly's and Mr. Curtis's seats. Behind me I heard Roxy say to Tom, "What do you think would happen to me if I ate just one?" and heard her jiggling the Pounce.

Little Life Lesson 49: When embarking on a day of crime fighting, take time to have a good breakfast. Because it takes a lot of energy, and you never know when you'll get to eat again.

If ever.

Mr. Curtis had his arm across the back of Polly's seat, which I knew she hated—it was almost like touching—but at least it made him stop fiddling with his watch, and it gave me a chance to check the time. Three twenty-five. No wonder I was hungry.

I was just starting to wonder if maybe there was a taco place we could stop at really fast, when we came around a bend and saw Lake Mead close by. Mr. Curtis pointed to a secluded spot by the side of the road and said, "This is it. Pull over right here."

Polly deftly maneuvered the Pink Pearl into a little clearing and turned off the engine. "Now what?"

"Now you stay here while I go—" Mr. Curtis started to say, but stopped short as the driver's side door was wrenched open and the muzzle of a gun was pressed hard against Polly's head.

Twenty-eight

Little Life Lesson 50: If you think there is anything worse than seeing your best friend with a gun pointed at her temple, you are wrong.

"What will happen now," a voice attached to the arm with the gun said, "is that you obey me." Even if I hadn't been able to see the hint of long brown hair, I would have known the Fabinator anywhere by his fascinating use of English.

Roxy's heartrending cry in the back merely confirmed the identification.

I glanced out the window. From what I could see, this was just the kind of place I'd pick if I were organizing a mass grave site, an overgrown area with a view of the lake. There was a rusted picnic table off to one side, some faded beer cans, and nothing else.

In the far back of the van, Jack started to snore.

"That is a CB?" the Fabinator asked.

Polly nodded.

And just in case any of us still harbored a hope, he reached across her with his free hand and ripped the cord out of the dashboard, ripping some of the pink leather with it.

Here is how brave Polly was: She didn't even flinch. Even though I knew she must have felt like he ripped out her heart.

"I've got a gun," Mr. Curtis said to the Fabinator now. "And I'm pointing it right at you. I'll use it. Drop your weapon and step away from the van."

The Fabinator cocked his head to one side but did no dropping or stepping. "I think no," he said. "Where you are sitting, you have no aim. Also, I can shoot first. No, I think you give the gun to me. Now. Or—" He pushed his own weapon harder against Polly's head and made a clicking noise with his tongue.

I swear, he was enjoying himself. I have never hated anyone as much as I hated that man at that moment.

There was nothing else for Mr. Curtis to do but hand over his gun. As he took it, the Fabinator said, "Mr. Curtis gets out first, hands up. This one"—pointing at Polly—"will follow. The rest of you after."

Before getting out of the van, Mr. Curtis turned toward me to say, "I'll try to distract him by fighting. If you can get away, run for the marina. There's a—"

"Quiet!" the Fabinator barked. "Move. Now."

We watched Mr. Curtis walk slowly around the front of the van with his hands up. I thought I heard him trying to negotiate, saying something about fighting to protect us, but I wasn't sure because at the same time Polly hissed, "I can't believe you got us in to this, Jas."

In the nearly thirteen years I'd known her, I'd never seen Polly really angry. Ever. I said, "I'm so sorry. I didn't mean—"

"Almost getting us killed and now you're making excuses to *boot*," she said, and her eyes met and held mine in the rearview mirror.

"I know. I'm sorry." I wrapped my arms around my shins.

"No talking," the Fabinator said. "Exit the vehicle. Now."

He pulled Polly out of her seat, while Roxy, Tom, and I lined up near the sliding door. Keeping the gun on Polly's head, Fab opened the sliding door and stood to one side. "Get out. One at a time, slow."

I looked at Polly. She looked at me. She nodded. I pulled the tube out of my cowboy boot, pushed my finger on the top, and—

—nothing happened. I was courageously brandishing . . . lip gloss.

"What—" the Fab one opened his mouth to say, and that was when Roxy hit him full force in the face with the Designer Imposters perfume. He choked and coughed and his eyes closed. As soon as Tom saw that, he grabbed the roof of the van and swung himself out, legs first, landing both feet right in the center of the Fabinator's chest.

The Fabinator staggered backwards, tripped over the shiny pink shoe Polly stuck out, and let go of her. Mr. Curtis was there to grab him and twist the gun out of his hand. But Fab was not so easily subdued. Oh, no. He stood up and started fighting back, and soon he and Mr. Curtis were pummeling each other like TV cowboys in a saloon brawl. You could almost hear the *Wham! Bang! Pow!* of punches hitting. Mr. Curtis got Fab hard in the gut, but the Fabinator came back with a sock to Mr. Curtis's jaw that sent him reeling backwards into Roxy. Roxy stumbled under his weight, and they went down, Mr. Curtis landing with his ankle at a weird angle. For a second I thought he was done, but he staggered back up and threw himself onto the Fabinator. Mr. Curtis grunted, said, "This time you're going down," and hit Fab with a left jab. It must have been the power of positive thinking or something, because the Fabinator jerked backwards, hung in the air for a second, and then fell to the ground.

Victory was ours!

But this was not the time for party hats and confetti. From the way his eyes were already starting to open, it was clear the Fabinator was only out for a little while. Mr. Curtis turned to me and said urgently, "I'll keep him busy. Take that pathway down to the marina and look for a boat called the *Payoff*. My sources say that's where Fred and Fiona are being kept. Be careful—there are probably guards all around it. I'll make sure this guy can't send up an alarm, but do your best to be quiet."

"What about Jack?" Tom said to me. "Do we just leave him?"

"In his passed-out state, he's totally defenseless. I think he's safer in the Pink Pearl than anywhere else. Besides, we should be back soon."

"Get out of here," Mr. Curtis said. "Now!"

We went. I felt bad leaving Mr. Curtis there to contend with the Fab one alone, but he seemed to be able to hold his own, and if it meant saving Fiona and Fred, it was worth it.

We found the *Payoff* moored at the end of a dock with a bunch of other fishing boats. It was by far the largest and fanciest. There was an upstairs section with a cabin, another enclosed space on the main deck, and portholes in the side suggesting quarters down below. We didn't see any guards. In fact, we didn't see anyone. It looked completely deserted.

"Mr. Curtis might have had bad information," Polly suggested. "This might be the wrong boat."

"We've got to check," I said. "If Fred and Fiona are on here, this could be our chance to get them away."

"We can inspect it faster if we divide up," Roxy said.

We fanned out. Roxy went upstairs, Polly and Tom took the main floor, and I walked around until I found a staircase that went below. Next to it was a hatch with a padlock on it. The padlock was unlocked, and the hatch opened easily when I lifted it. Inside was a wood ladder, going into the bottom of the boat. I felt like I had been working fast but when I looked at the shipboard clock, I saw it had been about ten minutes since we left Mr. Curtis and the Fabinator in the clearing. There was no time to waste deliberating. I looked from the wood ladder to the stairs, then back at the hatch. Yes, definitely. If I were stashing someone on the boat, I thought, this is where I would stash them.

I had my foot on the first rung of the ladder when I heard it.

Click clack, snap pop. Followed by the voice of my psychic scars saying, "Jas, are you here? Calamity? Jas, where are you?"

Evil Henches!! We'd avoided them all day and yet somehow they managed to find us here. HERE!

And they were shouting about it! In case there were bad guys lurking around who needed to be alerted to come down and find us.

"Alyson, be quiet!" I whisper-slash-shouted as I ran toward her. "Please, just shut—" And stopped cold.

Alyson and Veronique were standing at the edge of the gangplank. Actually, despite their white vinyl four-inch platform boots, they weren't standing, they were more like dangling. Each from one of the Fabinator's XXL-size biceps.

Superpower, apparently: To be unstoppable.

Which would be a handy superpower. If anyone who hands those things out is listening.

I was dismayed to see that the Fab one was fully functional, but he wasn't his usual dapper self. Whatever had happened to Mr. Curtis, and it made me scared to think of it, he hadn't gone without a fight. There were splotches of dirt on the Fabinator's clothes, a trickle of what looked like blood on his chin, and his hair had come out of its bow. As he pushed Alyson and Veronique onto the boat toward me, he said, "Now you obey."

Not a sparkling conversational opener, but it got his point across. Especially because I could see he had somehow recovered his firearm.

So when he said, "Call your friends. Now," I did.

"What are you doing here?" I asked Alyson as Polly, Roxy, and Tom joined us.

"Following you. Duh," she said. "Nice of you to go on a cruise without us."

"Why? Why would you follow us?" I meant it as a question but I think it came out as a whine.

Veronique answered for the Hench Collective. "We saw the Pink Pearl pulling out of the Venetian as we were on our way back from buying collars at the pet st—" A look from Alyson stopped her for a second. "I mean, when we were on our way back from shopping, so we told our taxi to follow you. You know, 'Follow that car,' like in the movies? Only we said, 'Follow that van.' And we didn't expect it to be so—" She looked over my shoulder and she started grinning. "Hi, Tommy!" She gave a little wave. "Anyway, it took us forever to find you. I mean, at first we thought it was because we stopped for those Diet Cokes for lunch but, you know, you parked in a really weird place. It was totally hard to see the van. We had to drive by like three times before we even noticed it. And when we finally did, you weren't even there. But that nice man was. He was looking for you, too."

"What do you mean looking for us?" I asked.

"Looking around the van. He said you were in trouble and needed our help and we came down here right away. But it doesn't look like you're in trouble."

"Oh, we are," I assured her. "Did you see anyone else?"

"No."

At least that meant Mr. Curtis had gotten away before the Fab one regained use of his gun. He'd probably left the Fabinator passed out and gone for help.

Alyson, who had been carefully checking her makeup in the mirror of her eye shadow compact during this exchange, snapped it closed and said, "Um, Jas, instead of twenty questions-slash-*Jeopardy!* could we like—"

"Enough talking," the Fabinator intervened. He looked at me. "Remove the boots."

"My cowboy boots? No way," I said, planting my feet on the ground.

But the Fabinator ignored me, turning instead to Polly to say, "You also. With the pink shoes. Take them off and—"

He didn't get to finish that thought because Tom went Chow Yun Fat[54] on him, spinning around and landing a kick in his ribs.

---

[54]Tom: Actually, Jas, it was more Jet Li.

Jas: Really? I thought it was more Prince Charming Saving His Lady Love.

Tom: I was, um, just, you know, doing what anyone would do.

Jas: Are you blushing? TOM IS BLUSHING. You guys, come down here and check this out. Tom is blushing.

Roxy: Jas, I think we have more important things to do. Have you noticed what is going on in your story? What is going on with Ivan? He was supposed to be one of the good guys, protecting Fiona. But he's not! He must be working for Red Early. And even worse, did you see how the Evil Henches were *clinging* to him?

Jas: Um, Roxy, I think —

I have to say, I was very impressed. The Fabinator once again found himself the victim of Tom's Feet of Fury, falling backwards, this time onto the ample bosom of Alyson.

"Eeew, get off of me! My manicure!" she screeched, pushing him back from whence he came and saying, "Tommy, get him!"

Tom was ready to unleash more FoF's, but before he could get off another kick, the Fabinator had regrouped and, being twice as wide and a foot taller than Tom, not to mention forewarned, grabbed him in an illegal wrestling hold and disabled him.

It was a valiant effort on Tom's part, which would have worked if Someone had been working for the team rather than protecting her nail tips. But this was not a time for finger pointing. This was a time for coming together. And mourning. Because the Fabinator had put Tom in handcuffs, and then moved to Part Two of his plan. Which was to grab Alyson around the neck and point a gun at her head. I guess if you have a good trick, you keep using it.

"Now you obey," he said, probably with the hope that enough repetition would make it true. "If you do not, this one feels pain."

Little Life Lesson 51: When selecting a member of a group to put on the Endangered Species List, it's probably best not to pick the least popular person, because there is always a chance everyone will shrug and be like, "Um, okay. Hey, anyone want pizza?"[55] and leave.

Polly: Less chatting, more butt-kicking, everyone. Places, people.
      (Tom, that was really cool what you did. Thank you. I mean it, it was really amazing.)
Tom: (It was nothing. Besides—)
Polly: (Shhh. Just say "You're welcome.")
Tom: (You're welcome, Polly. Anytime.)

[55] Roxy: Did someone mention pizza?
    Jas: No.

Little Life Lesson 52: On the other hand, it could be diabolically clever. Because everyone feels so guilty about their initial "Yes, pizza[56] would be great, half with pepperoni?" impulse that they immediately behave. And are tortured with the knowledge that they have brought this on themselves.

Little Life Lesson 53: And let me tell you, that is quite torturous. Especially if you haven't eaten in, like, twelve hours.

Little Life Lesson 54: And if the Endangered Species nominee turns to you to hiss, "This is all your fault, Jas. I swear, if he hurts me, I will kill you. Slowly."

Mmmm, pizza.[57]

But of course, I couldn't let Alyson get hurt. My father would never forgive me, and it would make Uncle Andy and Aunt Liz sad. And I am not heartless.

Much.

So we did what the Fabinator told us to. Tom, handcuffed, stood manfully by as Polly took off her pink glitter stilettos with the gold heels, and I took off my cowboy boots, and we threw them overboard. They were followed by all the cell phones we had among us. After an insufficient mourning period, we all marched toward the hatch I'd been inspecting in the back. I climbed down the ladder first.

[56] Roxy: There it is again!
Jas: Not really.

[57] Roxy: I knew it! I knew someone was talking about pizza!
Jas: Only figuratively.
Roxy: Can you talk about it literally? Because I don't want to scare you or anything, but *Lord of the Flies* is beginning to seem less like a novel and more like a cookbook to me, if you get my drift.
Jas: I think that is a drift I am going to steer clear of.
Roxy: Mmmmm, steer.

At the bottom there was no furniture and very little light, and I stumbled on the last step of the ladder. Which was why I flew forward into the room. And found myself nose to nose with a man.

Or rather, a murderer.

Red Early looked me over from head to toe and said, "Jasmine Callihan, I presume." He glanced behind me as everyone else came down the ladder. "How nice, you've brought some friends. I've always thought it would be so much more pleasant to die with others than alone."

Twenty-nine

His words would have been more ominous if I had understood exactly what was going on then. And if he hadn't been handcuffed to a pole.

Polly came to stand beside me. "Isn't that—?" she whispered.

"Yes," I said. "It's Red Early."

"But why is he—?"

"Handcuffed like a prisoner?" I filled in for her. "I'm not sure." Which wasn't exactly true. Because the moment I saw him stuck in the boat hold like we were, the moment I noticed there was some dried blood around his nose and a few drops on his clothing, I'd had a startling thought.

Maybe Red Early wasn't a murderer at all.

But there was at least one objection to that theory. I said to him, "Fred told me he saw you standing over Len Phillips's body, holding a bloody knife. Did he?"

"It's a pleasure to meet you too, Miss Callihan," Red Early replied. "How does a nice girl like you end up in a place like this?"

Apparently Red Early hadn't gotten the instructional memo that said if you happen to encounter a six-foot-tall girl who has just watched her cowboy boots get pitched into a lake, not to mention her best friend almost get KILLED, skip the clever bantering. It will be lost on her.

And it might cause her to want to bite you.

I said, "I just want to know—"

"Miss Callihan, I have never spoken about the events of that day, not even to my lawyer, and I'm not going to now," he said, like he had a copyright on Strong & Silent Behavior. Not to mention Lonely Suffering.

I thought I could bolster his spirits. "We've got someone on the outside with connections in the police who knows we're here. If we don't waste time, there's still a chance we can be rescued. All hope isn't lost."

"It is for me. I've lost everything that matters. Hope is the least of it."

And that is when *I* lost it. "Sir, I know we've only just met, so I probably shouldn't be this honest," I said. "But really? This is no time for a pity party."

"A pity party?" he repeated, kind of choking as he said the words.

"I recognize that you've probably had a bad day, but what I mean is—"

"A bad day?" he said, repeating after me again. I began to worry about his mental competence. "A bad DAY?" he did it again. "I beg your pardon, did you say—" And then to my complete astonishment, he started to laugh. "My dear Miss Callihan, I suppose that to some people, going to a hotel room with the hopes of seeing the woman they've been seeking for months, and instead being knocked over the head by an ape of a man, tied up, searched, and stowed in the hold of a boat could be considered a bad day. But being on the run from the law for a murder I didn't commit puts everything in perspective. I haven't had a bad day, Miss Callihan. What I've had is a bad year. A really incredibly lousy year." He looked up at me. "Although I do feel somewhat better now. I haven't laughed like that in a very long time."

Well, it was nice to know that my power to amuse unintentionally was still functioning.[58]

Tom said, "I don't understand. If you're innocent, why did you refuse to talk to your lawyer? Why didn't you stick up for yourself?"

Polly said quietly, "And why didn't Fiona stick up for you?"[59]

But Red just hit them with more Strong & Silent Behavior©, only this time with the added reminder that, "It's all about to be over, anyway."

---

[58] Polly: Oh, you don't have to worry about that, Jas. You are always *très* unintentionally amusing. I also like that little dance you are doing from side to side.

Jas: It's not a dance. I have to go to the bathroom.

Polly: I'm not hearing that. I'm hearing dance.

[59] Jas: Ah, young love. So idealistic. Don't you think they are cute, Roxy?

Roxy: I guess.

Jas: I'm sorry, Roxy. It was thoughtless of me to bring that up while your own wound is still so fresh.

Polly: Hello, ladies. Are you aware that there are people up there trying to have a conversation? Jas, you are being very rude to Red Early by whispering like this behind his back.

Jas: Sheesh. Love-sick Teens are SO BOSSY.

Polly: You take that back! I am not a—

Jas: Gee, I'd love to chat, but I've got to get back up to my story.

Thanks, Red! Now I see where Fred gets his fine conversational stylings from! I found myself thinking that if this was typical of his witty repartee, I could not really fault Fiona for having an "Alex, darling" on the side.

Despite the glad tidings Red's words offered, a distinct pall fell over those of us marooned in the boat hold. Roxy slid into a depression about the end of her crush.[60] Tom and I tried to figure out if Tom could pick the lock on his own handcuffs with our help (no) or somehow, working with his hands behind him, on Red's (double no). We checked Red's fingerprints just in case to see if he had tented arches (nope), and then wandered around looking for a way out (none). It was saved from being too peaceful by Alyson muttering, "You're going to be in so much trouble if we miss dinner, Jas," and other helpful things from time to time. She did, finally, relent and share her gum stash with everyone, which was good since I had begun hallucinating that she was a large and delicious dancing hamburger.

---

[60] Jas: Are you okay, Rox? I'm really sorry he turned out to be a bad guy.

Roxy: It's just my luck. All the good men I like aren't.

Jas: Aren't?

Roxy: Either they aren't good, or they aren't men.

Jas: Have you ever considered maybe you should look for another type?

Roxy: You mean like *Jack*?

Jas: No, for once I was actually not thinking about myself. I don't know, maybe someone who shares your interests. Or someone your age.

Roxy: I guess. Are you flossing?

Jas: Yes. There's nothing else to do. Want some?

Roxy: Sure. I wish it were flavored, I'm starving. Do you think I would have to kill Alyson to get a piece of her Bubble Yum, or could we just hold her down and take it?

Jas: I like the first idea best. Plus, it would be something to pass the time.

Roxy: Yeah. But we could probably have more fun tormenting her while she's alive.

Jas: Good point.

Roxy: So if Red isn't the murderer, do you know who is?

Jas: I might. I wish I could figure out why you would throw away two broken Oreos.

Roxy: Is that one of those Zen questions? Or are you—ouch!

Jas: Sorry, I didn't mean to hurt you. Is that your sore heart?

Roxy: No, it's the shoulder Mr. Curtis banged into. What are you doing?

Jas: You had something on your T-shirt.

Roxy: Is it edible? PLEASE say it's edible.

Jas: It's just some of those purple fibers from that car.

Roxy: Maybe if I pretend they are grape flav—hey, look at Polly and Tom.

Jas: No way! She's sitting near him! Six inches closer and they'd be touching!

Roxy: She's probably only doing it because he's in handcuffs, so it's safe.

Jas: Still, it's a start. Maybe one day they can hold hands.

Roxy: And after, like, a year, they could kiss.

Jas: A year and a half.

Roxy: Through a sheet.

Polly: That's not how I am! Plus, sheets hold a lot of germs. Do not roll your eyes at me, Jas. You're more picky about the TV you watch than the boys you kiss.

Roxy: And you watch a lot of bad TV.

Jas: I just want practice for when I meet the One. And I do not watch bad TV, Girl Who Has Subscriptions to Tabloids.

Roxy: Okay, Girl Who TiVos *Maury Povich*.

Polly: Once I caught her flipping between *Dr. Phil* and *Circle of Power Ministry* at the same time. It was like no bad TV could satisfy her. I think Jas may be a bad TV hussy.

Jas: Call me what you will, duckling. I interest myself in our modern culture, that is true. You can learn a lot from those shows. There is more human drama and pathos in one episode of *Dr. Phil* than—

Veronique: Hi, you guys. What are you doing down here?

Roxy: We're working on an escape plan.

Veronique: For real?

Polly: Shhh, not so loud. Top secret.

Veronique: I knew you'd be doing something cool. Can I be part of it? I want to help.

Roxy: Do you have any special skills we should take into account when formulating our line of attack?

Veronique: Well, I'm really good at macramé. You know, things with knots. If that helps.

Polly: It does. We'll definitely include some knots in our plan.

My piece had just lost its flavor and I was starting once again to see two smiling all-beef patties where Alyson's head had been, when she and Veronique had a disagreement. At first we couldn't hear what they were saying, just saw a lot of dangerous-looking, black belt–level Accusatory-Pointing-with-Nail Tips, but then Veronique got up and went over to where Red Early was sitting with his head against the post his hands were cuffed to.

"Can I ask you a question?" she said.

Red nodded.

"When we first came down here, you said you were glad to see us because you thought it would be more fun to die with people than alone." She picked at the edge of her white vinyl boot. "Um, what did you mean?"

For once Red decided to give a complete answer. "I'm fairly sure the original plan was just to kill me, but they can't do that in front of you, so you'll have to go too. I think they are going to keep us down here until dusk, then motor out to the middle of the lake and kill us."

Oh, that Red and his words of comfort and joy! More, please! And don't spare the details!

"But who is going to kill us?" Veronique asked. "Why?"

Alas, before we could see if Red had some other inspirational sentiments for us or was going to return to his old Strong & Silent© ways, Alyson jumped in.

"Did you say until dusk?" she demanded. "Great. We're going to miss our family dinner. Jas, you are so busted-slash-dead when we get out of here."

"Mission control to Allie," Veronique said. "That's the point. We're not getting out of here. Like I told you."

We all turned to stare at her. I'd never seen Veronique talk back to her Hench Idol before.

"I'm sorry, Veronique, did you just call me Allie?"

"Yes. I think Allie sounds cute and nice. I like it as a nickname."

"Anything else you've been keeping from me, Vera?"

"Yes. I think you should apologize to Jas. You blame her for everything just because you're jealous of her and her relationship with her dad, but it's not fair. She's nothing but nice to you."

I swear, if my own head had exploded at that moment, I could not have been more shocked.

"That is such a total lie-slash-lie!" Alyson shouted. "I am not—"

"Whatever," Veronique interrupted. She turned to Polly now. "And you. You know you love Tom just as much as he loves you. Why are you being such a baby and not admitting it? Personally, I think you have intimacy issues and are afraid to let someone get close to you because they might know the real you and reject you. But that's not going to happen. He is a great guy, and you two can make each other really happy."

We were all gaping at her, Polly included, but only she was blushing at the same time.

Then Roxy clapped and said, "My turn! Do me next!"

Veronique shook her head. "I can't. I'm only up to chapter three in *Psychology for Dummies*. I don't think we covered you yet."

Veronique and Roxy got into a deep speculative huddle over what Roxy's problem might be and what Veronique's problems were and somehow segued into Veronique's study of *Feng Shui for Dummies*.

I looked at Alyson, but she pretended I had already been vaporized under her gaze and ignored me. I felt like I had to say something, though, so finally I said, "Don't worry. I know that's not true. What

Veronique said about my dad and all. I mean, first of all, your father worships you. And secondly, my relationship with my dad is not something anyone would—"

"Uh, Jas? Just because Veronique is delusional doesn't mean you have to go all Dr. Phil on me. Of course she's wrong. I'm *glad* my dad doesn't feel the need to spend every minute with me or take people on laps of the Boring Grand Prix every time he talks about how smart I am, the way some people's dads do."

"Okay. Good." Clearly Alyson did have issues about someone's dad, but it wasn't mine. He'd done many a lap at the Boring Grand Prix, but never when I was the subject; of that I was positive.

Across the way, in the last glimmer of light from outside, I thought I caught Polly slipping her hand onto Tom's lap.

That made me smile, but feel a little sad. I mean, what if this really were it? What if we were all destined to die on a ship called the *Payoff*?

What kind of a name was that for a boat anyway? *Payoff.*

I tried to think of happier things, like all that L. A. Curtis could be doing to save us . . . if he'd been able to exit: stage out-of-there. Since Alyson and Veronique didn't see him, he must have had enough strength to get away before they came by to "help."

"Do you really think my dad worships me?" Alyson whispered, interrupting my thoughts.

"Yes."

"Are you sure?"

"Yes."

"Because—"

All of a sudden, my brain, which had been taking a commercial break, started to function again. Fast. "*At*, not *for*," I said. "The finger. And the window."

"Hello? I was talking?"

"Allie, look, yes I am sure he worships you, yes he thinks you fart perfume, can we discuss this later?"

"I do not fart!" Alyson said.

"Yes, you do," Veronique chimed in.

"That is so—"

But I ignored the rest of it, repeating to myself "finger, window, aliens, broken cookie, *Payoff, look at the whole picture.*"

I slid over to where Tom and Polly were sharing their first and last precious moments together. "Do you still have those envelopes I gave you in Fiona's room, Tom? 'Evil boy hairs from deathmobile'? And the matchbook?"

"Yeah, they're in here," Tom said. He half sat up so Polly could reach into his back pocket (!!!!)[61] and pull them out.

"What's going on?" Roxy asked. "Are we going to—hey! I like all my little hairs. Where are you taking them?"

"I need a control sample to burn," I told her.

---

[61] Polly: Um, Jas? Punctuation alone doesn't mean anything. You need words.
Jas: Oh, really? Then why are you BLUSHING? Did you FEEL something?
Polly: I'm sorry, I cannot hear you over the pleasant tunes I am humming to block out your untoward suggestions.
Jas: I bet you felt his big, thick, smooth—
Polly: STOP IT RIGHT NOW!!!
Jas: —wallet.
Roxy: Heh. Good one.
Polly: Never. That is when I will speak to you two again. Mark it on your calendars.

"Did you say burn?" Roxy said. "As in fire? Goodie!"

"Uh, Calamity," Alyson chimed in with her usual supportive tone, "we're in a wooden boat here. I know you may feel your life is so boring-slash-pointless there's no reason to go on, but, hello, some of us have things we want to get back for, and not with burns over eighty percent of our bodies. Think about someone else for a change."

"Actually, it was you who gave me the idea," I told my darling cousin. "You said the person driving the car that tried to run me over had a beard 'like a religious freak.' That's right, isn't it?"

"Are you calling me a liar?"

"No, I'm *asking* if you're a liar. It's totally different."

"He had a beard. Why does that mean you're going to go all pyro on us?"

"Fake hair burns differently than real hair." I lit Roxy's hair to show how real hair burned. Then I lit one of the samples we'd collected. It curled up at the end and gave off a sweet smell, totally different from Roxy's.

"Artificial," Tom announced. "Which means the beard was a fake."

"So?" Alyson asked. "What does that mean except that now it smells like a barn-slash-men's urinal in here?"

"For real? How do you know what a men's urinal smells like?" Roxy asked.

"If the beard is a fake, that means whoever was driving the car was in disguise," Tom said. "So it must be someone who was afraid of being recognized by Jas or Jack."

Caftan Man, I said to myself. Always popping up wherever Fiona was—or rather, wherever she had just been.

"Tom, what about that other envelope I gave you? The one with the pill bottle?"

"Side pocket," he told Polly, and she reached all the way in (!!!!)[62] and handed me the envelope with Fiona's sleeping pill bottle in it.

I wrangled Alyson's precious eye shadow compact from her so I could dust the pill bottle for prints. Given the not-exactly-ideal circumstances of being in a boat hold and the fact that Alyson was leaning over my shoulder the whole time to ensure I didn't do anything "gross-slash-typical" with her makeup (oh, the temptation. Horrible, drool-inducing condition, where are you when I need you?), it wasn't the best job I'd ever done.

And yet, it was good enough. Good enough to bring up a beautiful thumbprint, with a tented arch. A print that identified the mastermind behind all of this.

I'd been looking *for* explanations that confirmed what I thought I knew, rather than looking *at* the bare facts. I'd started with the story of Fiona being on the run from a murderous husband and looked for things that confirmed that picture.

But that picture was wrong.

[62] Polly: During which Polly felt NOTHING. No. Thing.
Jas: Taht eveileb I erus.
Roxy: Oot em sey.
Polly: What?
Jas: Oh, I'm sorry. I thought we were playing backwards day, where we say everything the opposite of what we mean.
Polly: Gniltrohc flesruoy truh t'nod uoy luferac eb.

The real meaning of my own words in the Pink Pearl earlier—"It seems obvious her husband would come after her"—hit me. Now that I knew the hairs from the car were fake, that someone was wearing a disguise, all the evidence clicked together. The purple fibers, the tented arch fingerprint, Red's silence, Fiona's unwillingness to help him. I knew who was under the Caftan Man disguise. I knew what Fred had seen the day Len Phillips died. I knew who the murderer was. I knew what the killer had been searching for. And—

"I think I know how to save us," I said. "We have a bargaining chip, but we'll need Mr. Curtis's assistance. We have to act fast, before we leave the dock."

Just as I said that, the motor started.

Thirty

This could still work, I told myself. And if it did—

Well, I might live to floss another day. And that would just be the beginning. Still, it was going to take everything I'd ever learned on TV to pull it off. Because the only thing standing between us and death would be my ability to hold everyone's attention, no matter what I had to stoop to.

I banged on the hatch door to get attention but nothing happened.

"I don't think they'll come to get us until they are ready for us," Red said.

I shrugged. "You're probably right. Still, a girl can dream." And dream I did, for the half hour it took us to get out to what I had to assume was the darkest and most vacant part of Lake Mead. When the hatch finally did open, I was sitting on the ladder, ready.

"Hi, Fabinator," I said cheerily. "Miss me?"

"Go stand on deck."

"You did!" I said. "Ivan, that's so sweet!"

"Did you just this instant decide to put a lifetime of clean living behind you and start taking drugs?" Polly asked as she followed me toward the back of the boat. "Because only someone on drugs could be happy at a time like this."

"Not true, my turtledove. I have a plan."

"Is it a good plan?"

"No. But it's the only plan we have. That counts for something, right?"

"By 'something,' do you mean 'some thing'?"

"You, my friend, are the beef. Filet mignon."

"You are on drugs," Polly said.

I was a little nervous as I walked forward. Everything hinged on what was waiting to greet us.

I came around the corner and saw our welcoming committee and let out a long breath of relief. Fiona was there, looking tense and exhausted. Fred was lying in a bundle of blankets next to her, fast asleep. And unless he'd grown the tail that was peeking out of the corner of one of the blankets, Mad Joe was in there too.

That was it. My final piece of proof.

I almost smiled to myself, but I knew we were far from safe. Plus, the reunion of Fiona and Red was not exactly a Kodak Moment. When Red came around the side of the boat and caught sight of her, his face was like an encyclopedia of emotion. His first impulse, you could tell, was that he still, somewhere deep inside, loved her. But then the anger came flooding over and turned into rage when he caught sight of Blankets of Fred.

He started toward the boy-blanket meld, but was cut off at the pass by the Fabinator. That was when his face went into pure hatred.

It was also when I had to stop watching. Because now that we were all assembled, I had a job to do, and only until they started weighing down our feet with the cement blocks I now noticed stacked alongside the deck in which to do it.[63]

We'd divided up into two groups along the Us–Them axis, with my crew, the Too Young to Dies featuring Red Early, and Fiona's crew, We're Man Enough for Bows, facing off. We had more people, but they had a gun, so things seemed to be stacked in their favor. Plus, two of our members were still handcuffed.

It was time.

I took a deep breath, moved past the Fabinator to stand roughly between the two sides, and said, "Can I have everyone's attention,

---

[63] Roxy: I can't believe they really got cement blocks. I thought that was just in movies.
Polly: I guess they work well because they're easy to tie people to. I wonder how many each of us get. Do you think it's better to sink fast or slow?
Roxy: I think it's better not to think about it at all. Didn't Jas say she had a plan?
Polly: She also said I was filet mignon.
Veronique: Did you say there's a plan? What should I do?
Polly: If you see any opportunities at all to macramé anything, take them. TAKE THEM!
Roxy: We'll be counting on you.
Veronique: Okay. What knot do you think I should do?
            Polly? Roxy?
            Wait up! Wait for me!

please?" Everything on my body that could be crossed for luck was crossed for luck.

"Get back," the Fab one said.

"Can't I talk to my friends for a second?" I asked him. "I got them into this. The least I can do is tell them what they mean to me."

"No."

From behind me, Fiona said, "Just let her speak."

I spoke. "Before we get started, I just wanted to say that I've really enjoyed meeting and getting to know all of you, and you've each taught me something in your own way." I drew a circle in the air around me. "This is a Bambi Circle. It's a circle of honesty and compassion. In here we only tell the truth, and we abide by the Bambi Creed, 'If you can't say anything nice, don't say anything at all.' I would like to invite two people to join me in the Bambi Circle. Can I have Red and Fiona up here, please?"

"Enough," the Fabinator objected.

Fiona said, "I want to hear what she has to say, Ivan," and took a step toward me.

"Jas, what are you doing?" Polly whisper-hissed.

"Benefiting from my knowledge of trash TV," I whisper-hissed back.

Alyson chimed in with her moral support, saying, "This is the lamest-slash-stupidest thing you have ever done."

But the jeers from my team felt to my ears like soothing dewdrops, because both Red and Fiona had come to stand in the Bambi Circle with me! It was like they wanted to work everything out and actually thought I could help. Those televangelists were really on to something.

I said, "Fiona, you've spent the past year thinking that your husband is a murderer. You're wrong."

Fiona looked at the ground and shook her head.

"Damn you, Fi, you know—" Red started to say, but I stopped him.

"No no no," I said. "Not in the Bambi Circle. Red, I want you to be honest. You've spent the past year hiding the fact that Fiona is a murderer, haven't you?"

There were appreciative gasps and a "no-slash-way" from behind me.

Red stared at me. Then, like it cost him a huge effort to move his lips, he said, "Yes."

"You came home the day of the murder and saw Fiona standing over Len Phillips's body with the knife. You took it from her, sent her away—"

"I sent her to bed."

"Then you started to clean up. And that was what Fred saw. You were standing over the body with the weapon, but because you were cleaning up. You were trying to protect Fiona. That's why you would never talk about discovering the body. And why you fled. You were afraid if you answered questions, you would say something wrong and implicate Fiona. And you loved her too much to do that."

"That's insane," Fiona said.

"My God, can't you drop the act now?" Red asked her, angry. "Can't we just admit what happened? Do you have to add killing all these kids to your list of—"

"Actually," I interrupted, "you were wrong too, Red. Fiona didn't kill Len Phillips." Before he could object, I said, "And I don't think she came out here on this boat to kill you or us. I'm pretty sure she has no idea of what is really going on. Do you?"

Fiona said, "What are you talking about, Miss Callihan?"

"Neither of you murdered Len. But through a combination of bad advising and bad judgment, you've both been encouraged to conclude the other person did it."

"This isn't a funny joke," Red said. "Not at all."

"I'm not joking. I have two pieces of proof."

Red looked past me now at Fiona, really meeting her eyes for the first time. "What are they?" he said.

"The Finger and the Window. The finger is Len Phillips's severed thumb. Murderers cut off fingers for two reasons: to take as souvenirs, and to menace victims into doing something. I believe Len's finger was cut off to get him to open the bedroom safe. The murderer was making good on a threat. Neither you, Red, nor you, Fiona, would have had to do that, because you both knew the combination to the safe. So I'm going to postulate it wasn't one of you."

"But it still—" Fiona started to say.

"Please hold all objections until the end."

She stopped. People were listening to me! This was so cool! I loved the Bambi Circle.

"Next, the window. The window in the bedroom was always kept closed by everyone in the household, right? Because otherwise Mad Joe ran out?" I looked at Red and Fiona and they both nodded. "But someone opened it that day and Mad Joe did run out, and his leg got hurt. So the window being open is suspicious on its own, but what makes it evidence is that there was a footprint outside it. A distinctive footprint, one that did not match either of you two, but showed a clear and unusual wear pattern. Which suggests someone else was in that room. Someone who entered with Len Phillips, killed him, and left through the window, leaving it open and allowing Mad Joe to run out. Someone who, disguised with a beard, tried to run me over the other night. And someone who, unlike either of you, had a motive."

"Who?" Red demanded.

I turned around fast and pointed toward the Fabinator. "Him."

"Ivan?" Roxy said. "That too?" Out of the corner of my eye I saw her take something out of her bra, drop it on the ground, and stomp on it.

Please let me have guessed right please let this have worked please let Mr. Curtis have done what I thought he did please please please—

A shadow moved from behind the Fabinator, and the murderer stood there. "Bravo, Miss Callihan," L. A. Curtis said,[64] showing no sign of a hurt ankle and coming into the light with his usual bouncy step—the one that wore the front of his shoes more than the back, leading *Weekly World News* to conclude the print outside the window had been made by an alien. "That is quite a story. I enjoyed it."

"You think Mr. Curtis killed Len?" Fiona asked. "That's impossible. He only got involved because of me."

"No," I told her. "That is what he wanted you to think. He *pretended* he was just trying to help you. The same way he pretended he was trying to help us today, just to get us here so he could keep us locked up. I bet Mr. Curtis got in touch with you and offered you the suite at the Venetian."

"He did," Fiona said. "But only to make it easier for me to get my life back. He told me that if I came out of hiding, I'd be safe there. That we could trap Red, and then, finally, Fred and I would be able to move on. And last night he told me that everything was all set and if Fred and I would just move to his house on the lake, he would capture

[64] Roxy: But I thought he was on our side! He fought Ivan for our freedom.
Tom: I knew that fight looked kind of staged. I bet he planned it when he made that call before getting into the Pink Pearl with us.
Polly: That traitor! I can't believe I let him ride in my van. He is in BIG trouble.

Red in our room at the hotel. He's been a good friend to me."

"He wanted you to believe that. But once you had Jack set up the meeting, he didn't need you anymore. In fact, you became a liability. That's why he moved you, and that's why he drugged Fred and Mad Joe with sleeping pills."

"What?" Fiona was aghast. "Fred isn't drugged, he's just tired. This whole thing has been such an ordeal for him, and he has a bit of a cold. I would never let anyone do that to my child."

"No, you wouldn't. But you'd let Fred eat Oreos and he'd share them with Mad Joe. So after you left your room at the hotel, Mr. Curtis crushed up your sleeping pills and sprinkled the powder over the Oreo filling.[65] It was insurance for him. He knew you would never go anywhere without Fred, and if he were asleep, it would be impossible for you to carry him."

"He did give Fred Oreos, but—but that's impossible," Fiona said. "It's utterly—"

"I found a fingerprint I'm sure is his on an empty bottle of your

---

[65] Roxy: So that is what Jas meant about throwing away a broken cookie!

Polly: What are you talking about?

Roxy: You were too busy making Fawn Eyes at Tom to hear it, but Jas was wondering why you would throw away a broken Oreo. It's because you'd want the cookie to look absolutely one-hundred-percent normal if you drugged it. Which is why I always eat broken cookies. Perfection is suspicious.

Polly: That explains a lot about your taste in men too. And by the way, I was not making Fawn Eyes at your brother.

Roxy: Of course you weren't, deer.

sleeping pills. I bet he offered you some reason why it would be better to talk to Red in the middle of the lake than on land. Why you should put off calling the police."

"He said this way I could finally get Red to tell me the truth, without worrying about being interrupted by anyone. That afterward, if I wanted to, I could let Red escape again without the police ever knowing." She looked at Red. "I never wanted to believe you were guilty." Then she moved her eyes to glare at L. A. Curtis, and for such a beautiful woman, she looked really scary. "You drugged my son and you—you used me."

But Mr. Curtis was not paying attention to her. He was looking at me, shaking his head with wonder. "You have quite an exciting imagination, Miss Callihan. Pity you have nothing to back your stories up."

"That's where you're wrong," I said. "I have proof. In fact, you're wearing it."

"What?"

"There's a brown-colored thread caught in the watchband you've been pulling on all day. I noticed it earlier but I didn't realize what it meant. It's from Jack's jacket. You remember Jack? The guy you hit over the head last night outside the club, then tossed into the car you borrowed from one of your employees? Who is going to say no when the boss asks for a favor like that? Anyway, you must have gotten your watch caught on Jack's coat. If I had to guess, I'd say the real reason you went back to Fiona's room this afternoon was to finish Jack off. Too bad we got in the way. You also had a few purple threads on your back from being in that car. Some of them rubbed off on Roxy this afternoon when you fell against her. That proves not only that you were the one who grabbed Jack, but that you were driving—and that you were the Caftan Man. Following Fiona, trying to kill me. I should have realized it earlier, it was all so theatrical with the fake explosions and the disguises. Even the way you acted like you were on our side this afternoon—you just love playing the good guy, don't you?"

He smiled. "I am a good guy. And unless I misunderstand, your proof to the contrary hangs by a thread?"

"Threads," I corrected.

"The thing about threads," he said, tugging hard at the one in his watchband until it snapped, "is that they are very hard to hold on to." He gripped it between his thumb and index finger, then let it be carried off by the wind. "Oops."

"The threads were just to prove to you and everyone here that I know the truth. Each of your ploys to scare me away from Fred left traces behind. I've written everything down in a letter I left in my room, and enclosed several pieces of tangible evidence, such as fingerprints—fingerprints the police will identify as yours as soon as they run them through their computer.[66] If I am not back by nine tonight, my father will find it, read it, and call every security force on the planet to hunt you down." I smiled sweetly.

"This is getting more and more amusing," Mr. Curtis said. "Do you really think I'd fall for that dime-store detective novel ploy? And fingerprints! I can only imagine how you think you lifted those. Even if you have written a note, you'll be at the bottom of Lake Mead by the time anyone finds it, and there will be no link to me."

"But there is. I was stumped for a little while about what you would want that was small enough that you might think it was on Red Early's body and have the Fabinator search him when you couldn't

[66] Roxy: Wait, is that true? Did she really leave a note?
Polly: No, Rox. There is no note. Jas is lying out her ear holes.

find it in Fiona's room, but then I figured it out. It was so obvious. The negatives."

"Negatives? Now you've really lost me."

"The ones you killed Len Phillips to get."

Mr. Curtis gave a little laugh that showed his teeth, but it sounded forced. "Why would I care about negatives from a fashion photographer?"

"Sometimes the most interesting parts of a photo are in the background," I said.

He frowned. "What are you referring to?"

"I'll tell you. On land. In fact, I'll show you. I happen to have the negatives."[67]

"I really don't see what—"

"The police won't need more than the shots of you with Adam Nightshade.[68] You remember him, right? What was he blackmailing you for that made you kill him? Was it the illegal payoff you named this boat after?"

---

[67] Roxy: Is that tr—?
Polly: No.

[68] Roxy: Who is Adam Nightshade?
Polly: It's that guy Mr. Curtis the Big Evil Liar was telling us about on the way here. The blackmailer who was killed in Vegas. I'd totally forgotten.
Roxy: But Jas didn't! Way to go, Jas!
Veronique: You guys, is this tr—?
Polly/Roxy: No.

Suddenly there was no more laughing. "Where are the negatives?"

"They are in my hotel room.[69] You can send your crack search team to look for them like you did in Fiona's room today, but they won't find them. My father will, though. He knows me."

Mr. Curtis grabbed my arm in a distinctly non-WWBD way. "Tell me."

"Take us back to the dock. You have no choice. I won't tell you until I see the Venetian rising up in front of me. And you can't shoot me until you have the negatives."

Little Life Lesson 55: There are some situations they don't teach you about on TV.

"That's not quite true, Miss Callihan," Mr. Curtis said. "It's you who don't have a choice." He swiveled his gun hand toward the sleeping form of Fred. "Tell me where the negatives are, right now, or I pull the trigger."

My plan came to a screeching halt.

"Just tell him where they are, Jas," Alyson said, in what was perhaps her greatest show of faith in me ever. "I want to go home."

Me too. And how. But now it didn't look like that was going to happen. I'd been close, but as long as Mr. Curtis had his gun on Fred, I was powerless. Gun on me—okay, I would take my chances. Gun on boy—my bluff was called.

Game over. Good-bye friends. Good-bye world. Hello murky depths of Lake Mead.

"Actually," a voice said from the shadows, "I have the negatives."

And saying that, Jack walked into the Bambi Circle.

---

[69] Veronique: You guys, is this tr—?
   Polly/Roxy: No.
   Veronique: Oh. Wow.

Thirty-one

There are times in a girl's life when she would like to faint, and that was one of them.

Even Mr. Curtis looked like he wanted to faint. I had the distinct impression that Jack had not been on the *Payoff* passenger manifest and had somehow snuck onto the boat.

Mr. Curtis turned to glare at the Fabinator, who said, "I told you. I looked all around the pink vehicle and did not find him." The Fab one frowned at Jack. "How do you come here?"

"Actually," Jack told him, "I followed you. You seemed to be having such a nice time with those two lovely ladies"—he nodded toward Alyson and Veronique—"that I didn't want to interrupt. So I just tagged along behind."

Mr. Curtis attempted a BriteSmile. "I'm really enjoying this little play, but I'm afraid it's time for the curtain call."

"I agree. Do you want the negatives?" Jack asked.

"Why? Are you going to tell me you've got them with you?"

"As a matter of fact, I do," Jack said. And reached for his belt buckle.

"What are you doing?" Mr. Curtis said. "I'm not bluffing when I say I will shoot the boy."

"The negatives are on my belt. I taped them there."

Drat my puritanical friends. I knew I should have stripped him entirely. If they'd let me take his clothes off earlier, none of this would be happening. I would have found the negatives and solved the whole thing and gotten to have lunch and—

On the plus side, maybe now I would get to see him without his pants on.

Hello, inappropriate thought at life-threatening moment.

"Go back over with your friends," Mr. Curtis said to me, destroying yet another dream.

As I walked by him, Jack's eyes met mine and he said, "I hope you're feeling macho."

And my insides started to tingle.

I went and stood next to Polly and Roxy. Even from the sidelines, I watched Jack undress more attentively than I'd ever watched anything. Which is why I saw the split-second gesture when he reached into his pocket, brought his hand out clenched, and threw a fistful of what looked like pebbles at Mr. Curtis.

At first nothing happened and I thought I'd misunderstood, but then all of a sudden Mad Joe came wriggling out of the blankets with the kind of determination he'd shown the day I'd met him, and leaped on Mr. Curtis, making strange crunching noises. Apparently, Pounce had the superpower to revive cats from the dead. I didn't get to think anymore about that, because as Mad Joe jumped on him, Mr. Curtis's gun hand flew away from Fred, and I decided it was time for action.

With precision honed by hours of practice, Roxy and I got our wrists together, Polly jumped onto them, and we swung her onto Mr. Curtis's back. She clung there with her hands over his eyes, and he started to turn around to try to smash her against a wall to get her off. But he floundered and tripped over his feet, going down face forward with Polly along for the ride.

"What just happened?" I said.

Roxy pointed at his feet. "Veronique tied his shoelaces in a box knot while you were talking about letters and proof. Nice diversion, by the way. Very *Hogan's Heroes*."

"Thanks—" I started to say, but stopped when I saw the Fabinator heading our way and looking big and mean. Veronique was assisting Polly, who was sitting on Mr. Curtis's back saying, "And this one is for the Pink Pearl too"; Alyson was clinging to Tom and sobbing; and Jack was helping Fiona and Red move Fred inside; which left Roxy and me alone to contend with all million pounds of the Fab one.

Roxy and me and her heartbreak, I should have said.

"Bend down and leave this to me," Roxy ordered. A second later, something pink whizzed past me and then the Fabinator's head jerked back. When I looked up I realized that Roxy had made a weapon out of dental floss and gum, which adhered itself to his hair and then, by tugging on the piece of floss so his hair pulled, allowed her to distract him enough that I could wrap another piece of floss between an air duct and a cement block and watch him lose his footing just enough to make him ours.

Leaving Roxy to tie the Fabinator's hands up with his very own navy silk jockstrap, I turned my head to check on Polly and Mr. Curtis and was blinded by a bright light coming from next to the boat. I blinked and saw a figure in silhouette leaping over the edge and onto the deck like a comic book superhero.

Or superheroine. Because she was wearing a black leather corset and black leather pants and black boots and a black leather choker and wrist cuff.

It was my Sage Master! The Queen bartender from the Voodoo Lounge. And, I realized, the clumsy cocktail waitress at the roller rink who had raised my suspicions by distractingly spilling on the Fabinator. Only she was wearing an additional accessory tonight: the gold medallion of a police officer.

She was a cop!

Little Life Lesson 56: Just when you think there are no more surprises, there are more surprises.

Fiona came running out to her, threw her arms around the woman, and said, "Alex! Thank God you're here!"

Alex was a girl. When my Sage Master had disappeared from her place behind the bar at the Voodoo Lounge, I thought she was on a cigarette break—but she'd gone to call Fiona. This was *Alex darling*. This was the person Fiona couldn't be seen with. Alex, Fiona's best friend since third grade, now a Los Angeles police detective on leave, working unofficially in Las Vegas to offer her friend support in a difficult time.

"I should have listened to you," Fiona told her. "I never should have trusted Mr. Curtis. Thank you for coming to save us."

Alex looked around at the two men being pinned to the deck, chuckled when she saw the pyramid of cement blocks Roxy had erected on the Fabinator's chest, and said, "Actually, Fi, you should thank Jasmine for our being here. Her father found a note she left that described some threats against her and included impressively lifted fingerprints of the person who'd done the threatening.[70] He sent her note to the police, who ran the prints and matched them to Mr. Curtis's. But we wouldn't have found you so fast if a man named Captain Doom hadn't gotten worried when he couldn't raise the Pink Pearl and sent out an all-points bulletin for it. Still, I'm not sure you needed to be saved. It looks to me like this situation was pretty well under control. All that's left for me is the cleanup and the paperwork."

She pulled out a pair of handcuffs,[71] and took over where we left off, getting the Fabinator and L. A. Curtis properly cuffed and stowed.

Which freed up Jack to walk over to Red Early, give him a long hug, and say, "It's over, Dad. It's finally over."

---

[70] Polly: Wait, there WAS a note?

Jas: Everyone knows you should summarize your case as you go along, and leave it somewhere people could find it if something should happen to you.

Polly: You're saying you really left a note? With fingerprints? But we had all the evidence with us.

Jas: Not all of it. I left — are you hugging me?

Polly: You are the beef, Jasmine Callihan.

[71] Polly: Did you see how Alex had her cuffs in a special pocket in her leather pants?

Jas: I know!!! I want some pants like that so bad!!

Roxy: And her wrist cuff was actually a walkie-talkie.

Jas: No. Way.

Polly: The bar on assignation chic has just been raised. Jas, prepare yourself for a whole new wardrobe.

Thirty-two

That's right. Red Early was Jack's father.

Which made Fred—

"My half brother," Jack said, coming over to me. "But we spent a lot of time together growing up. I was eleven when he was born, and he seemed like he was eleven when he was born, so even though I was in England half the year with my mother we—Jas? Is something wrong?"

I guess maybe the stress of almost being killed for the second time in two days got to me and I cracked. "He's your dad? Fred is your brother? Why didn't you just tell me? Why did you play all mysterious and lie to me? I would have helped you if you'd explained. You said you trusted me."

"I did it to protect my father and Fred. Fiona had told Fred not to speak to me, afraid that I would somehow get in the middle and get hurt, which is why he ran away from me in the casino. I couldn't tell *anyone*. It was nothing personal about you."

I really wanted to believe him. But I was too tired and fed up and confused. So I—well, let's just say I'm not proud of what I did.

Little Life Lesson 57: Be prepared for surprises, because if you're not, you might act really stupid and ruin the rest of your life.

Little Life Lesson 58: For example, upon finding out that the guy of your dreams was sort of lying to you the entire time you knew him—possibly for a good reason—calling him a trash-talking moldy Monchichi and saying you never want to hear another word from his lying mouth again may feel cathartic at the time, but in the long run only ensures you will never hear from him again and therefore lead an existence of unremitting pain and loneliness.

Little Life Lesson 59 (one to go!): Also, if you happen to be involved in a life-threatening situation that you get out of unscathed, and police in two states praise your quick thinking and even say they would not have solved the case without you; if the police department of the city you live in makes you an honorary deputy, and offers you a chance to go on a ride along with Alex, the coolest woman you have ever met, and a part-time job, you might think your father would be pleased, proud even.

You would not, however, be thinking of the Thwarter. Or, as I have taken to calling him, the Grounder.

Yes, Air Jas was grounded for the rest of her life and beyond, parked forever at Little Life Lesson 59. I was pretty sure my father was researching options in cryogenic grounding, enabling grounding from beyond the grave. Some of his best lines, which he would periodically pop into my room to repeat, were, "The next time you set foot outside this house alone will be to go to my funeral," and, "Our species has evolved for thousands of years to avoid the kind of situations you cavalierly waltz into," and, my favorite, "You could have drowned. Drowning is supposed to be the worst way to die." A real hit parade.

Although I guess the fact that he hugged me every time and sometimes I would hear him whisper really softly, "I was so scared I'd lost you, little one," kind of took the sting away.

The only people it ended worse for than me were L. A. Curtis and the Fabinator. It turned out they had met doing community theater, and had actually performed that little fight scene they did in the clearing for an audience during a run of *West Side Story* before showing it to us. Mr. Curtis will stand trial for the murder of Len Phillips in Los Angeles, after he's tried for the murder of Adam Nightshade in Las Vegas, captured entirely—and accidentally—on film by Red Early. Len Phillips had been with Red that day, and Mr. Curtis spotted both men. His plan had been to get rid of them both and the negatives by murdering Len and framing Red for it. When that didn't work, he enlisted Fiona's help to lure Red out of hiding and into his lap, by convincing her that getting Red recaptured would help the police and was the only way she and Fred could have a normal life.

The Fabinator is looking at some time for trying to kidnap us, and dealing with a series of smaller lawsuits brought by the firm of Prentis & Prentis *in re:* destruction of one pink leather dashboard; destruction of one pair of pink sparkle pumps with gold heels.

Red and Fiona were making up for lost time playing happy family. I got an email from Fred saying they were all doing "really good and Mad Joe says hello."

I didn't hear from Jack.

"Should I call him and apologize?" I asked Polly on the phone.

"No. You have nothing to apologize for."

"I called him a moldy Monchichi," I reminded her.

"Hang on, let me ask Tom's opinion." Muffled noises that did NOT sound like talking. !!!!!!!!!!!!!!!!!!!. Then a little laugh. "Tom says you shouldn't call him."

"Thanks."

The capture and arrests made the news big-time, and although my father would not let me talk to any reporters, Sherri! started a scrapbook of clippings about it. I also started getting a lot of emails from people asking me if I could help them find their dogs or solve the unsolved murder of their daughter or lend them $10,000 at a very good interest rate. In among them, a few days after we got back, I found this one:

To: Jasmine Callihan <Drumgrrrl@hotmail.com>
From: J.R. <JR_211@hotmail.com>
Subject:

Congratulations on your heroic work in Las Vegas. You truly are Winnie Callihan's daughter. Your mother would be very proud.
I will be watching you.

I wrote back and got no reply.

But I didn't really have time to think about it, what with obsessing about Jack and whether Jack would call and if I should call him and apologize and if—

It was totally stupid. He was going to be a sophomore at UCLA, I'd discovered. I was in high school. Oh, and I had told him he was a Monchichi.

Or rather, a trash-talking moldy Monchichi.

Yeah, I'm sure I was very much on his mind. But what if he was The One and I'd blown it forever? What if I were destined to a life-time of broken dreams and one-night stands because of this? I couldn't even consult with Polly over what kind of clothes I should start laying in for my new chaps-and-cheap-motel life because she was always busy in Tom's room—although Roxy reported the door was always open and mostly she saw them sitting on opposite ends of the bed reading *Hot Rod*.

Still, it was a start.

Roxy was too busy to be any help either. Ever since Veronique diagnosed her as being slightly paranoid, she'd been so excited that she spent all her time at the UCLA medical library looking up her symptoms.

Why couldn't I have normal friends?

Why would someone send me an email saying they were watching me?

How was I supposed to learn my sixtieth Little Life Lesson if I was stuck in the house?

Why were the only things in my Meaningful Reflection Journal haikus?

Could I write a haiku college essay?

And, speaking of college, what was Jack doing?

And why did I care?

I didn't care, I told myself. Especially tonight. It was the last Friday night of the summer and somehow Sherri! persuaded my dad that I should be allowed one night of fun before school started, so he was letting me go out with Polly and Roxy and Tom to a club to hear some band Roxy was crazy about. As long as I was home by 11:30. "And that means without a police escort or handcuffs," he said, and laughed like he'd said the funniest thing in the world. Ha ha. It's only MY LIFE we're joking about.

The club was packed when we got there, but Polly and Roxy managed to talk our way into a section near the stage, possibly qualifying for yet another superpower, while my total remained at zero.[72]

"Who are we hearing play again?" I asked as the warm-up band finished their set.

"The NASCAR Dads," Tom said. "It's the band that did that song

---

[72]Polly: This is a joke, right, Jas?
Jas: Why would I joke about not having a superpower?
Roxy: Because you totally have one, sweetie.
Jas: I do? What is it?
Polly: There's dancing in Kermit underwear, of course.
Jas: I'm serious. Just tell me what it is. Please?
Polly: Hate to chat and run, but the band is about to start.
Jas: Please? Superpower? Me? Please? Please? Fine. Be like that. I don't care anyway. At all.
Roxy: That's the spirit.
Jas: TELL ME WHAT IT—Ouch! That thing you're pulling on, Polly, is attached to my body. It's called my arm. Okay, I'm coming.

about the piñata I told you about."

"Right." The truth was, I didn't care. I was out of the house and with my friends and alive. And in many respects, as the Thwarter enjoyed pointing out, that was a lot more than I had any right to expect.

The lights went down and people started screaming and an announcer said, "Let's welcome to the stage the NASCAR Dads."

And then the stage lights went up and I was staring at a pair of worn-in green Adidas just like Jack's. And a pair of jeans like his. And a green-striped shirt like the one he'd been wearing in the gondola. And then I looked up and it was Jack. ONSTAGE. Behind the microphone and with a guitar.[73]

He said, "This song we just wrote and recorded for our next album. It's called 'Super Girl.'"

And he started singing and it was a totally adorable song, all about how this girl lived in disco-ball motion, and how she was too smart for his own good, and listening to it made me want to laugh and cry at the same time. Because it was awesome.

And because it definitely wasn't about me.

I looked around at the beautiful girls crowded by the stage and tried to guess which one was his girlfriend. It would take someone special to be the girlfriend of a rock star and inspire songs like that. I hoped it was the really pretty brown-haired girl standing in front of me with the cute necklace and the perfect skin because she seemed like she was nice and would smile at him and be a lot of fun to hang out with. She totally looked like a super girl. I bet she had

[73] Jas: Did you guys know about this? That Jack was in a band?
Roxy: Not at first, I just thought he looked familiar. Then I saw a picture of the NASCAR Dads in *Spin* and I realized why.
Polly: What are you doing down here? Get back up there. The band is about to start. Up up up!

a dozen superpowers, half of them sexual.

"I'm going outside for some fresh air," I yelled in Polly's ear. Which was code for "My heart is breaking in one million zillion pieces and I am now going to sob very, very hard for a long time."

"No, you're not," she said, grabbing my arm. Which was not code.

"I really think I should—"

"Pay attention!" Polly said.

Jack sang:

She has the power to make you wish her
With you all the time so you could whisper
About how just much you've missed her
And how badly you want to
Take her out for dinner bring her flowers chocolate see what
socks she wears under her cowboy boots make her smile so
you can see her dimples—those dimples, God—while you . . .

And as everyone in the audience sang KISS HER, he dropped his guitar, jumped off the stage.

And said, "I've missed you, super girl."

And kissed me.

ME!

ME!!

SUPER GIRL!!!!!!!!

Little Life Lesson 60: If you meet a guy who is six feet three inches of perfect manly splendor with green eyes and a British accent and a slight scar on his cheek and warm soft hands and a nice-smelling chest who laughs at your jokes and has lovely manners and makes you melt inside when he kisses you and he is named Jack and is perfect in every single way, keep your distance.

He's mine.

Over and Out[74]

---

[74] Veronique: *Saluton!* That's hello in Esperanto. Am I late? Did I miss the band? Hey, where is everyone? Jas? Roxy? Polly? Tommy?
Hello?
Saluton?
Anyone?
Drat.

And they lived....

....happily....

```
                                            \    |    /
                                             \  /|||\  /
                                          _   {(|||)}   _
                                             /  \|||/  \
                                            /    |    \


              |'#'| @@              ,......,
             @@@@@@@             ///|/VV V
              @ @    @@@@       ///|/
             @@@  .  .@@@@      ///
             @ @@ ~   @@@     __/\  /\__
                    ##_               \   /   / /
             /____/\ \            |   \ /   / /
                   | | |          /   |    / /
                   | | |         /   /|   / /
            * ******      ()    /___/ |  / /
            *********     /____|    /  / /
          ************* |>>>[-]<<   |  \ \
          ***************|          |   \ \
             /| | |     / | | \        \  \
            | | | |    /  | |  \        \  \
            | | | |   /   | |   \      >  |  >
            | | | |  /    | |    \    /  /  /
            |^^| \^^\     |^^|   |   /  /  /
           / |  \  \ \    / |    |  /  /  /
          ---/|-|- ---\-- /,//|_|_ |_/|,//|_|
```

...ever after.

Whoever locked >
us in the bathroom
is going to be so
sorry-slash-dead!
I mean it! This is
totally not Visa!

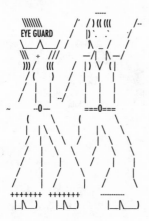

Ha!

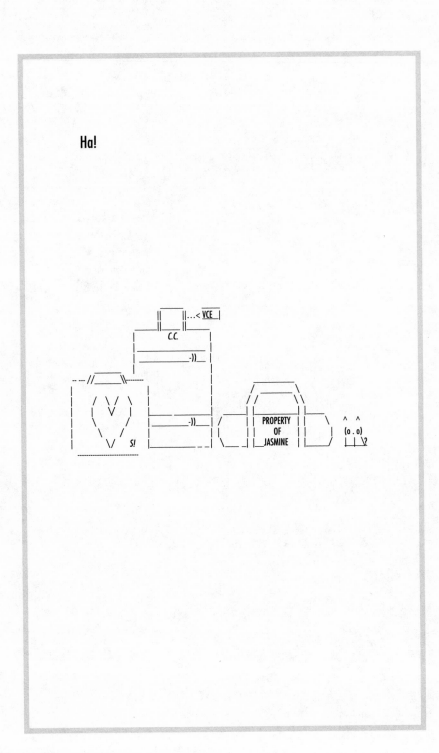